The Substitute Bride

The Marquess stood before her. He had loosened his shirt and she could see the hard, flat planes of his chest. "It's not what I had in mind for a bridal bed, but I am sure you will find it adequate."

Once again he gripped her shoulders and put his mouth on hers. He pulled at the ribbons on her gown, widening the neckline, causing it to slip down off her shoulders. Lily gasped and made a move to cover herself.

"Come, come. There's no need to act the blushing maiden. You are a more than married woman."

If only he had known the truth. But she must not reveal it. So she yielded to his caresses which was not difficult, since the mere brush of his fingers over her flesh left a trail of fire.

In a swift move he scooped her up and laid her on the bed. He pulled down her nightgown and the thin slip beneath it, exposing her nakedness to him.

Lily heard the Marquess draw in his breath. Did something about her appearance offend him? But he had moved over her, his hands taking much greater liberties...

THE SUBSTITUTE BRIDE

Noël Cades

First Printing, 2016

ISBN: 0-6480874-3-3

ISBN-13: 978-0-6480874-3-4

This book is dedicated to Aunty Carolyn

1. The swap

"But you'll do it? Oh please, Lily, I'll die if I have to go through with it. You are my last, my only hope."

Lily Cosgrove looked at the distraught, tear-stained face of her cousin Betsy. She was pale in the candle-light, her eyes dark hollows from sleepless nights. Outside the wind howled and a tree rattled against the window panes.

It was a wild night for a wedding.

But wilder still was Betsy's plan. For Lily to swap places with her, and marry the unknown man who was coming that night to save her family's honour. He had never met either of them: how was he to know if a substitute Elizabeth Cosgrove stood before him at the altar?

Lily wanted to help her cousin but she was conflicted.

"What if we were discovered? Would it even be a valid marriage?"

"I am sure it would. Oh, Lily, if I am forced to marry him it means I can never, ever be with Tom. I simply couldn't bear that!"

No thought was given to Lily's own fate, but then she had never enjoyed the same expectations as Betsy. Orphaned and penniless, her uncle had reluctantly taken her into his household, avoiding spending a farthing more on his niece than required.

Lily didn't care if Sir Robert was cold and indifferent to her, for she loved Betsy and was grateful for a home. She reminded herself that he was her father's only brother and had done his duty by her.

So the two girls grew up together, Lily a year younger than Betsy. They had been happy enough. But then Betsy had her first Season - there were no such plans to waste money debuting Lily in Society - and met the Honourable Tom Farrington.

She had allowed herself to be seduced by him, and worse, got caught *in flagrante delicto*. The less-than-honourable Tom had bolted to the continent at the first opportunity, leaving Betsy bereft.

Although it soon became apparent that there wasn't going to be the complication of a child, Betsy was nonetheless ruined and her family's name tainted with her.

Darkness descended on the household. Invitations were cancelled. Weeks followed of furious silence from Sir Robert and hand-wringing and recrimination from Lady Maud. She even managed to cast blame on her niece despite Lily not even being there. Not being out in Society, Lily had never even met the infamous Tom Farrington. But her aunt was too distraught to acknowledge this. How could her beloved daughter have had this happen to her? Others must surely be at fault!

The servants, well aware of everything that had gone on, remained tight-lipped but they cast one another glances and Lily knew they must gossip about the scandal behind closed doors.

Poor Betsy. One foolish mistake and she carried all the burden of censure and condemnation. And despite Tom running out on her she still adored him. She was still convinced he would come for her, though Lily feared this was very unlikely.

Then a surprise offer of help arrived. Tom's cousin, the Marquess of Westford, had written to Betsy's father proposing marriage to save her family's honour. A very private man who rarely left his country estate, he had expressed shame and embarrassment at his young relative's actions and wished to make good the situation.

Sir Robert was only too glad to take the Marquess up on his offer. The marriage would be held in the chapel of his own home. He and his wife were away at the time the correspondence took place. Lady Maud was taking a "rest cure", unable to bear the proximity of neighbours and staff who knew all about their dishonour.

"We will remain at Buxton due to my wife's condition. It is desirable that this event takes place with the least delay," Sir Robert wrote.

He preferred to distance himself from the entire affair and his daughter's disgrace. If in time her reputation were redeemed in the eyes of society, he might again acknowledge her.

So Betsy would get married alone. The local curate would give her away. There would be no wedding gown, no trousseau. It was purely an arrangement.

Lily smoothed the worn muslin of her own gown over her lap. It was a cast off of Betsy's, she was rarely given new clothes of her own. Her uncle considered that she didn't need them as she wasn't out in society. Now she almost certainly never would be.

The candles flickered. The evening drew on. Tonight the Marquess would come for his bride.

"They say he's a confirmed bachelor, he must be ancient, Lily! And I know Tom means to return. He loves me Lily, I am certain! This horrid cousin and his disapproval are the very reason we had to keep our love secret, and why he had to flee abroad."

As inexperienced as Lily was, she doubted this. But she did not want to upset Betsy further.

Betsy's accusations against the Marquess hardly encouraged Lily to agree to take her place, but she knew her own fortunes were very different to her cousin's. Lily had no money for a dowry, so with his duty done, her uncle planned to send her to live as the companion of a distant relation. This lady, an elderly dowager of irascible temper, lived in the remote Highlands far away from society. A bleak and gruelling future lay ahead..

Maybe to be the mistress of a household, any household, was better?

But it was not this consideration that made Lily finally agree to her cousin's desperate plan. It was out of genuine concern for Betsy, and the faintest hope that Tom might yet return for her. Since there was no prospect of love in Lily's own life, it was surely but a slight sacrifice for her to be confined by matrimonial bonds?

Still, she wavered. What if this was the best outcome for Betsy? Even if this Marquess were elderly, he was a rich and noble man and Betsy would want for nothing. She would regain her place in society and perhaps even bear children if the Marquess were not quite so decrepit as feared.

"Very well."

As she spoke the words, she had the strangest sensation that the walls were at once closing in and crumbling down around her.

"Oh Lily!" Betsy was in raptures amid a fresh outburst of tears. Her relief, that saw her breaking down even more than before, vindicated Lily's decision. Marrying this man was almost a matter of indifference to her, but to Betsy it was a prison sentence.

Now all she had to do was go through with it. Approach the altar, speak her vows, and leave for she knew not where.

***

Betsy was as accommodating and as generous as she could be in the limited time left.

"You must take any of my things you like. I won't need them and I shall have new ones when I eventually have my own marriage," she offered.

Lily was reluctant to take any of Betsy's possessions. Her own were embarrassingly poor and shabby so she would at least need to borrow a newer gown for the deception to be convincing.

The Marquess couldn't imagine that Sir Robert's daughter would wear frayed cotton or patched silk.

"This muslin might do for a wedding," Betsy suggested It was one of her newer ones, she had worn it to a ball last spring. The fabric was thin for these cooler, autumn nights but Lily agreed that it was elegant.

There was something she wanted to know. Something a mother might have talked with her about, or at least given tactful hints towards. Here, there was no one she could ask except Betsy.

"What happened with you and Tom Farrington, what exactly... I mean the wedding night," Lily started. In the freer years of her childhood, before her father died, she had played in stables and around the estate. She had some sense of mares being sired and that certain things happened, though it seemed absurd to imagine it could be anything quite like that among people.

Still she knew there was something. Snatches of conversation from the giggling of a newly betrothed maidservant about the Wedding Night. An unguarded remark from the cook to one of the kitchen maids about bedchambers, within the young Lily's earshot. She knew that men and women were different for she had caught a glimpse of men bathing in the river once or twice. Her nursemaid had gasped and quickly ushered her young charge away when this happened.

Betsy blushed. "One doesn't possibly talk about such things, Lily."

"I know. But what exactly does it involve? Surely I need to know, if I am to be married?"

Her cousin remained tight-lipped. "The man takes care of all that."

"But is it... is it bearable?" Lily had heard older women speak of "duty".

"When you are with someone you love, you won't mind anything," Betsy told her.

This was hardly reassuring. Lily might be going to promise to love and honour a husband before God, but since she had never met him she could hardly feel that she loved him. She didn't even know what he looked like.

She clearly wasn't going to get any more out of her cousin. Betsy was busy arranging her own affairs. A letter had rapidly been dispatched to her former governess. Anne Carter, a weak soul who had adored Betsy during the years she had attended to her education, would now be Betsy's refuge while she awaited Tom's return. She lived in a tiny cottage in the countryside, on a small pension, but it would be safe enough for Betsy.

"Of course my mother and father will think that it's you who are staying there. I don't think they'll ask many questions, since you were going to be leaving anyway."

Lily's aunt's and uncle's indifference to her made the whole deception much easier. They would simply be glad she had gone, even if it meant the Scottish relation lost out on her promised companion.

As Lily packed her few, pitiful belongings into a small trunk and slipped into Betsy's muslin, her cousin assisting her with the fastenings, a maid knocked on the door.

"Oh Miss Betsy, Miss Lily, the visitor has arrived."

2. The nuptials

Scarcely able to breathe from nerves, Lily tried to gather her courage as Betsy helped adjust the heavy lace veil over her face. Lily's own hand trembled as she pinned her hair with a pearl ornament, a wedding gift from her cousin.

"I can't take that, it must be valuable. Aunt Maud will notice it's missing," Lily protested.

"She won't. She'll think I wore it, remember?"

They stood back to review the finished ensemble. Lily felt like a white ghost and was sure her face was even paler than her gown.

"You look lovely," Betsy told her. "The gown fits you perfectly, it suits your figure much better than mine." She could afford to be generous now that her younger cousin was relieving her of this terrible fate.

Lily's head was in such a spin that she barely gave a thought to how the gown looked or felt. But with the veil to disguise her face, they might just get away with this. It wouldn't deceive anyone who saw the two cousins side by side, but were the servants to glimpse Lily by herself they might be satisfied that she was Betsy.

"What will you do?" Lily asked Betsy. "They'll expect you to attend me."

"I'll stay quietly up here. You can mention to John that I - that Lily - is unwell and wishes to be undisturbed. He's so hard of hearing that he won't recognise it's the wrong voice behind the veil."

John was Sir Robert's steward, an aged retainer who had managed the other servants and household for many years. He was a kindly old fellow, assiduous in his duties, and Lily hated to deceive him.

But needs must. Feeling very alone, she made her way down the staircase and crossed towards the chapel. The house was cold and draughty: fewer fires were lit when Sir Robert and Lady Maud were away.

John met her and bowed. "Miss Elizabeth." He had always seemed the least censorious of Betsy's dishonour, his eyes saddened rather than scandalised when she had returned home in disgrace. He had known her since infancy: were it not for the uncrossable boundaries between family and servant, he might nearly have been a kindly great-uncle.

He had shown kindness to Lily too when she had first arrived there, grieving her father and missing her home, and assailed with constant, pointed reminders of her uncle's charity in taking her.

"Your cousin is not with you?"

Lily mumbled the untruth about a severe headache. It was unsettling to be lying about herself.

John paused for a moment. His white hair had grown sparse but he still stood upright and kept his black uniform as impeccably smart as possible. "It's not my place, Miss Elizabeth, but…"

He seemed to waver and then straightened, extending his arm. "I can't have you walk up there alone. Let them say what they will."

It was the most defiant he had ever been, but this was the last time he would probably ever see his young mistress. Lily felt a pang of guilt that it was the wrong young woman that he offered to escort.

Gratefully she took his arm and they stepped together into the chill of the chapel. The altar at the far end glowed softly with candles. There were no flowers.

Lily kept her head bowed, hardly daring to look up. She had suddenly realised that she might have to lift the veil up at some point and what then? John would doubtless see, what would he do?

For now she had to brazen it out.

It was only a small chapel but the walk up the aisle seemed the longest ever. Reaching the altar Lily looked up to see a tall, dark figure standing there.

The man turned to her and she suppressed a gasp, thinking for a moment it was the wrong man.

He wasn't elderly - he was perhaps little more than thirty-five, she guessed - and his dark, chiselled features were set in a rigid fury. He nodded abruptly to her, more an acknowledgement of her presence than any form of greeting.

Lily was so terrified that she closed her eyes as the curate read the solemn words. She and the tall man were both facing him, but Lily's mind wandered from the Book of Common Prayer and she looked up at the profile of the stranger who was about to vow matrimony to her.

She was both relieved and troubled that he was so much younger than they had imagined. Troubled because perhaps if Betsy saw this man, she might not be opposed to marriage with him as a respectable future. Lily agonised over whether she should speak up and perhaps fetch her cousin. It would cause shock and outrage to reveal the deception now, but far less, perhaps, than a month hence with the marriage irrevocable. For the truth would be revealed eventually.

Troubled, also, because her secret hope had been than an elderly husband might be less inclined to require of her those duties that older women alluded to in hushed remarks. But this man was clearly… virile. If only Betsy could have given her better advice about those duties.

As if he sensed her gaze on him the man turned slightly to her and Lily quickly lowered her eyes again. Not that he could see where she was looking through the dissembling lacework.

"I, Gervase Revelston Dainard, take thee, Elizabeth Ann Cosgrove..."

His voice startled her. It was deep and eloquent. He might be angry but his tone was measured, perhaps in recognition of the solemnity of the vows.

Given the set of his jaw and the muscle that clenched in his cheek, Lily had expected him to speak with an icy fury. But he spoke with resolve, not anger.

All too soon it was her own turn. She tried to keep her voice steady. "...to love, cherish, and to obey, till death us do part, according to God's holy ordinance; and thereto I give thee my troth." Her voice broke on the last words but she held her head up and did her best.

Now a ring was slipped onto her finger and a strong, warm hand took hers. Having imagined a thin, elderly claw with papery skin - or worse, something soft and clammy like that of Aunt Maud's unpleasant brother - this grasp was a comfort. Lily's own fingers felt ice cold but she returned the grip with a gentle firmness.

Those whom God hath joined together let no man put asunder.

The rest of the curate's words passed in a blur, until the words "Man and Wife". It was done. It was too late to confess now, to change her mind, to run away.

Old John, satisfied that Elizabeth was now passed properly into her husband's care, bowed to them both and departed. Lily felt loss and relief. Her last friend was gone, even though he had not known who she was. But at least he could not now expose her.

"Now we are Man and Wife there can be no need for this curtain between us." The voice was dry, the tone deep and masculine as before. Lily started as the Marquess lifted her veil and looked upon her for the first time.

Something momentarily flared in his eyes and for a second Lily was terrified that he had realised her deception. But how could he? He had never met either of them, nor seen their portraits. Lily might have dark golden hair where Betsy's was a light brown, but both girls would have been described as "fair" if anyone had been asked about their appearance.

"Dark" was a term used for the colouring of this man who now stood before her. With her lace removed and a candle shining more directly on his face since he had stepped towards her, Lily could see him clearly.

His hair was jet black with no streak yet of grey, likewise his brows, and his eyes were the colour of stormy skies. Lily was of a good height for a young woman but he towered over her. His dress was immaculate: his coat of a flawless cut that accentuated broad shoulders tapering to lean hips.

Surely Betsy would have admired this man, or come to admire him? Her Tom could not have been so very much better looking than this? Lily had rarely been in the society of men outside her family but she was quite certain that this man would be considered extremely handsome.

This man. Her husband. She had to start thinking of him as that.

"Madam."

Realising she had forgotten herself and was staring, Lily quickly lowered her head and curtseyed. "My lord".

"I do not require that of you, now that you are my wife. An address will suffice."

Confused, Lily nodded.

"We make for Westford Park tonight. If the servants have arranged your things, we leave immediately."

Lily had hoped - expected - to return upstairs and farewell Betsy. But the trunk that she had packed was already in the hall. Having let down her veil once more on leaving the chapel she accepted the congratulations and well wishes of John and the housekeeper, and was escorted by her new husband into his carriage.

She was utterly alone, utterly friendless. Lily was glad of the privacy of her veil. It hid the tears that welled in her eyes and slipped down her cheeks as she farewelled her uncle's house and her girlhood.

Everyone she had ever known and loved had been taken from her. The man at her side was a stranger - even a hostile stranger, from the way his gaze had narrowed as he looked at her. The reluctant bridegroom, only to become more furious if and when he discovered his impostor bride.

3. The roadside inn

Gervase Dainard, Marquess of Westford, hardly knew what he had done.

He had, he decided, bailed his feckless young fool of a cousin out for the last time. Over the past few years, since Tom had been sent down in disgrace from Cambridge, Gervase had frequently paid off his gambling debts and dealt with several women with whom Tom had embroiled himself.

A pregnant chambermaid had been discreetly dispatched to a house in the North of England, to marry a widowed gamekeeper. An actress, who claimed breach of promise, was appeased and dismissed courtesy of a large cheque. A notorious French courtesan who tried to blackmail the young Farrington with letters stolen from yet another of his indiscretions - this one a married lady - had likewise been paid off.

For as long as Tom had confined himself to the *demi-monde* it was one thing. But to dishonour a young woman of his own class was insupportable.

And worse, the niece of the man that Gervase owed his life to.

The Marquess could see no other means of redress, with Tom now fled to Italy and refusing to answer correspondence, than to offer marriage himself.

Gervase cast a glance at the veiled figure beside him. He had no need of nor desire for a wife, he had dispensed with any such notions years ago. He had no idea what he would do with her.

A strange little chit, sitting there covered by her veil. Doubtless it was a show of modesty to conceal the shame that she must feel.

Well, he had restored her honour now. She was the wife of a Marquess, a Marchioness.

He had been momentarily surprised when he had seen her face. Pale and terrified, indeed, but that was perhaps to be expected. But also a beauty. He had even felt a flicker of admiration himself, which he immediately quelled as he recalled her folly.

Remembering the sly charms of the actress and the dusky, sultry allure of the French girl, Gervase thought this latest piece a break from form for Tom. She had a quiet grace, a fineness to her. Were she to bear him heirs - unexpectedly he found himself stirring at the thought - they would be fine looking children.

Gervase had had no plans of having offspring. Tom, for all his faults, was his heir and he had formerly hoped that the young man would eventually settle down and lead a respectable life. Gervase himself had been wilder in his youth, albeit not to the extent of Tom's debauchery. Nonetheless he had felt sympathy towards his younger relative, growing up without a father as he had done, with only a weak and indulgent mother to mould his character.

He had formerly thought Tom redeemable. But as the years passed he had become increasingly concerned that the boy's behaviour was escalating: and now this.

It was the final straw. Gervase now had grave concerns about the family title and property passing to his cousin, which in the absence of his own issue it would do.

Issue. Heirs must be begot, of course, which might mean closer marital relations than he had anticipated. He had vaguely considered that it might be a legal or moral requirement to consummate this marriage, but before meeting the girl had felt no interest in doing so.

Gervase's previous line of thinking was that they would simply lead separate lives. He owned several properties and Westford Park itself was sufficiently large that their paths need rarely cross.

It had been raining when they departed Sir Robert's house and the skies fell even heavier now. The wind had whipped up and the road was becoming slippery and perilous for the horses.

If the carriage wheel broke or a horse fell they would become stranded in this wild weather, far from anywhere, at the mercy of highwaymen who preyed on lonely roads.

Gervase called to the coachman to draw up the horses. "We will not make it safely to Westford Park this night. Is there an inn nearby?" Lost in his thoughts, he had not noticed if they had recently passed one.

"There's one not far away, perhaps two miles further," the coachman told him. He had remembered passing one on the journey there.

"We'll stay there." Even if it was a rough place it would be shelter. Not somewhere the Marquess would have chosen for his wedding night but circumstances required it.

The carriage continued on at a slower pace, the coachman taking the utmost care that the horses should not stumble. The road was particularly bad here: narrow, with many potholes It threw them all about the carriage even though it was a fine and expensive vehicle, well-sprung.

A lantern glinted from above the inn door as they approached. The Marquess ushered his bride into the warmth and shelter within while the coachman attended to stabling the horses.

Arrangements were made. They were simple premises but seemed clean enough, and the patrons inside looked not significantly more villainous than those in any other such establishment. Gervase now felt relief that the girl was veiled.

The lecherous glances directed at her slim figure might have been cruder still if they had been able to view her face.

The landlady led them up to what she described as the "best bedroom". She lit the fire and left them, having promised to send up a tray of supper. Lily's trunk was brought up and placed at the foot of the bed.

There was just one bed. One chair. A small washstand with a chipped porcelain ewer.

Gervase was a man of the world, he had served in battle and camped in rough terrain. The basic room did not faze him. He wondered about his bride: she would be used to finer accommodation.

But she should be grateful even for this, he reasoned. After all her family could have thrown her out, or sent her overseas far from the lap of luxury.

"I will dine downstairs," he told her. "You can arrange your affairs here. It is only for one night."

He did not indicate when or if he would join her, though the landlady had made it clear that no other rooms were spare. The coachman would sleep by the fire downstairs, where the stable hands also slept.

Gervase left the girl, still veiled, alone in the bedroom.

***

Lily was exhausted. All she wanted to do was get beneath the eiderdown and sleep. She opened her trunk, finding some small comfort in the familiar items inside.

There was a knock on the door and the landlady - for most of the other servants were in bed by this late hour - entered with a tray and set it down on the small table by the chair.

"Here you are, my lady. Is there anything else you need?"

There wasn't so Lily thanked her.

The tavern woman was curious about this nervous looking girl, arriving with such a rich and titled husband. She had first thought the worst but glancing at Lily's hand, saw the ring there.

"Newly married, are you?" The girl was so young and tense, she didn't have the assurance of a long married woman.

"Yes." Lily couldn't bring herself to say "earlier tonight". It seemed indecent, as though it still lacked propriety for her to be sharing a room with a man. "Recently."

"My belated congratulations, my lady." She saw a shadow pass over Lily's face and interpreted it as the typical bedroom fears of a new bride. It took a while to get used to these things, after all. As like as not the man downstairs was a boorish beast when it came to taking his rights. Titled or not - and the landlady had entertained both in her time, make no mistake about that - they were all the same. They needed a firm hand, but what mere woman's strength could counter a man's lusty force?

The landlady had given her own daughter some choice advice on her nuptials, as well as the recipe for a brew that would cool the ardour, quell the loins and hasten sleep. But it was not her place to suggest any such thing to this girl. A marchioness she must be, fancy that! Staying in her own humble inn.

Wanting to do at least something for her the stout tavern woman lifted another log onto the fire and gave it a good poke, sending a shower of sparks up the chimney. The young bride wouldn't freeze to death at least.

"Good night then, and anything you need, you let me know," she said, taking her leave.

Lily was alone once more.

On the tray lay a dish of stew with a rich gravy, a hunk of bread and a tankard of weak ale. It smelled appetising and she should have felt hungry but something constricted her throat. She could barely manage a morsel.

Oh Betsy, Betsy, what have we done? How can I bear this alone?

She drew out of the trunk a nightgown made of fine lawn. It was Betsy's, her cousin must have slipped it in there as a gift. The filminess of the fabric was like silk compared to Lily's own plainer cotton one. Quickly she undressed before the fire and put it on, folding away her muslin dress as best she could. She loosened and removed her own stays.

It was lovely to have her own fire, even in these circumstances. Sir Robert never allowed them in bedrooms and in winter there was frequently ice on the inside of Lily's window pane.

Despite her exhaustion she was too wound up to sleep so she took a book of verse she had packed, sat in the small chair, and started reading.

She was lost in the poetry when there was a knock at the door. Startled, she said "come in!" and then rose to her feet in shock as the Marquess entered. Her husband.

4. The wedding night

Whatever Gervase had expected to find when he opened the door, it was not this. He had imagined that his new bride would be long asleep, and to ensure this state of affairs he had delayed as long as possible over his supper. He was feeling strangely uncomfortable about the whole situation himself.

But he found himself greeted by a slim figure, the firelight behind her thin robe rendering it nearly transparent, which being the wanton she obviously was she did not seem to care about. He would have expected a more modest woman to have wrapped something around herself before admitting someone to her room.

Instead he could see every slender line of her body, nearly as though she were naked. He clenched his teeth, frustrated at his body for not being as indifferent to this sight as he would have liked. No wonder she had snared young Tom.

"You are not asleep?"

It was obvious that she was not but Lily did not draw attention to this. "No my Lord, I was reading."

Gervase noticed that she had been holding a book which she placed on the table as she stood up. He was surprised to find her reading anything: Tom's usual bits of muslin had little in their heads.

Doubtless it was some frippery romantic novel such that women always seemed to go wild over these days. He picked it up and was more than surprised to see "The Eclogues of Vergil" inscribed on the cover.

"You read Latin?" he asked.

"My father taught me Latin and Greek."

She saw his eyebrows rise in wonder and remembered that her father was supposed to be Sir Robert, who was the last man on earth to know or teach the Classics. "Through a tutor," she quickly added.

"And you enjoy Vergil?"

"Very much, my Lord."

Then we have something in common, he was about to say, but stopped himself.

Gervase found himself taken by a sudden fury that this girl, a girl intelligent enough to read Latin, should have let herself be seduced by his feckless cousin yet feign nervousness and reserve in his own presence. By rights she should have been as welcoming and willing as any tavern maid.

Not knowing what overcame him he strode over to her, gripped her shoulders and brought his mouth down on hers. She stiffened in shock for a moment then - as he had surely known she would - softened in his embrace. They were all the same, these hussies. A brief pretence of chastity and then the true wanton within was revealed.

Yet the embrace shook him. Her lips were sweet and soft and while he had invaded her mouth to assert some angry right, he now found himself deepening the kiss in a desire to explore her.

She had put her hands on him, as if to push him away, but now she held onto him as though for support.

Despite every effort of will, Gervase could not stop his own hands from running down her body. He felt the slender hollow of her waist, the curve of her buttocks.

He was on the point of crushing her against his unparallelled hardness when he managed to recover his senses. He broke off and stood back from her.

His bride - Tom's chit - stood there, her face flushed, her parted lips swollen from the force of his kiss, her grey eyes managing to display both confusion and arousal.

She was a brilliant little actress, he afforded her that much.

And as he drank in the figure he could see through the thin garment: the firm, rounded breasts, the graceful neck, the dark gold tendril of hair that had escaped its pins, Gervase knew only one thing.

He had to have her. She was legally his, but even if the curate had rushed up to declare the marriage void, he could not have held back.

***

Lily had been shocked to her core when the Marquess kissed her. First at the fact he did it and at the harsh force with which he bruised her lips.

But then - and this was the greater shock - with the way that her body had responded to him.

She had wanted his embrace.

Lily, who had never before danced with a man, never even flirted with a member of the male sex unless you counted fencing off the creepy gropes of Aunt Maud's brother, found herself welcoming the touch of this man.

She knew what a kiss was. But she had had no idea that he would open her mouth and invade her with his tongue. Taste her and drink her in.

Nor that the actions of his lips would send strange bright throbs to the lower regions of her body.

Was this, then, why Betsy had done what she had done with Tom? Had she felt this powerless to resist?

For the moment the Marquess - her husband, she must remember - began to run his strong, warm hands over her body, she was helpless. Instead of trying to push him away she wanted him closer. She wanted the comfort and warmth of his skin, his masculine aroma of musk and bay.

Then he was standing back from her, a mocking glint in his eye.

"So, the charade of modesty vanishes as quickly as it came? There is no need to dissemble with me, my dear. We both know all too well the circumstances that led to our union."

He thought she was Betsy of course, and he needed to keep thinking that at least for now. What would Betsy have done? Was there something Lily was failing to do that might give the game away?

"The man takes care of all that" Betsy had told her.

"I am at your disposal, my Lord," Lily said and instantly knew it was the wrong thing when the Marquess's eyes widened and for a second he looked as if he might laugh.

But her response seemed to have defused the veiled aggression in his previous remark. "That's a novel way of putting it." He seemed almost amused. "Your cooperation will be significantly less tiresome than a continued semblance of prudishness."

When the Marquess had pressed her to him, Lily had felt the outline of a hardness that was not his thigh. She had pieced together what she knew of men and stallions and mares, and her own body, and was coming to some worrying yet surely absurd conclusions.

Did her cooperation mean that…? But surely, no, women were not built like horses. Such a thing could not be possibly be accommodated. But women also gave birth, Lily thought. Albeit she had assumed that doctors and midwives did something to facilitate this, though she knew not what.

Inwardly she cursed her ignorance. She would have no choice but to let him take care of everything and hope that he did not guess it was entirely new to her.

She shivered although the room was warm. The Marquess was pulling off his cravat. Lily wondered for a moment that he had not travelled with a valet. Sir Robert's man was indispensable to his toilette and she remembered with fondness her father's man, William.

The Marquess stood before her. He had loosened his shirt and she could see the hard, flat planes of his chest. "It's not what I had in mind for a bridal bed, but I am sure you will find it adequate."

Once again he gripped her shoulders and put his mouth on hers. He pulled at the ribbons on her gown, widening the neckline, causing it to slip down off her shoulders. Lily gasped and made a move to cover herself.

"Come, come. There's no need to act the blushing maiden. You are a more than married woman."

If only he had known the truth. But she must not reveal it. So she yielded to his caresses which was not difficult, since the mere brush of his fingers over her flesh left a trail of fire.

In a swift move he scooped her up and laid her on the bed. He pulled down her nightgown and the thin slip beneath it, exposing her nakedness to him.

Lily heard the Marquess draw in his breath. Did something about her appearance offend him? But he had moved over her, his hands taking much greater liberties.

Then his lips were kissing down her neck, over her breastbone. Towards her… Lily had to muffle her response as he enclosed her right breast in his mouth, suckling on it.

At the same time she felt his hand slip between her thighs. She was astonished to feel him reaching for the very core of her modesty yet finding that her body wanted his touch there, her hips involuntarily moving towards him.

"More than ready. To be expected perhaps, given your past experience."

Not fully understanding what he meant, Lily was shocked as the Marquess moved directly over her, pushing his own breeches aside, and feeling a long hardness press against her upper leg.

"My lord…" She wasn't quite sure what she was frightened of, though she knew she was frightened.

For a second he paused and she imagined she saw a flicker of concern in his eyes, of doubt, even. But his hands pushed her thighs apart and she felt him position his maleness at the place where his fingers had just been.

In one long, smooth move he plunged inside her and she cried out in genuine discomfort, closing her eyes and clinging to him because she had nothing else to hold on to.

Again he paused but if he looked down at her she could not tell, for her eyes were closed and she bit her lip to bear the sharp pain.

Fortunately, as he moved in and out of her, the edge wore off to be replaced by a dull throb, abating into a sense of heat and fullness. The more he slid himself in and out of her, the more it seemed to ease the discomfort and change it to something quite different.

The Marquess shifted and the new feelings intensified. His hand cupped her breast, his mouth silenced her murmurs, and her body was in the complete control of her new husband. Unable to do anything else she gave herself into the sensations, until something built and built within her. Bright and tender and sharp all at once.

Then, fearing at the back of her mind that she may be dying, that her body was having some kind of fit, she found herself spasming uncontrollably as he ground into her.

Finally she knew no more. Exhausted from all the physical exertions and emotion of the day, Lily passed out into slumber.

5. The first morning

Lily awoke, now a bride and a wife in every sense, to the furious gaze of her new husband.

Her body ached from his ministrations the previous night and she was thirsty. Still so tired and so thirsty.

The Marquess's voice held a dangerous softness. "This was some sort of plot, was it? This deception practiced upon me?"

Lily opened her eyes wide in fear. How had he guessed? What had she done wrong? Or had her aunt and uncle returned early and discovered the switch? All sorts of scenarios raced through her mind.

He was satisfied by her reaction. "I see this is no surprise to you. How did you imagine you might get away with this?"

"My Lord, I..." she started to explain, to apologise but her mouth felt so dry that the words stuck in her throat and he cut across her speech, impatient.

"Answer me this, lest there be any further misunderstanding. Were you or were you not inviolate when I took you last night?'

Inviolate? The confusion showed on her face.

"Were you a maiden? Had you still your maidenhood when you lay with me?" His furious expression and tone demanded an answer.

"I - yes, my Lord." Lily didn't know enough about what he was referring to try and lie.

There was a faint, fleeting guilt that passed over his face. "Had I known, I might have…" But the anger returned. "Whose idea was this? Your parents, to entrap me into this unwanted marriage?"

"To trap you?"

"Pretending that your honour had been wrest away by my cousin, when in fact it remained intact?"

She was starting to understand his question but wasn't fully sure why it mattered. Betsy was still disgraced, even if she hadn't gone so far as what had just happened to Lily. Though Lily knew that her cousin must have done so since there had been the worry of a baby.

"My Lord, I did not know."

Once again he surprised her by tracing his finger down the side of her face, almost tenderly. "Regardless of your role in this scheme, as a maiden you deserved gentler than my treatment of you last night. For that I express my regrets."

But as soon as the kindness appeared, the cold, angry formality returned. "Were there any way to dissolve this and free us both, I would do so. But I fear that you and your family have outwitted me with your machinations, and given last night, annulment is now out of the question."

He stood up. "I will breakfast downstairs. A tray will be sent up to you. Be ready in one hour."

***

It was after he had gone and Lily rose from the bed that she was horrified to see blood staining the linen. But it was not the time of her monthly courses. What he had done to her last night must have wounded her in some way. The area still ached.

She bathed herself as best she could with the ewer of cold water, wincing as she touched her bruised skin.

She now understood what the matrons meant about submitting and bearing one's husband's attentions, though it had not been entirely an ordeal. There had been as much pleasure as pain, more so, by the end.

The landlady rapped at the door and entered with the tray. Her eyes fell on the ruined bedclothes before Lily had a chance to pounce on them and conceal them. She stood there, frozen with horror and shame.

The tavern keeper realised the situation instantly and felt a welling of pity. This girl's mother, whoever she was, had not done her duty by her. It was hard to speak of these things but a young girl deserved better than to be wed in complete ignorance.

Tactfully the woman bundled up the sheets such that the stains were concealed inside. "Nothing that lye and hot water won't fix," she said.

Lily felt like weeping.

The landlady hesitated. "You gave me to understand you had been married a while, my lady."

"We were married last night."

It was not her place but she spoke anyway. Someone had to. "Forgive me if I speak out of turn, my lady, but it's usually only the first time that…" she left the sentence unfinished. "It's not so bad later on. And you'll have such pretty children to occupy yourself with."

She departed, leaving Lily with a much better comprehension of what the Marquess had seen and realised. As well as the conclusions he had drawn from the situation.

The wrong conclusions, but he was not wrong in his suspicions of being deceived. Lily was beginning to realise the enormity of what she and Betsy had done. But there was no going back. She must make the best of it.

She steeled herself. Remembered her courage. Her father had been a soldier and she would not dishonour him with cowardice.

She, Lily Cosgrove and now Elizabeth Dainard, Marchioness of Westford, had chosen this path. Somehow she would travel down it as best she could.

***

Horses always calmed him down. Their magnificence, their intelligence compared to most other animals. There were times that Gervase preferred them to people. Most of the time, if he were honest.

He had been dishonest with himself and with his bride that morning. Despite his shock and anger, despite his sense of remorse, he had lied about one thing.

After last night he had had no intentions of a speedy dissolution of the marriage. What his mind and body had felt as he possessed his young bride had been absolutely unforeseen. A part of him had felt awakened for the first time in years.

Not just that part. The girl had got under his skin in some deeper way.

Her beauty, her intelligence, her grace. He almost admired young Farrington for his distinctly improved taste.

Yet she had lied. She was no different to nor better than the others. She had flirted and fallen for one man, and then fooled another into restoring her honour.

Had the Marquess not been so filled with fury at being misled, he might have questioned why his cousin had fled to the continent when he had not even ruined the girl. But his thoughts did not go there.

He would have liked to think that his new wife was somehow a mere pawn in this. That the plot to snare him in marriage was cooked up and coerced by her family. God knows her father had nothing of the reputation and regard that his brother was held in. Gervase felt again the regret at the loss of his friend and former military commander.

Sir Robert was held in no such high renown. He was known to be ungenerous and abrasive. Might he be suffering financial troubles that had compelled this stratagem? Gervase determined to investigate.

But despite whatever parental pressure she had been under, there was no doubt that the girl had gone about with Tom Farrington in a shameful manner and compromised herself badly. There were multiple witnesses. Even though it now appeared that complete dishonouring had not fully occurred, her behaviour could not be absolved from censure.

She was his wife now, however, and in time could be taught the modesty and dignity required of one in her new position.

**

Gervase was surprised to find his bride ready to leave when he re-entered the bedroom just before the end of the hour. Her trunk was packed and her cloak was once again around her shoulders.

He was more used to women dawdling and delaying so her punctuality was welcome.

"You are ready to leave?" he asked her.

"Yes, my Lord."

Two of the tavern workers came in to haul the trunk downstairs. Gervase noticed the lightness of it as the men raised it. He imagined it held but a few possessions necessary for travel, doubtless his wife would send for the rest of her belongings once established in her new home.

The atmosphere was uneasy between them. Gervase was aware that he had been less than kind the night before, and Lily was in agonies of guilt and panic at discovery.

He tried to redeem himself by helping her into the carriage with more care and courtesy than he had shown the previous day and Lily felt some faint hope at his changed attitude. Perhaps his anger with her and the situation might eventually be somewhat appeased.

The coachman drove the horses on and they continued the journey if not in a companionable silence, then at least a less hostile one.

6. The arrival

Lily had dozed off during the journey. The steady motion of the carriage lulled her and one night's sleep had not been nearly enough to compensate for the emotional exhaustion of the previous day.

Gervase watched her. With her eyes closed and the sweep of a lash on her ivory-pale cheek, yet flushed with a faint rose, she looked as innocent as an angel. More a girl than a married woman.

If only she hadn't allowed herself to fall into such folly. She might have made a good match, he thought. Even if Sir Robert wasn't amongst the richest in the land they were an ancient and noble family.

He reminded himself that she had, in fact, made an excellent match. The position of Marchioness of Westford had been highly sought after, part of the reason that Gervase had kept largely to his country estate in recent years. The scheming of matrons and the gauche flirtations of their daughters had wearied him.

Gervase had typically preferred a woman who was closer to him in age and more educated in her tastes. This was another reason for his extended bachelorhood, because such women tended to be long off the market and he was not interested in married mistresses. Unlike his cousin.

It was perhaps ironic, then, that he had ended up with a girl so ignorant and virginal that she had barely understood what he had demanded her earlier that morning.

Although she was not ignorant in all respects. He remembered the volume of Vergil. If she liked to read, she could avail of his library at least. That might keep her out of mischief and give him some peace.

Looking at her now though, she was the very image of tranquillity.

As the carriage swung into the driveway of Westford Park Gervase touched his bride's arm. "You may wake, we have arrived," he told her. He was nearly moved to add "my dear" as an elderly uncle might. Something about her youth and vulnerability, her scheming apart, aroused an odd sense of protectiveness in him.

He tried to shake this off. Despite her appearance, he was certain that she knew exactly what she was doing. He would also make this known to Sir Robert. The Marquess had already prepared some choice words for that gentleman.

Lily opened her eyes and gasped in delight at the beauty of the house they were approaching. Bathed in the late afternoon autumn sunlight, the leaves turned to red and gold on the trees, it was the largest and most magnificent building she had ever seen. Of course she had visited few great homes in her life, but she had seen many paintings and drawings. One childhood tutor had been a keen student of architecture and had given her some introduction to the art and its terminology.

She could barely take in that this place was to be her new home. Her own family home had been lovely but small, and Sir Robert's pile was a grim grey mausoleum.

"It meets with your approval, madam?"

Lily was too awestruck to detect any nuance in his tone. "It is magnificent, my lord."

Gervase noted her parted lips and the genuine wonder in her eyes. She was truly impressed with his home and this moved him.

He had loved it himself since boyhood and felt pride in its heritage and maintaining its rooms and grounds for future generations.

Generations that this girl might well beget.

He helped her down from the carriage. They were met at the front door by an assortment of servants headed by the steward and a formidable looking housekeeper. These were later introduced as James Pelham and Mrs Hollis, the former never married and the latter a widow.

For now Gervase had business matters to attend to. He left his new wife in the care of the housekeeper and departed to his study. He also wanted to clear his head.

***

It was all overwhelming for Lily, trying to remember so many new names and faces. Her father had taught her through his own example the importance of recognising staff as individuals.

"Your own maid will be following you, my Lady?" the housekeeper asked her as she showed Lily to her chambers. "We have a room prepared for her."

Lily almost laughed. As if she had her own maidservant! Even the girl that attended Betsy had other duties than being a lady's maid. Only Aunt Maud enjoyed the ministrations of a dedicated servant.

"I had not arranged to bring a maid," Lily said. She wasn't sure what else to say.

Fortunately the housekeeper did not appear disconcerted. "That's probably as well. These girls often struggle to resettle so far from their homes. With your permission I will appoint a girl with suitable references and experience, and for now Sarah will attend to your needs."

Sarah, a parlourmaid who was hovering in the background, brightened at this. Promotion to lady's maid had long been a goal of hers but there had been no lady here for many years.

Mrs Hollis turned to her. "You'd best be off to take Nanny Noakes her tray, my girl. She frets if she's kept waiting."

"Nanny Noakes?" Lily had not thought there were children in the house.

"The nursemaid for young Master Tom, and his Lordship before him. A very elderly person now, and without charges for many years, but his Lordship wouldn't consider turning her out. She suffers from rheumatism and mostly keeps to her room," Mrs Hollis explained.

Lily thought that it was nice to give such a valued old servant a home, and said so. Mrs Hollis smiled approvingly.

"Old Nanny Noakes won't give any trouble. You'll find this quite a quiet household perhaps, depending what you're used to. His Lordship rarely entertains, though I expect that will all change now that you are here, my lady."

The housekeeper clearly had no idea of the circumstances that had led to the Marquess's marriage, or if she did she was being supremely tactful, Lily thought.

"Other changes too, of course. You must let me know how you would like things to be from now on. His Lordship has tended to leave things as they are, so Mr Pelham and myself..."

Lily interrupted her as politely as possible.

"I am sure the house is very capably managed by both of you. I have no intention of making any changes to a happy and well-run home," she said. The thought of this older and experienced woman having to defer to her over household matters that Lily had no knowledge of made her feel very uncomfortable. She had been a poor relation for so long that it was hard to realise, let alone exert, any authority of her own.

There was relief in the housekeeper's eyes. "You can trust that it will be so, my Lady." She had noticed the youth of the girl and guessed her likely ignorance in such matters. But she was impressed by her grace. Like the tavern woman before her, she felt that she wanted to help this child in some way. Whatever had led to this sudden marriage, for his Lordship was not given to whims, was as yet a mystery though some nasty rumours had hovered within her earshot.

For now she chose to discount them. Whatever this girl was, she was very much a lady.

"For tonight I took the liberty of choosing upon a menu, but from tomorrow I can present them to you each morning after consultation with the cook," she told Lily.

Lily couldn't imagine being able to choose food. She also had no idea what the Marquess preferred.

"I am sure it will be well, thank you, Mrs Hollis. You must know the preferences of the household far better than I," she said.

From what she gathered the "household" in terms of dining menus was only the Marquess, and now herself. But she might be required to entertain guests in future.

The housekeeper nodded and left her, promising to send Sarah back up to her.

Lily sat on the edge of the bed and looked around her. It was an absolutely beautiful room, decorated in pale blue and gold. The windows had a southern aspect and looked over the grounds. There was a lake beyond with what appeared to be a small island on it. Lily's first thought was whether there might be boats, or even if it was fed by a river. She couldn't tell from the thickness of the trees in the surrounding parkland. And in warmer weather, might she even swim there?

The bed itself was large and looked comfortable. She longed to sink down into its pillows and sleep for a week but she had things to attend to. Her pitiful wardrobe for one. She now realised she had scant outfits suitable for dining with her husband each night, assuming he required that of her. She had worn Betsy's good muslin for her wedding and to travel in, so she must find something else.

Nor would any more clothes be following her, any more than her own maid. What was she to do? Unless Betsy's clothes were sent on to her, before the deception was realised. Albeit Betsy would surely have taken the best of her remaining gowns with her to her former governess's house. She was still expecting to be reunited with Tom Farrington and would undoubtedly want most of her fine outfits for that encounter.

For now Lily would have to pick the best of the worst and make do. Her own best gown was a faded rose silk that was long out of fashion. She had grown since it was made for her, and after it had been let out the neckline had become immodestly low. She could sew on some lace, perhaps? But she had brought nothing with her save a small sewing case with needle and thread.

She was holding the silk up to shake out the creases just as Sarah re-entered the room. "Oh my lady, let me attend to that for you." Sarah put down the tea tray and was carrying and took the garment from Lily, smoothing it. "What a becoming colour!" The maid looked at it more closely.

"My lady, there is a tiny tear here. I am proficient with a needle, might I attend to it for you?"

Lily realised that Sarah wished to prove herself and acquiesced. She had planned to spend the next couple of hours fixing it herself. It was strange to realise that with her new status she might no longer be expected to perform such tasks. Indeed, it might be looked upon oddly if she even tried to.

Consider the lilies of the field, how they grow; they toil not, neither do they spin.

But she had never been that kind of Lily. Other than her love of reading she preferred to keep busy.

She hadn't even got around to exploring her room yet. There were doors on each wall. Lily approached one of them. "That's the bathroom, my lady," Sarah told her. "Mrs Hollis arranged for water to be heated for your bath. She thought that after such a long day of travel…" Sarah was unsure how to end the sentence, not wishing to imply that her new mistress was unclean.

"Thank you, Sarah, that's very thoughtful," Lily told her. She cast a glance to the other door, hesitating to ask where it led.

Sarah also hesitated to respond to the unspoken question. Blushing, she said: "that leads to his Lordship's chambers, my lady."

Now Lily was the one who felt utterly disconcerted. She should have guessed her husband's rooms would be adjacent. The implications of this made her blush deeper than the maid and they both stood there, in extreme awkwardness.

Lily broke the silence with a soft laugh. "Forgive me, Sarah. I should have realised. Today has brought many changes."

Sarah understood and welcomed her mistress's confidence. She had wondered what it must be like, marrying a man as formidable as the Marquess. He inspired respect and loyalty in the staff and he was extremely handsome, but so severe!

Sarah also wondered how the couple might have first met, though she knew it was not her place to speculate on such things. But her master spent so much time at his country estate that she marvelled how their acquaintance might have developed. Through letters, perhaps? His Lordship had barely been in London for the Season. Unless it was an arrangement?

She thought on these things as she helped the kitchenmaid carry pails of hot water to the bathtub. It was something she would enjoy discussing with her friend Ellen, a parlour maid at the neighbouring estate.

7. The dinner

Gervase felt impatient as he entered the dining room. He never usually had to wait, dining alone each night as he did, but now he would be forced to await the arrival of this girl.

He had planned to dine separately only to find that arrangements had already been made, with the staff wanting to offer him a wedding supper. More candles than usual burned on the table with fresh flowers also in abundance.

But mere moments after he had arrived, there she was. He caught his breath.

Whatever else his new bride was, she was ravishingly lovely.

The soft candlelight hid the age of Lily's gown, allowing it to deliver only a soft pink sheen that complemented her ivory complexion, the low neckline revealing the swell of her breasts. Clear, beautiful eyes fringed with dark lashes met his. Her dark gold hair had been twisted skilfully into a becoming style by Sarah's deft hands.

Her figure… well he had already appreciated her figure. But the setting of the room enhanced the poise and elegance of her slender form and upright bearing.

Gervase felt his loins quicken. He marvelled at his cousin ever having abandoned this piece. She was like a rare jewel and he felt the first stirring of pride that she was his. It conflicted with everything else he wanted to think of her, and would cause unanticipated complications, but there it was.

He knew better, however, than to be bedazzled by beauty. So he resisted his first instinct which was to take her in his arms and carry her to his bedchamber, and instead got her to take her place at the table with him.

Lily found her appetite restored. Through nerves and travel and all the other upheaval she had barely eaten for two days. The bath had revived her aching limbs and done much to ease the tenderness from last night.

Wine was poured for her and dishes put before her, and she ate at least a little from most of them. The Marquess was strangely silent during the first courses. Eventually he spoke.

"I trust that your needs have been attended to satisfactorily?"

"Yes thank you, my lord."

"Your room is sufficiently comfortable?"

"Indeed, my lord."

It was an absurdly stilted conversation for two people who had supposedly been joined in the closest and holiest of unions. Lily hoped that the servants would not pick up on the tense atmosphere between them. She could hardly ask him about his rooms, so she tried a different topic.

"The lake outside, does it connect to a river?" she asked.

"It is fed by two streams. My great-grandfather had it dammed and the island built. There's a bridge across from the back, but you can't see it from the house. You can also take a boat there."

Lily wasn't sure if she was disappointed by the bridge: it destroyed the image of romantic isolation, but she was pleased that the Marquess appeared forthcoming about his grounds.

"And the parklands surrounding it? From my window there appeared to be some trees I did not recognise," she said.

Equally pleased at her interest in his estate, Gervase began to tell her at length about the history of the gardens and the trees that had been planted there. He used the term "arboretum" which she had not heard in that context before, but guessed its meaning from her knowledge of Latin. "Arbor" meant "tree".

Lily was genuinely fascinated by what her husband was telling her. He was eloquent when describing different features and spoke with some passion. She found that she enjoyed his company and did not, at least for the duration of that meal, feel anxious about him. The wine she drank also eased and relaxed her.

She kept her wits about sufficiently to find out some information she needed. "My lord, may I ask who our neighbours are?"

The Marquess did not appear to find the question unusual. "A mile to the west at Leominster Hall, the widow of the late Lord Leominster, Lady Leominster. To the northeast at Grantlings, Sir Stephen Seton. The Westford estate borders his grounds, with the hill that you can see beyond the forest forming the dividing line. Grantlings lies in the valley beyond."

Lily wondered if Lady Leominster was old or young, and whether she had children. And was Sir Stephen married? She didn't like to appear inquisitive so determined to find out some other way. She urgently needed to ascertain whether Betsy had ever met either of these people in London. She hoped very much that they were both recluses who shunned the *ton*.

"I dare say you will meet both in due course," Gervase continued. "Sir Stephen dines here on occasion and Lady Leominster is a most gracious hostess."

There was something in his tone on his last phrase that Lily could not put her finger on but found unsettling. She was probably being foolish and letting her imagination run wild. She buried it for now.

All too soon they had finished the final course and the time to retire for the night fast approached.

***

The Marquess went to his study to finish a letter after supper and Lily mounted the stairs in the great hallway alone. As she turned on the first landing she was startled to see a figure before her on the next set of stairs, blocking her way.

Momentarily fancying it was a ghost, she realised it was actually an elderly lady, white haired and stooped.

Mrs Hollis came running up alongside Lily carrying a candle. "Oh Nanny Noakes, it's very late, let me help you back to your room. Was there something you needed?"

The old woman didn't respond but fixed Lily with a beady eye.

"Forgive me, my lady, not to have made introductions." The housekeeper was apologetic. "This is Nanny Noakes, whom I spoke of to you before. Nanny Noakes, this is his Lordship's wife, Lady Westford."

Nanny Noakes was apparently unimpressed by this. "My regards to you," she said to Lily, using no proper form of address. Not that Lily minded. The old nurse seemed befogged, as the elderly so often became.

Mrs Hollis managed to escort her back up the stairs and hurry her away down a corridor. Lily wondered if Nanny Noakes frequently wandered about the house at night, carrying no light with her. She was concerned that the old woman might stumble in the darkness and fall.

Still, there was nothing that she could do at present and Mrs Hollis seemed to have her well in hand. Lily determined to pay her a visit the next day. While Nanny Noakes may have been a servant, Lily had gained the distinct impression that she, despite being mistress of the house, was the one who was expected to pay her respects.

***

Lily had no idea how marital affairs worked. Her mother had died in Lily's infancy and her father had never given her a stepmother. She knew that Sir Robert and Lady Maud had adjoining chambers but had no idea how or when the door might be opened between them.

She assumed the man would make the approach. Would he knock? What if she fell asleep, should she try to stay awake for him? What if he didn't come? Did men always require to pay their attentions, or was it only on occasion?

Amid this uncertainty she slipped on her nightgown, delighted to find that the fire still burnt in her room, a wonderful luxury. She felt a pang of conscience that she was enjoying these things while Betsy was probably shivering in a tiny cottage somewhere in far less comfort. She must write to her tomorrow, she had Anne Carter's address written down. Any letter would of course need to be addressed to Miss Carter, not Betsy.

Lily dismissed Sarah who had attended to her disrobing and brought her fresh water and other items.

"Sleep well, my lady. Don't hesitate to call if there is anything you need."

Lily slid into her new bed. It was as comfortable it had looked, with fresh, clean linens, a warm quilt and downy pillows. She was still thinking about the letter. She must seal it very carefully, for if anyone peeked at its contents - given what she planned to write - it would be disastrous.

Perhaps if she genuinely wrote it as though to Anne it would be safer. She could still impart what she needed to by maintaining a literary pretence of being Betsy. Until she was more certain of how things might eventually stand it would be far wiser to be cautious. She would try to write in such a way that Betsy could read between the lines, and hopefully reply to her in similar form.

You can't get away with this forever, a small voice told her. At some point, someone was going to recognise one of the cousins and expose them. Or worse, her aunt and uncle might eventually visit Westford Park.

The prospect of this was so horrific that Lily could hardly bear to countenance it. For them to come and discover their impoverished niece taking the place of their daughter - no, it could not happen. How she would avoid it she knew not, other than that she must.

As these thoughts kept her from sleep there was a knock at her door.

The Marquess, her husband, entered.

8. The awakening

She was still awake. For this Gervase was relieved for the girl had seemed tired by the end of supper and he had not wished to disrupt her sleep.

Even though, given the ardour he felt for her, it would have been a sore temptation.

"Elizabeth." He used her name for the first time. By the light of the candle on her nightstand he saw the apprehension in her eyes.

"Do not be afraid. As I have said, I regret our misunderstanding of last night. What happened was not… how it should have been between us."

"My lord."

"Tonight I would like to show you how it can be between husband and wife. I will not cause you pain, Elizabeth."

He saw the conflict on her face: anxiety mixed with a desire to trust him.

"My lord, I… I am willing."

He had not directly asked for her consent though she had given it to him.

As Gervase lifted the bedclothes to lie with her, seeing her slender form beneath the thin fabric and smelling her faint rose scent, he knew that it was going to take all his control not simply to ravish her again.

It was no more than the scheming minx deserved, a darker part of his mind told him. But she had after all been a maiden, and could not have known the full bargain she was making when she took part in her parents' devious plans.

If they were to remain together, he would prefer mutual enjoyment from their nuptials. His original plans to shun her bedchamber and make this a marriage in name only had dissolved the moment he first tasted her sweetness.

He ran a hand over her breast through her nightgown and she trembled at his touch. He caressed it, swirling his thumb over her nipple. Lily half-closed her eyes and Gervase correctly interpreted this as arousal already beginning in her. She was responsive to him, he could say that much. It would make tonight and future nights easier for them both.

He kissed her gently, tenderly, opening the kiss and trying to encourage her to explore him as he explored her. His lips moved down her neck and over her breastbone. In a smooth movement he loosened and lowered the neck of her gown, cupped her breast in his hand and brought his mouth down upon it.

Slowly, languorously, suckling and teasing her.

His other hand slipped low, below the hem of the gown, travelling up her thighs to feel between them. She started when he touched her there; he hoped it was not from pain. Trying to be as careful as possible with his touch he felt the heat and wetness that was already there.

He desired to take her, but he also wanted to draw this out. Releasing her breast he worked her gown down, pulling it past her legs so she lay fully naked before him.

He kissed her again, back down her neck and over her stomach. Then lower.

Lily, trusting herself to his embraces, was uncertain what he was doing. She adored the feel of his lips on her body but where was he moving to? Surely he could not... but she felt his hands gently but firmly move her thighs apart and then his head was between them.

Why would someone do this? But when she felt his mouth over her most sensitive place, she knew. She could not restrain a cry as his tongue swirled over the crest at the core of her sensation.

He slid one finger inside her and though she initially tensed, she found that it did not hurt and was able to relax again.

He teased her like this for what seemed like ages. Her breathing grew rapid. She clutched the sheets in her hands, she wanted to clutch his dark hair but did not dare.

As he brought her over the edge she cried out, involuntary sounds that told him he had fully succeeded in his efforts. Not that it felt like any effort to do this to her, he could have tasted her for hours.

With any other woman Gervase would have moved up and plunged inside, taking his own pleasures, but he sensed it was still too soon for this one. He could wait one more day.

He had intended to return to his own chamber for sleep but chose to hold her for a while.

When he awoke the next morning he was astonished to find himself still there, his arms wound around his sleeping wife. He was not a man who fell asleep easily or quickly.

He blamed it on the recent journey and other issues pressing on his mind. He could not let himself believe that he had been lulled to sleep by the warmth and sweetness of the girl he held.

***

Lily woke alone, wondering if she had dreamt that her husband had lain with her throughout the night. She also wondered whether she had dreamt of what he had done to her before she slept, but surely her imagination could not invent such things.

Tea was brought to her on a tray for which she was glad, since it meant she did not immediately have to go downstairs and could thus write her letter.

She had paper and ink with her, packed into her trunk specifically for this purpose. If she had had to request these items she might have been compelled to write her letter downstairs, with people hovering in the background. Lily wanted absolute privacy.

My dearest Anne, she began.

I am settled into my new husband's home and all is well. Westford Park is quite magnificent and I am being very kindly treated by everyone in the household.

She wrote this mainly in case someone intercepted the letter, though she truly thought that the house and grounds were beautiful, and had been glad of the kind attentions of Sarah and Mrs Hollis.

Our neighbours, whom I have not yet met, are a Sir Stephen Seton of Grantlings and Lady Leominster, a widow, who resides at Leominster Hall. In all the whirl and blur of the Season I fear I may have met these people but their faces escape me. I am so often hopeless with names as you know, Anne dearest.

Lily underlined "hopeless with names" hoping that Betsy would realise what she was asking. She needed to know if she was supposed to have made the acquaintance of these people. God forbid that Betsy had met them because the ruse would be quickly unravelled if so.

I am not sure when my other belongings will be arriving I fear my husband will quickly tire of the few gowns I have with me!

Please understand this and somehow arrange for more clothes to be sent to me, she prayed. Surely Betsy would read between the lines: Lily would never write anything this vapid and foolish in the normal course of events.

She regretted not accepting more of Betsy's generosity at the time. But she had taken nothing but the muslin and the pearl hair ornament, having felt too guilty with everything else to take Betsy's other proffered clothes. How foolishly short-sighted she had been!

Yours with all my fondest love,

Elizabeth Dainard.

Here she nearly wrote "Cosgrove" and blotted the ink in changing the C to a D. Elizabeth Dainard. It looked well, but she felt a pang at the loss of her father's name. It was one of her last links to him.

Lily folded the letter and went downstairs to find Mrs Hollis. She realised she had no idea where to go. The only rooms she had seen so far were the dining room, her bedroom and the hall.

Uncertain what to do she lingered in the hall and was relieved to see the steward, James Pelham, arrive.

"Can I be of service, my lady?"

"I wished to speak with Mrs Hollis."

"I will have her brought to you. You might prefer to wait in the morning room, my lady. It is this way."

Pelham ushered Lily to a charming room at the end of the house, with windows to both the south and east. The day was overcast but the room was still wonderfully light. It was decorated in yellow and light green and looked to be very much a woman's room. She noticed a small bureau in the corner where she hoped she might find sealing wax.

She had just sealed the letter as Mrs Hollis arrived. "'Good morning, my lady."

Lily greeted her likewise. "Mrs Hollis, if it would not disrupt your duties, I wondered if you might take me on a brief tour of the house. I was not sure of Lord Westford's schedule." She broke off, hoping she had not exposed herself in some manner. Whose duty should it be to show her around her new home?

"By all means. It would have been done yesterday but for the hour of your arrival. I was sorry to learn of the difficult weather for your journey. It is, as you have seen, a house of some size and best viewed in daylight."

Lily expressed thanks and the housekeeper continued.

"At this hour Lord Westford usually visits the estate, and conducts his other affairs after breakfast with his secretary and estate manager, Mr Duncan Ross."

He sounded safe enough. Scottish, Lily presumed. It was the neighbours who worried her.

9. The tour

Mrs Hollis showed Lily around the main areas of the house. The west wing was closed off at present as repairs needed to be carried out to the roof. "The work should be carried by the end of next month. The ballroom is in the west wing, and occupies two storeys with a gallery above. It suffered some water damage from a recent storm," she informed her.

The east wing and central section of the house were ample enough to visit for now. The wings stretched back from the house, forming a courtyard with a fountain at its centre. Trellises of rose and wisteria surrounded it and clipped box hedges were planted in a geometric pattern. It was lovely and Lily said so.

Mrs Hollis looked pleased. "Her Ladyship - that's his Lordship's late mother - had the trellises planted. She preferred to sit and read there in fine weather than stay indoors. You'll find it nicely sheltered from the wind, my lady."

The more they saw the more Lily burned with questions about the Marquess and his life, questions that she could never ask the housekeeper. He was her husband but he was an absolute mystery to her, just as she was to him. Even more so in her case, due to the deception she had practised upon him.

All these people were so kind to her. How they would shun her if they knew.

Mrs Hollis indicated the position of the library and the Marquess's study but did not open the door to either room. They climbed the stairs to the landing where Lily had seen Nanny Noakes the previous night.

She mentioned this and the housekeeper wavered, as if considering something.

"If it wouldn't be too much trouble, my lady, it would be a great kindness if you could look in on Nanny Noakes. She doesn't see so many visitors these days, except when Mr Farrington is here."

Lily replied that she would be only too delighted to visit the elderly servant.

The housekeeper led them both down the corridor that led off to the left and knocked gently on a door before opening it.

"Nanny Noakes, Lady Westford has come to see to you."

The old woman looked as mild as milk today, sitting in an armchair by her window with a large piece of knitting. She looked like a benevolent old grandmother, Lily thought.

"You'll forgive me for not rising, Lady Westford, but the stiffness has come upon my limbs this past hour," Nanny Noakes said.

Lily assured her that it did not matter, and clasped the claw-like hand proffered.

"A new mistress for the house after all these years. You'll be getting me busy before long again, I expect."

Lily blushed and Mrs Hollis stepped in, gently chiding the old woman. "Now, now, Nanny Noakes. Shall I have Mary bring you some of your tonic?"

Outside the room Mrs Hollis apologised to Lily. "Her mind wanders sometimes these days, and she can be outspoken. No harm is meant by it. She forgets what she says soon afterwards. '

Lily, who the previous night had admittedly considered the old woman addled, had been left today with the distinct impression that she was as sharp as a tack. But she felt sympathy for her ailments and resolved again to visit her when she could.

* * *

Lily was reunited with the Marquess at breakfast. There could be little intimate conversation between them as Mr Duncan Ross also joined them.

Lily had wondered if he might be a young man, or no more than the Marquess's age. But he looked to be in his fifties, spare of build, with red hair speckled with grey. From his voice she had at least been correct in surmising his Highland origins.

She might expected to have felt ill at ease with the two men but the atmosphere was companionable and the Marquess and Mr Ross talked of general matters, from which Lily was not excluded in understanding. The expected weather, the repairs to the west wing which she already knew of, and a new winter crop that some of the farmers were trying this year.

As they finished the repast, the two men prepared to retire to the Marquess's study to carry out their business. Lily plucked up her courage just after Mr Ross went first out of the room.

"My lord, I thought I might take a turn around the grounds this afternoon."

The Marquess looked almost surprised, perhaps not having realised that his bride had been left at a complete loss for something to do. Sarah had taken care of her sewing and she had no fine embroidery to occupy herself with. She had none of the small duties that her aunt had endlessly required of her. Nor was there anyone else to whom she might write a letter. Mrs Hollis had already put her letter to Anne Carter and Betsy with the other correspondence to be sent out. Everyone else in the house was busy with their own tasks.

Other than read the books she had brought, Lily faced nothing but idle hours until supper.

"By all means. Would you prefer to ride or walk? Do you ride?"

"I do ride, my lord, but I would be happy to walk today." She wanted to explore the lake and the island, and doubted she could cross the bridge on horseback. She suspected it would be a narrow and ornamental affair.

The grass was thick and damp around the lake and the hem of her gown was soon soaked. But it was merely water, not mud, so it would dry. She discovered that the trees near the water were an orchard of apple and pear and imagined how lovely their blossoms would be in spring. Now they were hung with fruit that was already starting to fall.

Lily plucked an apple and bit into it. It was more sour than it was sweet but the flavour was fragrant. Carrying it with her, she wandered the perimeter of the lake clockwise until she was at the far side, by the bridge.

As she had guessed it was a dainty affair but seemed in good repair. She walked over it and onto the small island, where she was delighted to find a bench tucked away from view beneath a willow. What a perfect place to sit and read on a hot summer's day! Even now, if she brought a warm shawl, it would be a delight to sit here.

Ducks swam past and she saw a rabbit leaping over the undergrowth. For a moment she allowed herself to delight that it was all hers: her own place, in her own house.

But the realisation that she was an impostor who had no real right to be here soon quelled her joy.

At the edge of the lake facing the house she stooped to pick up a shining duck feather, the iridescent blue of a mallard's wing. As she turned back up again to look towards the house, she thought she saw a swift movement from one of the windows. Despite the distance she felt sure it had been a face looking out at her and for some reason fancied it was Mrs Hollis. But why should the housekeeper be looking out upon her in a furtive manner?

Lily scolded herself. It was doubtless a trick of the light, or if it was a person, a mere coincidence that they should step away from the window the moment she turned towards that direction.

Still, she tried to memorise the position of the window. She found herself curious as to whose room it might be.

***

When Lily returned to the house later in the afternoon, she found the Marquess wishing to see her.

"I'm afraid I have urgent business to attend to in London. I'll need to leave before nightfall."

Lily was surprised to feel disappointment. She should have been relieved, she thought.

"You'll be in good hands here," he told her. "Ben in the stables will saddle a mount for you should you wish to ride. My library is also at your disposal. Mrs Hollis will be on hand for anything else you need."

Lily hadn't even seen the library yet but didn't mention this.

Keeping her expression neutral for she did not want him to think she minded him going, she said: "Travel safely, my lord."

He gazed at her and for a moment she thought he might kiss her but he nodded abruptly and departed.

She would be alone in her bedchamber tonight. After the wicked and wonderful things he had done to her the previous night, Lily found herself feeling some regret.

10. The absence

Gervase had no wish to disclose that his urgent business concerned his cousin, up to his neck in trouble once again. Damned idiot. He should be long past the follies of boyhood by now.

He was also reluctant to mention Tom's name to his wife, apprehensive of the reaction he might see there. They would meet again eventually, he supposed, and it would be a test for both of them.

Strange child. He had imagined a wife would spend her time parading about the place and pestering him and the servants. But the chit seemed to prefer hiding herself away with a book. He faced years of peace if such behaviour persisted.

He rather felt he might need to be the one distracting her.

As the coach carried him towards London - he had brought Duncan Ross with him, to attend to some other estate matters - the thought came to him that she may simply be avoiding him. After all, this marriage was but a scheme for her, a lucrative convenience. She had played her cards brilliantly, the little devil. He might almost admire such a stratagem except that he was the one ensnared by it.

***

Though her conscience nagged her, Lily found much to enjoy in the following days. Her lack of gowns and the shabbiness of those she did own no longer concerned her.

"I will take a supper tray in my room, now my lord is absent," she told Mrs Hollis and this appeared to meet with the housekeeper's approval.

She spent much of the daytime outside, save for a couple of rainy spells, for which she might be expected to wear an older gown anyway. She did possess a riding habit, one that Betsy had gratefully passed on to her as she disliked riding herself. Aunt Maud was not fond of horses and Sir Robert indifferent save for their function in conveying his carriage. So Betsy had not been raised with the same love of the animal that Lily had. Lily's father had been a keen horseman.

A fine bay mare was saddled for her, named Dido, and Lily was able to explore the parklands at her leisure.

The Marquess's library was a revelation to her. He had given her permission to use it, though she had at first felt a sense of intrusion on opening the door.

Once inside, she felt transformed. Her father's own library - for Edward Cosgrove had been a scholar as well as a soldier - was eclipsed by the Marquess's collection. There were endless volumes she had heard of and longed to read. But her uncle was uninterested in books and had not thought them worth the investment, let alone for a mere niece.

Lily was delighted to find a recent edition of the Metamorphoses of Ovid, and spent many hours lost in the myths of ancient times.

At times she had the sensation that someone was watching her, but who? All the servants seemed to be occupied with their various tasks. Pelham and Mrs Hollis were in the closest proximity to her, but she found their manner frank and respectful whenever she had dealings with them.

The little voice pricked at her. *It's your conscience,* it told her. *For you deserve none of this.*

Towards the end of the week she received a letter from Betsy, addressed to The Most Honble. The Marchioness of Westford.

While it brought her some peace of mind regarding the neighbours of Westford Park, she found it worryingly unguarded and was concerned at her cousin's distressed tone. There was little attempt made to present the writer convincingly as the former governess, and anyone intercepting it would have been bewildered by some of its contents.

Dearest Lily,

The days pass slowly here and we wait anxiously for any news. I am sure that you will send any as soon as you hear anything of special interest to us. ["special interest" was underlined carefully].

I do not know what is become of your gowns if they are not yet sent. Your father [here, "your" was hastily scrawled over what had begun as "my"] *may consider that your husband has furnished you with new ones.*

Regarding Sir Stephen Seton and Lady Leominster, I do not remember your mentioning either such person on your return from London earlier this year. It is possible that you were pointed out to them, but no formal introductions were made.

Lily dearest, do write soon and let us know immediately any news that you hear [there was again much underlining here]. *It becomes more and more unbearable waiting and waiting for the news that I long for.*

Your fondest friend [one could detect that "cousin" had been begun, overwritten by "friend"]

Anne Carter.

Lily decided that it would be best to destroy the letter. She was glad of its assurance that Betsy was probably not known to either Sir Stephen or Lady Leominster. Even if Betsy had been pointed out to them across a room, a mistake could be claimed.

***

Sarah returned from visiting her friend Ellen burning with some quite scandalous gossip about her Ladyship. She could scarce believe it. Her Ladyship seemed such a good and gentle girl, but there it was.

Ellen was very thick with Lady Leominster's French maid, Marie, who neither knew nor cared that a lady's maid closes her ears and seals her lips when it comes to the tittle tattle of her lady's circle. Thus whenever Marie and her mistress returned from a visit to London, Marie was always brimming with news which was soon passed to Ellen and eventually Sarah.

It was through Marie that Sarah and Ellen knew all about Mr Farrington and his wicked ways, and the Marquess's troubles on his behalf. Not that Sarah was unduly surprised by this for Mr Farrington had a gleam in his eye that warned a girl to beware of such a gentleman.

Her Ladyship though, that was something else. Sarah thought of the young Lady Westford. She was inclined to believe that there must be some truth in it, for Marie's information rarely erred. Sarah didn't believe all her stories, in particular her "secret" that she was an escaped French aristocrat, for in Sarah's view the lady's maid didn't have very ladylike ways.

But this piece of scandal had an uncomfortable credibility to it. As shocked as she was, Sarah found it hard to condemn her new mistress. She herself had allowed Ben to steal a kiss with her in the stables once or twice, though she had refused further liberties until the banns were read. It was unwise for a woman to trust a man too far, for it was never the men who suffered the consequences.

Poor Lady Westford. Sarah felt a welling of sympathy for her and determined to hold her own tongue on the matter. Mrs Hollis didn't approve of gossip anyway, and Sarah feared being given her notice if she was deemed to be scandalmongering.

***

Until now Lily had avoided riding too close to the boundaries of Westford Park, as Ben had mentioned that she might meet their neighbour out riding of a morning.

Today she let Dido lead her to the upper ground, to open fields where Ben typically exercised the mare when there was no one else to ride her. The Marquess's preferred mount was a black stallion named Orion. Lily had seen him in the stables. He was one of the largest horses she had ever seen.

Lily was a natural horsewoman, feeling as she did an empathy with the creatures. She had no fear herself and she was patient. Dido mounted the hillside and broke into a gallop when they reached the plateau.

It was exhilarating. All her fears, troubles and guilt were suspended for now. Lily knew only the power and grace of the horse, the rhythm of her gallop and the wind that braced and invigorated them both.

If only this could be for always, she thought, I could be perfectly, utterly content. If all she had in the world was food, shelter and a mare such as Dido, she would want for nothing.

Then the memory of the Marquess's attentions in her bed stole into this image and flushed deeper roses in her cheeks than the wind had caused to bloom.

Some company might be a welcome addition to her otherwise solitary vision.

As she turned the mare to ride back towards Westford Park, another rider appeared from the western side. She guessed at once that it was Sir Stephen. He was perhaps a few years older than the Marquess, with long sideburns and a pleasant countenance.

"I have the pleasure of meeting Lady Westford, do I not?" he greeted her, smiling.

"And I, likewise, our neighbour Sir Stephen Seton?"

Lily suddenly realised she was riding astride and felt embarrassment. She knew that it flouted convention but her father had taught her this way so she could more easily keep pace with him. His own mother had suffered injury falling from side-saddle and he disliked it. "The women of the ancient world rode astride, Lily, and who are we to condemn their custom?"

So Lily, alone as she was in the house, had requested that Ben saddle Dido conventionally.

Perhaps guessing her discomfiture, Sir Stephen remarked upon it. "I see you ride in the progressive style, Lady Westford. Let us hope you set a fashion. I would that more of your sex likewise chose a safer seat, and were spared the many tumbles and injuries they presently suffer."

"Here in the country, I had not expected to encounter anyone," Lily said to explain herself. She realised it delivered the impression that she rode sidesaddle in town, when in truth she was never in town and did not ride there sidesaddle or otherwise.

"I must apologise for intruding on your excursion," Sir Stephen said. His eyes held a friendly light.

"It is I who should beg your forgiveness, sir, for I fear I trespass upon your land," Lily said.

The neighbour smiled. "The dividing line runs some yards to the east of here, so as yet you remain within the estate of Westford Park. But I beg you to discount the boundary, as both Lord Westford and I frequently do. The horses enjoy the greater freedom."

Lily thanked him.

"Lord Westford does not ride with you today?" Sir Stephen asked. "I have not seen him this past week."

"He was called to London on urgent business."

Sir Stephen, knowing well the smooth running of the Marquess's estate and the unlikelihood of his needing to travel to the capital for business related to it, correctly surmised the true reason. There was one cause which saw Westford not infrequently hasten to London, and it was certainly not broken culverts nor the repair of labourers' cottages.

He made no comment however. Scandal related to this hasty marriage had of course reached his ears, but he found nothing to condemn in the person or manner of the young woman before him. He was also of a liberal mindset and aware of society's uneven censure of the participants in these matters.

There was Farrington, as free to roam and raise the breeze as before, and there was this girl who faced ruin had Westford not done what he had done.

Looking at her though, he felt the same surprise as the Marquess that such an intelligent creature should have swooned at Farrington's addresses. Still, these young chits thrust into the Season and the company of young men for the first time might easily have their heads turned.

As he departed, he even found himself musing that Westford even owed gratitude to his cousin for unearthing such a jewel.

11. The neighbour

The new Marchioness of Westford was not what Lady Leominster expected, based on descriptions she had been given of her. When she deigned to visit towards the end of the week, aware that Westford was away and intending to take her own stock of his bride, she had had a clear picture in mind of the article in question.

"Pretty enough, rather vapid," had been the general consensus among those of her circle who had met the piece last season. Elizabeth Cosgrove had not distinguished herself from the crowd of debutantes by her wit or her beauty: any fame was solely derived from her disgrace.

This notoriety made it all the more irksome to Lady Leominster that the hussy had managed to thwart her plans.

Having finally buried Leominster last winter, her late husband having been some decades her senior, the widow had considered her path now clear to her richer and greatly more handsome neighbour. Indeed, even without the attraction of his purse, the attractions of his person might have been enough to engage her affection.

But now there was this bizarre and hasty marriage, reportedly conceived from some misguided notion of honour. Why the Marquess should consider it incumbent upon himself to serve as his cousin's scapegoat, Lady Leominster knew not. That rapscallion Farrington should have been brought to account and made to marry the girl, not Westford.

She would have easily contrived such a thing herself. Men were ultimately fools, Lady Leominster had always thought. Now here was Westford bound to a girl who was vastly his inferior in rank, assets and reputation, and Lavinia Leominster forced to retain her widow's weeds.

So it was with some surprise that she eventually beheld his bride, having finally deigned to call on her after curiosity got the better of her.

Far from the silly bit of muslin described, she found a young woman with a quiet dignity, an uncommon beauty, and most unexpectedly, a keen intelligence. Lady Leominster, no fool herself, was quick to appreciate this last quality in others of her sex.

Lily received her in the morning room and accepted her congratulations on the marriage.

"Lady Leominster, how very kind of you to call. Won't you be seated? Will you take some tea?" Lily nodded to Mary, the tweeny who was enjoying promotion to parlourmaid while Sarah occupied herself with her new mistress.

"Lord Westford is not presently at home?" Lady Leominster knew already from her sources that he was not. She suspected, and hoped, that there may already be marital discord.

"He is in town on business."

"I am sorry to hear that he has abandoned you so soon, he must be thoroughly scolded when he returns! And he must bring you to dine at Leominster Hall."

As Lady Leominster made the invitation her sharp eye caught the title of a book on nearby table. Gracious, was the girl some kind of bluestocking? From the little she knew of the girl's parentage - Sir Robert and Lady Maud did not enjoy the highest esteem in society - she struggled to imagine why their daughter would be immersing herself in the speeches of Cicero.

"Have you travelled to this part of the country before?" she asked Lily, suspecting that the answer would be in the negative. "You are not from here, I believe?"

"I am not, my lady. My father's estate lies in the west of the country, some twenty miles from Bristol."

"I trust that our county does not suffer too much in comparison with the charms of Somerset?" Lady Leominster asked her.

Lily felt the other woman's tone rang false. There had been a distinct note of sarcasm on the word "charms". "Most certainly not. From the little I have so far seen of Hampshire, it is very lovely indeed."

"Do you ride?"

"I do, my lady."

"And do you play, or sing?"

"Only a little. Not so well as to perform in company, I am afraid," Lily said.

She found it hard to warm to Lady Leominster. The woman was handsome and clever with ostensibly excellent manners, yet there was something about her that Lily disliked. Inwardly she scolded herself since the older woman had been assiduously polite and it had been courteous of her to call.

For her part, Lady Leominster was hoping that this chit might fall of her horse and be done for. She found it increasingly difficult to bear that such a young and comely young woman had usurped the position she felt was her own due. What could she possibly have in common with a man like the Marquess? It was intolerable. She decided to discount the Cicero. As like as not the girl was feigning to read it to impress her husband, or had mistaken it for a novel.

Well, he had married most unwisely, even under duress, and as he inevitably wearied of the superficial charms of his bride's youth and prettiness, he would greatly regret his rashness. This was the scant balm that assuaged Lady Leominster's ire as the maid brought tea and she was forced to grit her teeth and continue to make polite conversation with the new marchioness.

***

Feeling out of sorts after Lady Leominster's visit, and even more vexed that she would need to return the call the following week, Lily decided to make a visit of her own choosing.

Plucking some bright autumn daisies, she went to see old Nanny Noakes.

The eyes were beadier today. They followed the flowers as Lily put them in a vase on the small side table, but the old woman said nothing.

It fell to Lily to encourage conversation.

"Mrs Hollis tells me that you looked after both Lord Westford and his cousin," she said.

The beady gaze grew a little softer. "Young Master Tom."

"You must have fond memories of those days," Lily encouraged her. She admitted to herself being a little curious about the Marquess's boyhood. What had he been like?

"Such a young lad he was, Master Tom. The finest little fellow." There was a cackle of laughter. "The mischief he got up to! Never was there such a one."

Lily would have preferred to hear about her husband than his cousin, but she indulged Nanny Noakes by attending politely as the elderly woman chuckled over past reminiscences. She had clearly adored her last charge.

Many of the tales of Tom Farrington's boyhood did little to endear him to Lily. The picture painted was of a spoilt and unruly child, pampered by nurse and mother, with his "mischief" frequently bordering on acts of cruelty to both servants and animals.

It did not amuse Lily to hear such stories. Even had the young man in question not been her cousin's seducer, they were not to her taste. But any time she tried to turn the talk to the Marquess's boyhood, the elderly woman started relating yet another exploit of his cousin's.

"It's the way with young men, of course. They must have their wild ways." She fixed a sharp eye on Lily. "Sow their oats, as they say."

Lily was taken aback. Was the old servant trying to insinuate something to her? Surely she could not be aware of the incident with Betsy, or so indiscreet as to suggest that she did know?

But Nanny Noakes gave another cackle. "They settle down as and when they have to, and he's the heir of Westford. One day he'll walk in his Lordship's shoes, prouder and finer than all before him."

The old woman was growing misty eyed again, clearly unaware that she was speaking to a significant obstacle in Tom Farrington's hopes. Lily felt it wiser to humour the old woman. It seemed less than likely that this elderly creature would outlive the Marquess anyway.

She felt sad for her. It was a cruel thing when the mind started to fail and she perceived that Nanny Noakes' wit had lost much of the sharpness of its former days. Let her have her memories and dreams, they cost nothing.

12. The invitation

Occupied as she was with the new Marchioness's mending, Sarah had not failed to notice the scant quantity of her gowns nor their age and state of repair.

She had imagined that the wife of a rich man such as the Marquess would have had trunks filled with fine robes, bejewelled and adorned with Parisian lace. Or that new clothes would be ordered for her soon after her marriage. Sarah had looked forward to these arriving for she shared with Ellen an appreciation of ladies' fashion, even though they could never hope to wear such finery themselves.

But no gowns came, new or old. Sarah mended and repaired as best she could but she was conscious that such old raiments scarce befitted a marchioness.

Unwisely she let these concerns slip to Ellen.

"They are very worn, my mistress's gowns," she told Ellen when she visited her friend one afternoon. Ellen was attempting to arrange Sarah's hair in a French style that Marie had used on Lady Leominster. Like Sarah, Ellen aspired to promotion as a lady's maid and to be proficient in the latest hair styling was requisite skill that both girls desired. "I wonder that his Lordship has not provided her with new."

Ellen, who had not yet seen the new marchioness, already felt some prejudice towards her as Lady Leominster's dislike had filtered down to her via Marie. "A stuck-up piece," Lady Leominster had remarked to a friend and this was repeated with spiteful delight by the French maid to the other servants.

"You can't mean she wears rags, a lady of her station!" Ellen said.

Sarah, realising already her folly in mentioning it, strove to redeem herself. "Lawks no. Everything is mended very carefully indeed, I'm sure you would hardly know it to look at her, and she is very fair."

"But she must have some handsome ballgowns," Ellen said.

"None as I've seen," Sarah admitted.

"Not one! Perhaps they're being sent from London?"

Sarah was uncertain. Privately she thought this was not the case, but she said: "I expect so." She saw the gleam in Ellen's eyes and regretted being so indiscreet.

But it was too late. Ellen, already feeling no slight envy over Sarah's temporarily improved position, found herself unable to hold her tongue. She and Marie fairly feasted over the information: imagine, such a nobly titled lady in patched attire! and it was not long before the phrase "much-mended Marchioness" reached Lady Leominster's ears.

What could be meant by it?

She recalled that the chit had been wearing a relatively plain gown the day she had called upon her, but the marchioness had not been expecting visitors and her husband was away.

A small darn had caught her eye, she now remembered. Lady Leominster herself disposed of her gowns after the slightest impairment but nonetheless she accepted that not every woman did so

When Lady Westford had returned the visit she had worn a muslin of some style, in which to Lady Leominster's chagrin she appeared irksomely becoming. But it must be admitted that it was not a new garment.

The widow's mind began to work. Could there be truth to these tales, that the lady in question be suffering some genuine deficiency in her wardrobe? Lady Leominster recalled to mind the scandal surrounding the Westford nuptials. Certainly there would have scarce been time to prepare her a trousseau.

The girl must have had gowns though, for the earlier Season. What had become of them? Some loss or accident?

Whatever the reason, the normal course of affairs would have been for Westford to take his bride with him to town and have her properly fitted out. But he had not done so, at least to Lavinia Leominster's knowledge.

Slyly she dropped mention of this into conversation with Marie, as the lady's maid was fixing some new lace to one of her mistress's own ballgowns. "This is very fine lace, my lady," Marie had commented, appreciating the delicate embroidery.

"Indeed. But we must not be shadowed by the finery of our new neighbour!" Lady Leominster gave a light, artificial laugh. She disliked feigning such a concern to Marie, for in truth she could not care less how her wardrobe compared to any other woman's, confident as she was of its superiority and the superiority of her own bearing.

Marie gave a sly smile. "There's no finery at all, my lady, so I have heard."

Lavinia Leominster pretended to dismiss this as jest. "Any marchioness will have a myriad of gowns. Whether she has stretched her husband's purse as far as scattering them all with diamonds, we await to see."

"She has not one ballgown, the Sarah girl says."

Pondering this, the widow dismissed her maid to send for some tea. It seemed unbelievable, outrageous, that the bride of a Marquess would own naught but a few, patched gowns!

Outrageous yet advantageous. Lady Leominster mentally cancelled her plans for a dinner and despite the outrageously short notice, instead decided on a full ball given in the new marchioness's honour. She would send out invitations forthwith.

***

What could Lily do? The invitation lay on the tray that Pelham had placed before her. It was a thing of dread.

The Marquess was still away and she had had no word from him. Perhaps if he remained away… she could surely not attend alone?

It was impossible. Betsy's muslin might have done for a dinner, with a little trimming, but to appear at a ball in half dress? It could not be done. She did not cower from adversity for her own sake but she was conscious that she was not the equivalent of a Duke's daughter. Such a female might sport breeches at dinner and set a new fashion, for all she wished.

But Lily could not disgrace her husband's title. She had already done him a great wrong, now she must at least try to do what was right.

The invitation was not the only item troubling her that day. There was another letter from Betsy, sounding increasingly frantic. Lily was vexed at her cousin's impatience. Surely she had not expected the immediate reappearance of Tom Farrington at Westford Park? After all Mr Farrington presumably believed, as everyone else did, that his cousin had just married his lover.

Lover. Lily feared far less flattering terms for what Betsy had made herself would be bandied about in society.

So she did not expect an imminent visit from Mr Farrington, quite the reverse. She wrote, as tactfully as she could, to relate this to Betsy.

My lord is still away on business. We do not presently expect company at Westford Park, though we have received many kind congratulations on our marriage. It is strange to think that the name Elizabeth Cosgrove must have been on the lips of people I have never even met.

She hoped her meaning would be clear to Betsy. Society believed that Elizabeth Cosgrove, daughter of Sir Robert

Cosgrove, was now married to the Marquess of Westford. Thus Tom Farrington must believe likewise.

***

"I understand our neighbour Lady Leominster is to delight us with a ball, and in your honour," Sir Stephen Seton said to Lily as they met riding two days later. It was a fine morning, the sun already burning the silvered dew off the grass.

"Indeed." Lily was rather at a loss for what to say. "It is very kind of her."

Sir Stephen perceived her fears but misread their cause. "It is no easy thing, I imagine, to be presented with so many new friends and neighbours in one fell swoop."

No easy thing indeed, dressed with less occasion than a farmer's wife.

"You must think me very foolish," Lily said. From the few times she had met him riding, due to his easy manner and his close friendship with her husband, there was already a familiarity growing between them.

Sir Stephen thought quite the opposite but reserved his comment. "I must confess that I prefer the peace of my house and garden to a large social gathering. My neighbours doubtless consider me aloof but there it is. I have not a wife to compel me to conviviality, and can instead indulge my preference for solitude."

Lily laughed. "Your preference may well protect you from finding such a wife, sir."

She wondered that he had not married. He was a kind and intelligent man, and Grantlings was a large estate. He didn't seem like a rake but then she had never met a rake, so how could she judge?

They had ridden further south than previously and from this vantage point Lily could see another house, which from its position must be Leominster Hall. It was interesting to see it from this height after having travelled there by carriage some days earlier.

She traced the route from the Hall to Westford Park, and as her view fell upon the road she felt herself grow tense.

There was the Marquess's carriage, drawn swiftly along by his four Cleveland Bays. Her husband had returned.

***

"I trust your journey was comfortable and without incident, my lord?"

Lily greeted her husband having ridden back from the hill as fast as Dido could carry her. The grooms were already busy unshackling the four horses from the carriage.

She tried to smooth back the tendrils of hair that escaped when she rode and hoped that her riding habit was presentable. There had been no time for her to go and dress: she met him in the hallway.

"It was without serious incident." His eyes ran over her and Lily felt the flush rise from her breast. This was not how she had planned to greet him.

"My lord, I must change from my riding habit. I regret that I was absent from the house on your arrival." It had been a mere matter of minutes but she was anxious that she had transgressed.

"I regret that my business took me away for so long. Indeed, Ross remains in London to complete certain affairs," he added, explaining the absence of the Scotsman. "But I am sure, as ever, that Westford Park has been in most capable hands."

Pelham, standing nearby, straightened at the compliment.

The Marquess turned back to Lily. "I will be in the library. Come there when you are ready."

With these words he dismissed her and Lily fled, grateful to return to her chamber. She had forgotten how tall and commanding he was.

Yet she found herself not unhappy that he was returned to Westford Park, even if might mean her easy leisure was at an end.

13. The gift

The Marquess found himself unsettlingly glad to see his young bride again. While he went about London trying to resolve the latest indiscretions of his cousin, he had tried to push the thought of his marriage from his mind.

He had not succeeded. And when he returned he found her sweeter and fairer than he even remembered. Perhaps something might be made of this marriage, if and when she no longer hankered after Farrington.

The trouble this time had been a Spanish dancer, temperamental and threatening blackmail when she discovered she was cast aside for a younger woman, the wife of an Earl.

Standing with his back to the fireplace, Gervase thought of these things with exasperation. Why could Tom not confine himself to the bawdy house where the women held no such expectations? He must put a stop to this for once and for all.

Tom Farrington had fled, allegedly to friends in Sussex, as soon as he had got wind that his cousin was arrived in London. Thus Gervase had not even had the opportunity to confront him. Or pick him up by the scruff of his neck and shake him, something he sorely longed to do.

There had been the usual heavy gambling debts as well. At some point Gervase would be forced to abandon him to the Fleet. A spell within its walls might be the only remedy for his ills.

He had left the library door open so his wife entered without knocking. "My lord."

Gervase gestured for her to approach him, which she did.

"I trust that you have been well here, and that all your needs have been furnished," he said.

"Certainly so."

"I have a present for you." He saw the surprise and interest in her eyes, which grew as he handed her the slim volume. "It is a new edition of Theocritus. I did not know if you owned a copy, but you were reading the Eclogues of Vergil, which as you may know derive some aspects from these."

The girl was looking at the book and back at him with the same rapture as if he had made her a gift of fine jewels or pearls.

"I had not read Theocritus, though I had longed to. This is such a kindness on your part."

Her eyes were shining and Gervase felt but one desire at that moment, which could not be fulfilled in the library. Not with the door open, anyway.

"I learn that Lady Leominster is holding a ball to welcome you to the neighbourhood. This a very great honour," Gervase said.

For some reason his bride paled at this. She looked uneasy.

"I fear that I cannot go. I do not wish to inconvenience Lady Leominster, but I am very much afraid that I will be unwell."

Gervase felt a spark of anger. As his wife, she would surely not shirk her social obligations.

"You will indeed attend, madam. I see that you are in excellent health at this present time, with no reason for a deterioration in your state by the morrow. Let us have candour as to the true source of your reluctance."

"I would not wish to disgrace you, my lord."

Gervase assumed she referred to her own social disgrace. "It falls on you to redeem your reputation, Elizabeth. I have given you what rank and respectability I can. There is a price and a penance we must all pay for our follies. But I trust that no one would be so discourteous as to remind you of yours."

"It is not that." Lily summoned her courage and looked him directly in the eye. "I am reluctant to trouble you with this, but I have no suitable gown."

He was bemused. "No gown! You must have a dozen that would do." Surely any woman did? Particularly one that had so recently attended the Season and spent her time courting the attentions of young men.

"Whether by some accident or mishap, I know not what, I have but the few items I travelled here with, my lord."

Gervase remembered the lightness of the trunk. "That single trunk?"

Lily nodded.

"And nothing suitable among them?"

"I am afraid not."

Gervase was at something of a loss. Growing up without sisters, and never before having a wife let alone daughters, he had had no idea about nor interest in woman's fripperies. It began to occur to him that there may have been some deficiency in his own duty to his wife in this regard. On the rare occasions he visited his club in London and heard a gentleman groaning about a dressmaker's bill, he closed his ears. He was nonetheless vaguely aware that a man was supposed to furnish his wife with suitable attire.

"I suppose you could not borrow one?"

He saw from the horror on her face that this was an impossibility. The only likely candidate for a loan would be Lady Leominster, and one could hardly make such a request of the hostess without incurring shame and even derision, should anyone discover it. He wanted that neither for himself nor his bride.

"Then we will send for a seamstress and have one made."

"I do not think it can be done in a day."

"If a gown is needed by tomorrow evening, a gown will be made." He had no idea how, but surely stitching together one item of clothing need not take a week?

Lily bit her lip. If it could not be done, she would have to be excused attendance.

Gervase summoned Pelham and instructed him to have a needlewoman conveyed to Westford Park first thing the next morning. It was not a request that Pelham had ever been issued with before, but he set the wheels in motion accordingly.

***

Lily knew her husband must visit her that night, and she was half excited and half afraid.

Much as the Marquess seemed to distrust and dislike her much of the time - and she could not blame him for that - he had shown her a tenderness when he had lain with her the first night at Westford Park.

She bathed, letting the warm water relax her, using a soap scented with rose and lavender that she hoped would leave her skin fragrant.

She wasn't sure if it was seemly to want his attentions as much as she did, and she was sure that she should at least attempt to conceal it. After all people continually spoke disparagingly of "wanton" women.

But his earlier caresses had awoken an appetite in her that was as strange it was wonderful. Even if it was perhaps not her moral right to sate it.

She dried herself on the fresh linen that Sarah had laid out for her. Lily had told the maid to go to bed as she could manage her bedtime routine herself. She still hadn't become used to having someone attending her every need, never having had such assistance before.

Now she stood before the still-lit fire, already dying down to embers. Before she had even managed to put her nightgown on there was a light knock at the door and her husband entered.

Gervase drew in his breath looking at her there, illuminated by the soft glow. Her modesty was barely concealed by the fine linen she held against her.

"Let it fall," he commanded.

His tone was thick with heat but not harsh and Lily complied. She felt some self-consciousness standing there entirely naked. But he had seen all of her before and she trusted him.

Gervase drank her in. She was flawless. He simply wanted to make love to her. He had planned a longer seduction and education, following on from their previous encounter when he had managed to hold back from even penetrating her. But she must be long healed from his regrettable exertions on their wedding night, and he doubted his ability to hold back again.

He went up to her and took her in his arms. For now, all thoughts of her previous behaviour and her family's deceptions were dismissed from his mind. He would enjoy her - they would enjoy one another - just as they were.

His lips came down on hers and he kissed her long and tenderly, feeling his passion awakening in her as her arms wrapped around his body.

He broke off and took a step back. "Undress me. I want you know my body as I wish to know yours."

Lily bit her lip, hesitating. He wore only his shirt and buckskin breeches and she could surely not start with those. She reached up to the buttons at the top of his shirt. Her shaking fingers made unbuttoning difficult at first and she could not look at his face.

But she persisted. Once loosened at the neck, she lowered her hands to push the fabric up and he helped her, lifting it over his head. The firm muscles of his broad chest were before her and she could smell the heat and masculinity of his skin.

As if knowing she wanted to touch him but did not dare, Gervase instructed her. "Touch me, Elizabeth."

Lily put her hands on him and moved them smoothly over his body, up from his waist to where the dark hair spread on his chest.

For Gervase it was a struggle not to flinch at the sensation of her hands on his body. He had to brace himself: every muscle in his body tightened as he longed to grasp her and throw her on the bed. Her unschooled touch was the single most arousing thing he could remember. "Look at me," he ordered.

She raised her eyes to meet his. He saw the anxiety there and interpreted it correctly. "You need have no fear about touching the body of your own husband. Now unfasten the rest."

There were only his breeches left. Lily managed to undo them though she knew not how. To touch a gentleman in this way - husband or not - seemed so far removed from propriety that she struggled with it.

Gervase was suddenly struck by how young she was. She was far too young a bride for him: were it not for the circumstances of her former dalliance he would never have sought a wife so much younger than himself. He would never have sought a bride at all, truth be told. He had closed the book - or so he had believed - on that chapter of his life with some firmness.

Yet here he was, with this girl barely out of the schoolroom, requiring her to be intimate with him as he would normally have expected a far more experienced lover to act. She was nervous, he could tell, though she showed courage.

And desire, he thought. He hoped. The flush of her skin, the way her lips parted, the way she melded to him when he embraced her. He tried not to think of her past but he supposed he might take comfort that it was at least some evidence of her ripeness and willingness for such activity.

He took her hand and enclosed it around his hardness, mentally trying to delay what his body seemed ever on the brink of doing when he was around her. She was bewitching. He assumed she knew it and employed it to her advantage but at this point he no longer cared about her past indiscretions.

Scooping her up in his arms he laid her on the bed, ensuring her position was comfortable. This time she moved her legs apart for him, knowing what he wanted from her.

Gervase wanted to be sure that she was ready. He felt between her for the slickness and heat that told him that her desire at least in part matched his. Gently he slipped a finger inside her, marvelling at the warm tightness. She was not entirely relaxed, he felt, but it did not seem to cause her pain.

He positioned himself against her and slowly, as carefully as he could, entered her. He had to rest there for several seconds not moving. Partly to allow her to become accustomed to him, but also because he feared he had about as much control over his body as a drunken young cub visiting his first bordello.

Then gradually, with infinite care and self-control that strained him beyond measure, he made love to his wife. He noted how her breathing changed. How her body relaxed beneath him. How her hips eventually rose to meet his, how she matched his rhythm.

How she cried out and shuddered around him out as he finally spilled his seed within her, in quite the sharpest and sweetest release he had ever known.

They were, Gervase thought, one flesh.

14. The gown

A seamstress was conveyed to Westford Park the next morning, as instructed. A woman from the nearby town, she brought with her an assistant and as many fine fabrics as might be necessary.

To be summoned the very day of a ball to begin a new gown! It was unprecedented.

But she was a smart woman, and luckily for Lily, one with an eye for style that transcended the usual requirements of her provincial clients.

Mrs Mead was her name, and were it not for the proposal of Mr Mead in her giddier girlish days, she might have tried her luck in London and done as well as any French modiste.

On seeing the new Marchioness for the first time she drew in her breath. Here was a privilege to cut cloth for! She had fretted on the way over about the impossibility of obtaining rich brocades and ornaments as might befit such a high titled lady, but seeing the young woman before her she knew that these would not be needed.

It should be white and with minimal adornment. The cut and line would do the work, and the perfect proportions of the slim figure within it.

Swiftly she ordered the assistant to unfold the lengths she needed. White silk, the finest muslin, a new and impossibly delicate net.

For Lily it was a dizzying morning. She was measured from top to toe, made to stand on a stool, measured again. Cloth was draped around her, cut, pinned. She grew weary but did not complain.

"I thank your Ladyship for your very great patience," Mrs Mead said. "It is only the circumstances that require such."

"It is very kind of you to have come at such short notice," Lily told her.

The seamstress had no expectations of future custom, for she assumed Lady Westford would patronise London dressmakers in the usual course of events. So she attempted no obsequiousness, nor was it in her nature to have done so.

Neither did she question the emergency nature of the commission. She had been given to understood that a planned gown had suffered some mishap, and if a Marchioness preferred a brand new ensemble rather than to wear one of her existing gowns, it was not Mrs Mead's place to remark upon it.

She and Lily shared a single goal: to create a gown suitable for a ball by nightfall. Lily's anxiety was perhaps the greater, for she alone knew that there was no other gown waiting in reserve.

It was a long day. Sarah was summoned to assist as well as Mary, who was assigned the seams of the under-layer as her needlework was not so fine as that of the others.

Lily, who had never before owned a ballgown, was astonished and felt some discomfort at the extent of work involved.

She even offered to assist but Mrs Mead would not hear of it.

Unable to help with the garment, Lily ensured that refreshments were regularly supplied to the workers. Conversation consisted of Mrs Mead's instruction to and gentle chiding of the girls. She spoke of different fabrics and their properties, and notorious mishaps from careless stitching. Draping in the Grecian style was one of her topics, and sewing sleeves in such a way as to allow for their easy removal and interchange with other styles for a subsequent social occasion.

Lily, listening in, found it illuminating. This seamstress knew all the ins and outs of her craft and the history of its creations. The novel use of coloured lace by a visiting French aristocrat, the diamonds prised from the bodice of a princess to be surreptitiously replaced with glass by a light-fingered sewing maid, and an unnamed Duchess who reportedly commissioned a gown made entirely of peacock feathers.

Mrs Mead herself scoffed at this one even as she told it, but the young servant girls and Lily were transfixed by her tales.

The labour of the day gave Lily something else to fix her mind on than the fast approaching ball. The fact was that she had never been to a ball before. She was fortunate at least in that a dancing instructor had been hired before Betsy's debut, and had taught both girls the current dances.

The day drew on, the shadows lengthened.

Finally the gown was completed, and Lily stepped into it. Afforded the advantage of continuous fittings, rather than initial measurements and occasionally a final session of adjustment, Mrs Mead's gown fitted Lily like a glove. It had effectively been sculpted around her body.

The starkness of it: the straightness of the neckline, the fall of the skirt, softened only by the wisp-thin net, was remarkable. Yet Lily understood what Mrs Mead was trying to achieve.

No other woman would have a gown like this. So flawlessly white, so neat in its line. Save for a scattering of tiny seed pearls on the bodice, it was entirely unadorned. There was no lace, no fussy embroidery nor intricate tambour work. There had not been time for that of course, but it was nonetheless a conscious choice of design by the talented seamstress to create the gown thus.

"I hardly know how to thank you," Lily said. "It is a miracle."

Mrs Mead was more than satisfied with the results though she remained modest. "You wear it more than well, my lady."

Sarah and Mrs Mead's assistant echoed their own praise.

Lily hoped that she might one day be in a position to order more gowns from Mrs Mead. Since she did not at present feel entitled to make demands on the Marquess's purse she was unsure if or when this might be.

She instructed Mrs Hollis to have a very good supper prepared for the women before they were driven back to the town. The housekeeper nodded her approval at this, gratified to find the new lady of the house so considerate of her servants' needs.

"I will instruct the cook forthwith," Mrs Hollis said. "May I also add my admiration, my lady, for how very well that gown becomes you and for Mrs Mead's not inconsiderable skill." She too had noticed the sparse wardrobe of the Marquess's new bride and was both glad and relieved for her that she would be suitably attired at the ball.

She held her opinions of the Marquess's role in all this to herself. He was a very well-liked and respected master, but men were men, and his obliviousness to his wife's needs were not a point in his favour. He had brought her back a book of all things! Much good would that do to hide the worn fabrics and their darns.

Westford Park had been without female presence for too long, Mrs Hollis thought. With the previous Lady Westford some decades dead, no sisters or female cousins, and his closest friend a bachelor, she considered the Marquess completely out of touch with feminine requirements. It was not her place to say anything but something, somehow, must be done about it.

***

Her first ball. Would anyone suspect her inexperience?

Lily tried to push these anxieties from her mind as Sarah helped dress her. The maid's clever styling of her hair impressed her, and Lily had it in the back of her mind to request that Sarah remained her maid. She knew she was probably expected to take on a more experienced lady's maid, perhaps a fashionable French girl like the one who attended Lady Leominster, but Lily felt comfortable with Sarah.

She also felt that they were in some ways learning the ropes of their new positions together. That this might make Sarah more sympathetic to - or even unaware of - Lily's own missteps.

The problem was that Lily felt she had no proper authority to make such a request. She still felt as though she had no real rights here, even in matters explicitly permitted to her by the Marquess.

Every time she entered his library she felt as though she were an intruder. He had granted the privilege of access to his wife, the woman he thought was Elizabeth Cosgrove, daughter of Sir Robert Cosgrove. But the woman currently trespassing in his home was a different Elizabeth.

And some day he must find out.

Tonight even, if - God forbid! - anyone there had met her cousin Betsy. Lily prayed that Betsy's conventionally pretty looks had helped her blur into the general crowd of debutantes. Someone might merely suppose that they themselves must be mistaken if the former Elizabeth Cosgrove did not match their memory of the girl of that name.

Sarah fastened Lily's stays, pulling them a little tighter than usual but not to the point of discomfort or shortness of breath. She did not need to. Quite apart from the fact that the gown was cleverly cut to give a willowy-slim line without tight corseting, Lily had lost weight since arriving at Westford Park. The exercise of riding each day combined with the nagging guilt that dulled her appetite had certainly done nothing to increase her already slender curves.

The maid had noticed the scarcity of Lily's jewellery but was too tactful to make any remark. Sarah had imagined that a marchioness would be dripping with gold and diamonds, adorned by her husband. But as with the lack of new gowns, neither new nor heirloom jewellery had made an appearance in Lily's jewel case.

Lily had a few items that had belonged to her mother. Alice Cosgrove had not been a woman of extravagant taste nor Edward

Cosgrove a man of extravagant purse, though both were discerning. As a result the pieces left to Lily were pretty and elegant but not lavish.

Happily the gown called for the lightest additions only. A large set of family jewels such as the Westford sapphires would have overwhelmed it. Sarah had not seen the sapphires in person but they featured in a portrait of the Marquess's mother.

Instead, a tiny pearl cross on a delicate chain completed Lily's outfit. Both girls were very satisfied with the result of the day's labours.

"It looks very well, my lady," Sarah said, referring to Mrs Mead's gown.

"It does. How fortunate we were to find that woman," Lily said. "And also for your very fine and quick work, Sarah."

Sarah reddened. "Thank you, my lady. I owe my mother for teaching me."

Lily felt a pang for the loss of her own mother. "She must be very talented. You must let me know if she is ever available for work." She knew that Sarah had numerous siblings, which must be a strain on any family. The chance to earn some extra money would likely be welcome.

Sarah's reaction vindicated Lily's suspicions. "Oh, my lady, she would be very pleased to be given work. She formerly took on mending for Lady Leominster, but Lady Leominster's own maid does that for her now."

Marie had welcomed this duty no more than Sarah's mother had regretted its loss. But for Lavinia Leominster it had been a mere matter of economy to deprive one woman of much needed income and burden another with extra work. How different, Sarah thought, was her own mistress. She felt very grateful to be employed at Westford Park rather than Leominster Hall.

15. The dance

She was a maiden of snow, a young swan of long, slender neck and pure white feathers. Even the Marquess, who had not yet seen the gown as Lily had worn a cloak in the carriage, found himself disconcerted by her appearance.

Every eye was upon her as she stepped into the ballroom of Leominster Hall. Most were startled, many envious. All of them curious.

Whatever rumours had reached their ears, and there had been much gossip over the sudden marriage and the scandal surrounding it, the star-like beauty of the girl in question had never been mentioned.

A beauty only enhanced by the purity and simplicity of her gown, its starkly elegant line flawlessly shaped to her figure. More than one who beheld the new Marchioness at once regretted the fussy lace and ornate foibles of her own attire.

Yet there she stood, more than a prize for any Marquess if not a Duke or Prince, on the arm of her tall husband who scowled at the assembly with a forbidding glare.

For Gervase found himself wracked with such a possessiveness as he had never in his life felt before. People stared upon his bride and he saw the blatant admiration in other men's eyes.

"I would hardly call her plain, Lavinia," one of Lady Leominster's intimates whispered in her ear, with private amusement at the hostess's ill-concealed fury.

Lavinia Leominster had never found it so challenging to maintain her composure. She gritted her teeth. Her hope of shaming the chit had utterly backfired.

Where could the girl have got such a gown? The Marquess had only returned yesterday. Had she owned it all along?

It was unlike any gown Lady Leominster had seen over the past Season.

If only she had stuck to her original plans for a small dinner party. Now she must play the gracious hostess, unable to dance due to her position and situation, while her rival was sought out by every male in the room.

Not that they would get far with Gervase's glare upon them.

"Lady Westford is something of a bluestocking," she said aloud as she introduced Lily to some other guests. "I have it on the best authority - my own eyes, indeed - that she devotes herself to the Classics at any spare opportunity."

"Your Ladyship flatters me," Lily said, knowing full well that Lady Leominster intended nothing of the sort. "I have a but a small knowledge of Latin and very little Greek."

"A scholar of such modesty as well!" The sarcasm was barely disguised but Lily gave a genuine laugh.

"Would that my former tutor would hear me described as a scholar! I can only imagine his consternation. I thank you for your unduly kind opinion, Lady Leominster, but I would not wish to mislead anyone as to my ability."

Lavinia Leominster wished she could poison her guest's wine.

She wished it all the more so as she heard other guests complimenting the new Marchioness's gown.

"I hope you won't find it impertinent of me, Lady Westford, but I do greatly admire your gown. A Parisian model, is it not?"

This came from the wife of an Earl who wore a stylish lilac creation herself, bearing a large lace fan.

"Not from so far away, and I must thank you for your compliment on my dressmaker's behalf," Lily said, smiling. "She is from the town."

Mishearing "the town" for "Town" and making the assumption that Lily meant London, the Countess inquired as to whether the modiste was located in Knightsbridge or Mayfair.

"In the nearby town. It was made by a Mrs Mead."

The Countess nearly dropped her fan. A local needlewoman, such as sewed at most for the very lowest ranks of the gentry and more likely for wealthier merchants' and even farmers' wives! It was unthinkable. She was conflicted with a mix of condemnation and envy, as were others in earshot.

The instinct was to sneer at the notion of a Marchioness patronising a humble village dressmaker. In private, more than one lady planned to make inquiries and potentially avail herself of Mrs Mead's services.

"The line is indeed most becoming," the Countess said, rather at a loss for words.

There were a dizzying amount of names and faces for Lily to learn and remember. She was relieved when she finally had the chance to sit down for a few minutes in the retiring room, next to a pleasant faced young woman in a pale green silk who was introduced to her as a Miss Emma Sawthwaite.

Miss Sawthwaite's family came from the north, where her father had made his fortune in the textile industry. His eldest daughter, who had just had her first season, was a contrary mix of delight at the intrigue of the marriage mart, and a sage awareness that her own future was already mapped out for her.

Lily found her appealing and was glad to speak with someone of her own age. She had missed Betsy's companionship, even if it had admittedly been some relief to enjoy a reprieve from her cousin's endless tears and swooning over Mr Farrington.

After a few careful questions to Miss Sawthwaite made Lily confident that the other girl had never met Betsy - though she feared she must be aware of the scandal, for who could not be? - she was able to relax and enjoy her company and they returned together to the ballroom.

"There is Sir Stephen Seton, he is your neighbour, is he not?" Miss Sawthwaite asked Lily. Sir Stephen stood across the room in conversation with a stout elderly gentleman with white whiskers.

"Our nearest neighbour, yes," Lily said.

"His story is such a tragic one," Miss Sawthwaite remarked.

"Indeed?" Lily knew nothing of her neighbour's private history. But Miss Sawthwaite's tone had held sympathy and Lily was curious to learn more of the baronet. Most of their conversations had involved agriculture and its history with respect to the Grantlings and Westford estates.

Miss Sawthwaite lowered her voice and told her tale. "When he was quite a young man he was betrothed to the daughter of an Earl. Her beauty was so renowned that it is said she was painted by Sir Thomas Lawrence. But she died of a fever a week before the wedding. Sir Stephen was heartbroken and has never since looked at another woman."

The two girls were silent as they regarded the man in question and pondered his tragedy.

"Her hair was described as dark as ebony and her complexion of the finest porcelain. No other woman could ever compare." Miss Sawthwaite sighed wistfully at this. She herself had sandy hair and her own complexion was lightly freckled, though Lily found her very pretty.

"How very sad for her own family too. Did she have sisters?" Lily asked.

"Not as I have heard. A brother of course, the current Earl. Ah, well, I fear my own matrimony will be very much less romantic," Miss Sawthwaite said.

"Very much less tragic I would hope. Are you betrothed?"

"Not as yet, but there is an understanding between my family and the family of Lord Percival Elstone. Percy is good natured enough but I fear our children will have the reddest hair in England."

Lily had heard of Lord Percival through Betsy. He was as renowned for his flame-red hair as for the nobility of his line and the impoverishment of his family's fortunes. For him to marry Emma Sawthwaite, who boasted no title but brought money beyond measure, would be most advantageous to both parties.

How sad, though, that Sir Stephen's life had been haunted by his loss. He was such a kind and companionable man, Lily thought.

She found herself in conversation with him later, as the dancing started.

"Do you not dance, Lady Westford?" he asked of her.

"As an old married matron, I thought it wisest to leave the floor to others," Lily joked. She was not entirely sure of the propriety of her dancing, since it was usually only unmarried maidens who did so.

"As such a young and comely matron, I fear you will arouse much disappointment if you do not do so," Sir Stephen commented, the same humour in his eye. "Perhaps you will do me the honour, as my neighbour?"

Lily acquiesced and he led her onto the floor among the other couples.

Gervase felt his jaw tighten as he watched them. One outing into society and already she flung herself upon the attentions of other males! She was no better than her reputation, for all her appearance of grace and beauty.

Never having experienced jealousy before, he was unable to perceive the irrationality of his emotion. He saw only his wife and his oldest friend, talking and dancing in a familiar fashion together. Lily's face lit up as they laughed over something and Gervase felt such a violence within him as he had ever known.

At his side, his fist clenched.

"A considerable beauty you have snared there, Westford," an old acquaintance remarked, unwittingly adding fuel to the fire. "There's not a man in the room who wouldn't take Seton's place right now."

Gervase took a gulp of his wine. Lavinia Leominster, at that moment standing nearby, saw his tension. So this was the lie of the land!

It was not something she had expected, given her knowledge of the origins of this marriage, nor something she welcomed. Unable to administer poison to the woman in question's cup, she instead decided to drip it into her husband's ear.

"Indeed they dance most finely together," she said, keeping her voice light and as she hoped, playful. "They make a very handsome couple to lead the dance."

The Marquess's eyes narrowed and the widow felt a swell of satisfaction as the seeds of her spite took root. Due to her age, bereavement and position as hostess she could not dance herself, but this did not distress her. Men so often made themselves ridiculous on the dance floor and she had paid her dues in the days of her debut, trying to avoid tearing her gown as yet another young gentleman misstepped.

As the dance ended Gervase could bear it no more. He approached his wife, acknowledging his neighbour with naught but "Seton" and a cool nod. If that gentleman was taken aback by his friend's manner he was too wise to remark upon it.

"Westford," he returned in a far more cordial tone.

Gervase turned from him abruptly and addressed Lily. "Madam, perhaps you may now deign to dance with your husband?"

Lily was initially thrilled by his request. She found herself increasingly wanting his approval though he never spoke it to her. Given what people must believe about her nature, and given her own guilt at her different deception, she wanted to do him credit in some way.

If there was a deeper reason for her desire for his good regard, she did not yet admit it to herself.

The Marquess led his new marchioness onto the dance floor, with all eyes upon them. Lily was careful with her steps and comported herself with grace, aware of the attention. She pitied poor Miss Sawthwaite, partnered with a heavily perspiring fellow who frequently trod on her feet.

Gervase rarely danced. It may even have been years since he had done so. He did not remember ever feeling so aware of the physical presence of his partner, nor finding it so difficult to control the responses of his own body. Inwardly he cursed. This was a ball, not a bedroom! What ailed his self-control?

Lily tried to feel unconcerned that her husband's expression remained severe. She smiled at him but it was not returned. She supposed that he was concentrating on his dance steps. This was the first time she had ever danced at a ball, though it was her sincere hope that no one realised this, so her expectations were uncertain.

As the dance finished Gervase's bow to her was curt, yet her face was radiant as she looked at him. Yet he did not perceive this. They were adjacent to Sir Stephen once again, so Lily smiled at him, sending a hidden dagger through the heart of her husband.

Lady Leominster saw all, and was very satisfied.

16. The accusation

Lily was relieved when they finally departed as her head was swimming from the noise and bustle and she longed for the peace of Westford Park.

Tired as she was, she shyly hoped for a repeat of the previous night with her husband. He had looked so incredibly handsome at the ball, so much taller and more distinguished than all other males there, and his mere touch made her tremble. She had enjoyed dancing with him above all her other partners.

She wished she could have felt more liking for her hostess. There was something about Lavinia Leominster that she couldn't warm to. Lily was also well aware that the widow disliked her. She had no idea why, after all, Lady Leominster had arranged the ball to welcome her and introduce her to local society.

But she did not trust her. Lady Leominster had made more than a few pointed remarks throughout the evening: barbs dipped in the sugar of false praise. As inexperienced in company as Lily was, she recognised their true sentiment. Perhaps because Aunt Maud had so often made similar remarks to her. *"How like your great aunt Frederica you grow every day, Lily! Such a very distinguished woman."*

Frederica had been distinguished in appearance only by her plainness, despite the attempts of a portrait painter to soften her distinctly square jaw. Lily was confident she bore no resemblance to this ancestor. As her father had frequently observed, she took after her mother's side of the family.

But she had suppressed her thoughts and responded with tactful politeness to Aunt Maud, just as she did with Lady Leominster.

Lily was glad at least that these remarks had not been made in earshot of her husband. A slur against her was a greater slur on him.

The Marquess had been strangely silent as they departed Leominster Hall and in the carriage home but Lily put this down to his reserve. He had only returned from London the day before and likely he was still fatigued from that.

Once alone in her bedchamber with him, after Sarah had helped remove the exquisite gown and Lily had dismissed her, his demeanour changed. He grabbed her and kissed her so forcefully it was almost painful even as she felt herself melting in his arms. Gentle or hard, she loved it when he pressed her close to him.

But then he thrust her away, interrupting her growing arousal. Lily looked at him, startled. Had she displeased him?

Gervase misread her bewildered expression as a rejection of him, as a distaste for his advances. "Seeing as you court the attentions of other men, madam, perhaps you will not object to receiving your husband's attentions?"

Of course she would not object, but what did he mean? Had she made some faux pas in dance or conversation? Had she exposed herself in some way?

He continued. "This may be but a mere marriage of convenience for you, but you will not play me foul. You belong in my bed alone, regardless of your previous follies."

Lily had no wish to be in anyone else's bed and tried to express her confusion. "My Lord, I..."

"Silence!"

He pushed her down onto the bed roughly and she gasped in shock as he tugged at the neck of her nightgown with such force that it ripped. He reached in and cupped her breast, squeezing it just firmly enough that it was painful, though her nipple still tautened at his touch.

"You would have other men touch you here?"

"No!" She was at a loss for words. What had got into him?

As he fondled her flesh, albeit forcefully, she felt a throb in the pit of her stomach. Her eyes fell to below his waist to his close-fitting breeches, where she could see the fabric was strained. Knowing what was in store for her excited her even if his manner with her was abrupt.

His other hand moved between her legs, feeling the moisture that was already there for him. "Which man were you thinking of to cause this?" he demanded.

Lily remained silent. She feared it might be wanton in some way to admit that her husband caused this rapid response in her.

Gervase took her silence as guilty concealment. He flicked his fingers over her crest, making her throb and gasp. His thumb rubbed against her mercilessly.

"And here? Which man did you envisage touching you here?" He couldn't bring himself to mention Seton's name though he was sure it was their neighbour, if not still Farrington.

Lily realised he must be thinking of Betsy's behaviour and felt anxious. Had she herself behaved improperly at the ball? Had she disgraced him in some way? She had danced with other men, but this was normal, surely? She had been aware of a couple of other young married women taking part in the dances which had at the time relieved her doubts.

Sir Stephen had also encouraged her to do so and she was sure his behaviour would be all propriety.

The Marquess ripped her nightgown and slip from her, letting them fall on the floor. She was naked before him.

Once again he misread her confusion and apprehension as deriving from a guilty conscience. Yet gazing at her body he felt such a raging lust that he was determined to have her. He wanted to simultaneously punish her, to mark her as his territory, and demonstrate his prowess as compared to that of all other men.

He would subdue her, subdue her wanton desires. She would not stray from him.

In his desire to conquer her he turned her roughly around, bending her over the bed. The sight of her naked in that position, displaying what was his alone, nearly caused him to lose himself then and there. But he restrained himself.

Grasping her hips, he positioned himself at her core and drove into her: fast, hard and deep. Lily cried out and Gervase felt a faint twinge of conscience but his anger still dominated.

This hot, tight sweetness. This woman that fitted him as a lock fits a key: that another man should ever know her was unthinkable. Gervase felt gladder than ever before that he was in fact her first, he almost welcomed her family's deception at that moment.

His and only his. His, his, his.

His rhythm as he drove into her matched these thoughts.

Lily had been shocked at the position and his force. Was it normal for people to couple like this? She was more than ready for him but he plunged into her so rapidly that it had made her gasp.

Despite this she adored the feeling of him within her. Filling her, deeply, completely. Her body craved him.

That he still wanted her, even if he were angry with her, was reassuring.

Amid the fury he felt and his desire to take out his frustrations on her, Gervase found that he wanted his bride willing. He desired to possess her but something within him shrank from hurting her. Buried in his consciousness, below his rage, was the awareness that she was still an innocent, still very inexperienced.

Whatever her intentions and her behaviour may be, some of it could be attributed to her youth.

Though he felt he could not stop what he was doing - his body was no longer his own - he wanted to conquer her in another way.

Lily gave a soft moan as the sensations of his plunder of her rippled throughout her body. Gervase heard it and correctly interpreted it as pleasure, not pain. But in his madness he feared she was thinking of some other male.

He wanted to satisfy and exhaust his wife such that she would never need to look at another man. If this meant chaining her to a bed and ravishing her night and day, at that moment he felt quite prepared to do so. A kind of mania had overtaken him.

"You are mine, Elizabeth, mine and only mine!" His voice rasped as he approached climax.

He reached around between the front of her thighs and brought his fingers to the place that he knew would best control her sexual response. Sure enough she jerked as he first touched her, but as his finger swirled around firmly, unrelenting, he felt her hips grind back against his.

"Say my name!" he commanded her.

"My lord…"

"Say my name, Elizabeth."

What could he mean? He had used her Christian name so for the very first time she dared to use his. "Gervase." She found it hard to utter anything.

"Say it again. I want my name on your lips as I take you." His own words were thick with passion, he was seconds away from losing all control.

"Gervase. Oh - " Lily found herself suddenly tipped over the edge and her murmur became a cry " - Gervase!"

Hearing his wife call his name as she reached her peak and spasmed around him was more than he could take. His own orgasm shook him violently and he thrust into her, her cries and utterance of his name the sweetest of victories.

Beyond exhausted - she had collapsed beneath him - he remained inside her and rolled her over with him onto her side, pulling the bedclothes over them both. Still joined with her, Gervase fell into a troubled sleep.

17. The confrontation

Gervase awoke early the next morning, still troubled. He felt a gnawing sense of guilt and remorse that he at once attempted to bury.

He was not yet ready to let go of his anger, even if he could not yet admit that he was more angry with himself. Instead he determined to find some justification for what he had done. If he held fast to his suspicions and managed to substantiate them, he need not face the reality of what he had done.

His wife lay sleeping beside him. In the pale morning light she looked very young and very innocent.

Deceptively innocent, he reminded himself. Or tried to convince himself.

He extricated himself from the bed and tried not to be moved by the long lashes that swept in a curve against the cheeks, the golden locks that streamed over the pillow.

He crossed to his own room, dressed briskly not waiting to call his manservant, and strode down to the stables. A ride would clear his head.

The stable hands were already up and scrambled to saddle Orion for their master, since they saw the storm clouds brewing over his face. He was usually a man of an exceptionally even temper. His anger was typically only roused by the misdeeds of his cousin, misdeeds that were an open secret at Westford Park.

The huge black stallion welcomed his daily exercise at an earlier hour than usual. Such was his size that he could have borne a man twice the Marquess's weight with little strain. He was happy to go into a full gallop almost immediately, shaking off the confinement of the stables.

Surveying his lands, the window panes of Westford Park gilded by the bright wintry sun, Gervase did feel his thoughts begin to clear. But it brought him the opposite of calm. Instead he was becoming uneasily aware of his own hot-headedness and almost certain misjudgement of the previous evening.

He struggled with it. But he was so angry with himself, and struck with an increased sense of horror for how he had treated his wife the previous night - for he had never considered himself a man of violence - that Seton became the focus of his anger when he saw him appear on horseback over the dividing ridge.

His neighbour, unaware of the storms swirling in Westford's head, raised his hand in greeting.

Gervase did not return it and instead affected a frosty disdain. Seton was surprised but rode towards him, drawing his own chestnut mount up alongside his friend.

Gervase, more than half aware that he spoke irrationally and unjustly, could not restrain himself.

"For as long as I have known you, Sir, for you to play me foul with my own wife!"

Seton was utterly taken aback. "I beg your pardon?"

"I do not know what may have happened in my absence, but with my own eyes I saw the familiarity between the pair of you last night, and the looks you both exchanged."

Such anger and unfounded accusations were absolutely out of character for Westford, which shocked the baronet more than the sheer outrage of his allegations. He was silent for a while, unsure if he should even respond or merely cut him and ride home.

Looking more closely, he saw the turmoil on his friend's face and began to guess its true cause.

"Since I know that you can only have lost your reason, Westford, I will discard your last remarks. Suffice it to say that your accusations are absurd. Anyone with eyes and ears could remark upon the exemplary behaviour of your wife last night. And to imagine even in some fit of brain fever that I would play you foul, old friends as we are, speaks only for the temporary derangement of your senses." He paused for a moment as the thundercloud remained over Gervase's face.

"You know also my own history. To besmirch the memory of my own loss through some cheap dalliance with another man's wife, I would be pained to think you even imagined me capable of it. Only I do not believe you are capable of any rational thought right now."

Gervase did not respond. He sat erect on Orion, his jaw rigid.

Seton continued. "You know the circumstances in which you married, Westford. Circumstances that you accepted and a duty that you elected to carry out. If you made a bargain that you now cannot keep, then you must release her. But you must know that if you do so, you treat her no less foully than Farrington. More so, for you leave her all the more abandoned and all the more disgraced."

Seton took up his reins.

"Also know that should you pursue that course of action, you may consider our society at an end."

He rode off, leaving Gervase in a fury of shock, remorse and humiliation. The suggestion that he might release his wife had not even crossed his mind and he recoiled utterly at the prospect. But his friend's censure of his behaviour stung.

Riding for some time over the hills, with the morning air cooling his senses, the enormity of what he had done was starting to sink in. He felt nauseated as he caught sight of the distant rooftops of Leominster Hall, the origin of it all.

Gervase was no coward and did not shrink from apology when he owed it. But he did not trust himself to face either his wife or his friend again for now. Amid his current mental turmoil he might only exacerbate the situation.

He decided to once more depart for London, on the excuse of completing the estate business that Ross was taking care of, and conveying him back to Westford Park at the conclusion. With Orion stabled the Marquess gave the necessary instructions to the grooms and Pelham and awaited his carriage to be made ready.

**

"I must depart for London henceforth. My business there is urgent." The Marquess's tone was cold and Lily felt that he did not meet her eyes.

What, O what, had she done?

"When can we expect you back, my lord?" She tried to keep her own voice steady.

"I cannot say."

He was disgusted with her, she thought. This was the problem with never having been properly launched into society: she lacked knowledge of decorum. On the next social occasion, if there was one, she would have to be very much more careful.

She did not know when this might be, but Sir Stephen had mentioned a future dinner invitation. There had not yet been time for him to arrange this.

Lily was tired and strained with feeling like she must tiptoe on eggshells around her volatile husband. Had she felt less guilt over her deception of him, she might have even resented his brusque treatment. As it was, she felt that hers was still the greater fault.

Still, she found that she did not want him to go. "You will be missed, my lord."

Gervase raised his eyebrows but was startled to see sincerity in his wife's eyes. His gaze softened for a moment. "I trust Mrs Hollis and Pelham will attend to your comfort."

"I am certain they will."

Then the coach was ready, and he was gone.

Lily stood for a while in the hallway, feeling at a loss. It was only mid-morning and she had no idea what to do with herself. She had hoped that the Marquess might ask her to ride with him but he had gone out on Orion at dawn, before she had even awoken.

Now with him gone again she was completely at leisure. She could read, walk, sew. She did not have to worry about hunger, nor the sniping and endless demands of Aunt Maud. She should have felt entirely happy, she supposed. How fortunate she was compared to so many others.

But this leisure was not really hers and she knew that one day it must be taken from her. She shivered, imagining the doubtless spartan, draughty home of the distant Scottish relative. Perhaps thanks to the education her father had given her she might instead find a position as a governess. Such a post would put her beneath the society of Betsy and her other relatives forever, but she would nonetheless find some joy in it, she thought.

For now she must make the best of it. Lily went to the morning room at sat down at the writing desk, but came to the realisation that there was no one she could safety write to, except Betsy.

She toyed with a book. Then, still restless, went upstairs to fetch her cape to take a walk around the lake. She would sit and peruse the Theocritus that the Marquess had given her. She hugged the volume of verse to her. He had noticed what she liked to read and had been so kind as to choose this present for her. His alternating kindness and coldness were hard to understand.

Upon reaching her room she discovered that her cape was missing. Of course! Sarah had intended to resew a part of the lining where the stitching had become worn. She could walk without it but it was a chill day with the frosty promise of winter in the air.

Returning to the morning room once more Lily was just descending the main stair when there was the noise of a carriage drawing up outside. Puzzled, Lily tried to catch a glimpse of the passengers as they alighted.

Her blood ran colder than winter when she saw who it was.
Sir Robert and Lady Maud had arrived.

18. The guests

What could she do? What could she say? Lily was paralysed with terror.

They would give her away as soon as they spoke to her and addressed her as "niece" rather than daughter. She faced ruin.

Quickly, she escaped from the hall before the door was opened to them and fled as swiftly as possible to find Mrs Hollis.

"Sir Robert and Lady Maud have arrived," she told the housekeeper, trying to maintain her composure. She could not bring herself to call them "mother" and "father" but given her prior state of disgrace, some formality between daughter and parents might not appear exceptional. "Would you please have them shown to the drawing room and have rooms prepared in the east wing? My - " she nearly said "my aunt" but checked herself " - Lady Maud is very fond of the morning sun."

This was entirely untrue for Lady Maud was a later sleeper who resented being awoken by the early rays of light, but Lily needed her relatives as far away from her own room as possible. An idea had come to her and with the grace of God and a miracle, she might yet preserve her deception a while longer.

At her own dressing table she briefly splashed her face with rosewater, trying to cool the heat of anxiety from her cheeks.

Collecting herself, she made her way down to the drawing room.

A footman opened the door and as Lily saw Lady Maud's face crease in confusion, she rapidly dismissed Mary - hovering there in attendance - to fetch refreshments. She was aware that Mrs Hollis had likely ordered them already but needed to be rid of the maid. She was thankful that the Marquess did not employ an excessively large staff or there would have been more to stand witness. As it was, there was only the footman outside the door. Lily prayed his hearing would not be acute.

"Lady Maud, Sir Robert." Lily greeted them with the customary deference of the poor relation. They must not realise that she was mistress of this house.

"We did not expect to find you here," Lady Maud said. She looked most displeased at the sight of Lily.

"Not after your shameful and ungrateful flight," Sir Robert continued. "I always said that Carter woman was as sly as she was foolish. When your aunt and I were so considerate to have arranged such a suitable position for you."

"I was most grateful, sir, but Miss Carter had found another post which was more pleasing to me."

Sir Robert grunted. "Selfish and ungrateful. We nursed a thorn within our breast these many years, wife."

Lily lowered her head, making no reply. She was long immune to their carping and censure.

"Where is Betsy?" Lady Maud demanded. "And Lord Westford?"

"I regret that they are both in town, madam. Had they been aware of your visit, but there was no letter…"

"Then how came you here?" asked Lady Maud.

Lily's thoughts were in a rapid whirl. "My cousin wished me to pay her a visit to assist her in settling into her new home. As the family with whom Miss Carter has found a position for me are yet away, rather than trespass further on Miss Carter's hospitality, I came here."

This was at least plausible. Betsy was the kind of girl to make such a request.

"To trespass instead on your cousin's hospitality. Yet why do you not leave since they are gone?"

"My cousin wished me to stay, sir."

Lady Maud sniffed. "Most unusual." She knew her own daughter, however, and privately felt it was perhaps more of a surprise that Betsy had not also insisted that Lily accompany them to London.

"When do you expect them back?" Sir Robert inquired.

"I cannot say, my lord. However Lord Westford indicated that they may be gone some weeks."

This news displeased both Sir Robert and Lady Maud. They had had no intention of making a long visit, returning home as they were.

"I see. Then we will stay but one night, and leave on the morrow."

Lily nodded. "I will take my leave of you, I have some tasks to attend to."

Giving the impression that she was still a dogsbody who fetched and stitched and whatever else satisfied Lady Maud all the more. She detested the idea of Sir Robert's niece being here even as a guest, thinking herself above her station. She had resented the girl ever since she had been forced to take her into her home, partly for the largely imagined expense of her upbringing.

And even more, though she shrank from admitting it to herself, the painful fact of the girl's superior beauty to that of her own daughter. There was no way she would have allowed the penniless Lily to outshine Betsy in the Season, even had her gowns been the cheapest and the plainest that could have been got away with.

Lily encountered Mrs Hollis as she crossed the hall. "If you would be so very good as to arrange for the needs of Lady Maud and Sir Robert. I am afraid that I am unwell and must retire to my room."

Mrs Hollis's eyes met hers. They both knew there was another truth behind this. Mrs Hollis guessed that Lady Westford wished to escape the scrutiny and censure of her parents. This did not surprise her since the housekeeper had disliked the pair at first sight. She had already nursed a prejudice against anyone who would force their daughter into such a speedy marriage and not even be in attendance. Even if the groom, in Mrs Hollis's estimation, was more than a prize, it was not the way of things. Even more now that she knew and liked the young Lady Westford and felt increasing tolerance towards her rumoured indiscretion.

"I will have Mary bring your lunch to you, my lady. I will ensure that Lady Maud and Robert are made comfortable."

Lily thanked her, the relief apparent in her eyes. "Sir Robert has indicated they will leave on the morrow."

"Their coach will be prepared."

There was an understanding between them, almost a conspiratorial one. Not for the first time Lily sensed the housekeeper's growing loyalty towards her and she was both grateful and relieved by it. Mrs Hollis held such a key position in the household that to have her as an ally was very valuable.

Returning to her room she met Nanny Noakes on the stairs. Lily was glad to see the old woman's arthritis was troubling her less that day, for much of the time she was unable to move unassisted from her chair.

"Visitors, I see?" Nanny Noakes, as usual, included no formal civilities in her question.

"Sir Robert and Lady Cosgrove. My parents," Lily said, the lie sticking in her throat. She loathed to have to acknowledge them as any kind of relations, let alone her closest kin.

Nanny Noakes' expression was inscrutable but Lily had the distinct and uncomfortable impression that the old woman saw straight through her. While she surely couldn't have guessed the Cosgroves' true identity, she perceived that their visit was unanticipated and unwelcome, and that Lily wished to avoid them.

"You must excuse me, Nanny Noakes, I am afraid I must lie down."

The beady eyes flicked over her. "You'll be wanting some of my tonic. Always revived the little master, it did."

She spoke of Tom Farrington, Lily guessed. "If you have a remedy I would be most grateful to try it." She had no actual intention of imbibing anything that the old nurse provided, for she suspected it would be some syrup of laudanum, which she was in the habit of avoiding even when she was genuinely sick.

"Mary will bring it," Nanny Noakes said. "Do you the power of good, it will."

Lily thanked her and escaped to the sanctum of her room. She still found it hard to get used to the fact that such a large and beautiful room was hers, at least for now. Her aunt and uncle would likely have put her in an attic were they not all occupied by the household servants. Even then she had been given the meanest and most shabbily furnished of the guest rooms. It faced north and the panes of glass rattled in the wind.

But here was comfort and a fire. Soft pillows. Beautiful furnishings. A looking glass that was not cracked and tarnished like the previous one she had sat before. She regarded herself now and saw that she was paler than usual. While she did not truly feel unwell she was very tired and was glad to be able to lie down.

Just as she turned to the bed there was a light knock at the door and Mary entered with a tray. Lily thanked her and had her set it down before dismissing her. She was not hungry, her stomach churned too much from the stress of her aunt's and uncle's presence in the house and her fears that they would discover her true position at Westford Park.

Only intending to close her eyes for a few moments as she sank back onto the pillows, when she finally opened them she realised she had slept for an hour or more. The soup on the tray was cold, likewise the tea had lost all its heat. Lily poured a cup but found it to be over-brewed and bitter, so drank some water instead.

Now she must come up with some convincing reason to avoid dining with her aunt and uncle that evening. Otherwise one of the servants was bound to give her away by using her new title before them.

She would have to feign sickness once more. She would also need to tell Sir Robert and Lady Maud herself first, lest one of the servants announce to them that "Lady Westford" was indisposed.

This was all becoming so very complicated. Lily looked around at the luxury of her bedroom once again. There was a price to pay for all of this, and it was growing heavier.

19. The club

Every jolt of the journey to London shook more guilt from Gervase. He felt such chagrin over his actions that he welcomed every discomfort as a form of mortification.

What a fool he was, to have suspected and accused his oldest friend! Seton, of all people. He knew in his heart that Seton would forgive him, which only added to his shame.

And the young woman he had taken as a wife and treated so appallingly. He remembered her still grace, her starry beauty as she appeared before all his friends and neighbours. The memory of her image wrenched his gut. He couldn't think straight around her.

Was he going mad?

Deciding the only remedy lay in getting as blind drunk as his body would permit, Gervase headed to one of his clubs. He belonged to several and the one he chose that evening was by far the most exclusive and usually the least frequented. But right now, he did not seek company.

As exclusive as the club was, the Marquess easily ranked among its top members and was greeted with due deference by staff. It was only a short time before he sat before a fireplace, alone in the room he had chosen, downing a very large brandy.

The firelight lit up the amber liquid in the glass like a lantern. Gervase toyed with it, wondering just how drunk he would need to get to blot everything out.

He groaned inwardly as one of his acquaintances entered the room, accompanied by another man. Claude Belvedere, his godmother's son, with his close friend whose name forever escaped Gervase.

"Westford." Claude greeted him. He was about a decade older than the Marquess, a bachelor with a round and pleasant face. "I hear congratulations are in order."

There was neither guile nor insinuation in Claude's expression. For all his eccentric tastes - what was with that appalling waistcoat in royal purple and fuchsia? - he was a sound fellow.

Gervase raised his glass with an ironic lift of his eyebrows, but said nothing. He was well aware there must have been avid gossip these past few weeks about his loss of bachelor status. He had become so renowned for his apparent celibacy that his discarding of it provided plenty for the ton to pick over.

"Mother will be keen to see you," Claude told him.

Gervase winced. He suspected Lady Diana would have a few choice words for him, she always did. She had been a dear friend of his mother and he had great respect for her. Not that this made her frequently sharp remarks any less piercing.

"Father too, of course," Claude added, more as an afterthought. "I should visit Mother tomorrow, if I were you. She knows you were recently in town."

Claude didn't need to say any more. Gervase had failed to pay his usual respects to his godmother on his previous visit. He was in London so infrequently that she expected to see him each time he came. "Dashed busy last time, I'm afraid."

Claude raised his eyebrows. "The usual?" He exchanged a glance with his friend. Luis, that was the man's name, Gervase remembered. He was half Spanish.

"The usual," Gervase confirmed.

"Really not your responsibility any more, old boy," Claude said. "Certainly not since recent developments."

He meant since Gervase's marriage made his cousin unlikely to remain his heir.

Gervase swirled his remaining brandy around the goblet and drained it. "I'm beginning to think you're right."

"I should cut him off. Let him do a spell in the Fleet. Not that it's any of my business, of course. You know Crockford's after him?"

Gervase did not know but was not surprised by this further news of his cousin's gambling debts.. Pretty soon he was going to have to make a choice about Farrington, one way or the other. He hoped he could manage it dispassionately, but the very thought of his cousin and his wife coloured his thinking.

Before marrying the girl he had been irritated by the affair. Now, he felt an icy fury when he even so much as contemplated it, at the back of which lurked a fear that he could not bring himself to admit.

***

"Why you felt you must take it upon yourself to take on that wretched boy's burdens, I'll never know." Lady Diana Belvedere straightened in her chair. "Still, it was high time you married, Gervase, and the family is an old and noble one. Far better an heir by a Cosgrove than Westford should pass to Farrington."

Gervase, who had only recently been considering this possible change in status for his cousin, received his godmother's customary candour with some deference. The force of her presence was such that he felt more like a small boy scolded for letting loose his father's horse than a man of wealth and title, well into his thirties.

"It was for Edward Cosgrove that I did it."

Lady Diana saw the shadow that passed over her godson's face. He had admired, even adored, Edward Cosgrove with all the zeal of a young man new to arms, as had all of Cosgrove's men. Many had owed their lives to his exceptional leadership and courage.

It had been some surprise when Edward Cosgrove eventually resigned his commission and retired to the country. He had been tipped for grander command, a generalship, even.

But he had preferred to live quietly with wife, devoting himself instead to his family and his scholarly interests. The wife had had money, Lady Diana remembered. Gone far too young, of course. And her husband not so many years after her.

"There was a child, wasn't there? A girl?" she asked Gervase.

"Taken with typhus along with her father." He remembered the blow it had given him when he had paid his respects following Cosgrove's death. *"Dead and buried, and the poor little girl with him."* Leaving Robert Cosgrove and his daughter Elizabeth - now Gervase's wife - the last of the Cosgrove line.

"Naturally I've heard what I've heard. But I'll suspend my judgement until I meet the girl. You've brought her to London with you, of course?"

Gervase was taken aback by the question. "No, she remains at Westford."

"Is she unwell?"

Gervase read his godmother's meaning. "As it turned out there was no risk of that."

Lady Diana raised her eyebrows. The two of them were not unaccustomed to such candid talk, since the topic had arisen before in relation to Tom Farrington's profligacy.

"Indeed. Still, a reputation is ruined even by the imputation of such." She gave a sudden laugh. "I'll admit I'm relieved that Farrington's bastard won't inherit Westford. You can sire your own line."

The elderly woman summoned her butler with a wave of her hand. "A glorious cause for celebration, Padgett. Bring the '57 brandy."

Gervase considered that his godmother would be more at home in a gentleman's club than her shy and retiring husband was. He wondered aloud where Sir Clarence was.

"Out," came the unilluminating reply. "You'll be joining us for dinner?"

Gervase hadn't planned to but accepted nonetheless.

"So, if the new Marchioness of Westford is not in the delicate condition that wagging tongues might have had us believe, why do you not bring her to town? As irregular as your nuptials were, she must have the needs of any new bride."

Since Gervase had never even considered bringing his bride to town he had no real answer to offer. He referred instead to his previous visit and the troubles over Tom.

"There was some delicate business…"

"Which you've dealt with. Surely not the same again already?"

"I just hadn't really considered it, madam."

Lady Diana made a noise that in less polite society might have been referred to as a snort.

"You can't leave her buried at Westford. You married her to redeem her reputation. That means having her at your side in public. Fitting her out as befits the wife of a Marquess."

This last phrase gave Gervase a feeling of unease which his sharp-eyed godmother instantly perceived.

"Some problem there, my boy?"

Gervase was reluctant to say anything. Even having grown up without a mother for most of his formative years, nor sisters nor even female cousins, he was yet aware that the situation over the ballgown was somewhat irregular. "Nothing of note."

But he hesitated as he spoke and the answer did not satisfy Lady Diana. "Out with it."

Briefly he mentioned the last minute dressmaking arrangements. His godmother, as he had anticipated, was astounded.

"No clothes? But the girl just had her first season, there must be a full wardrobe. Certainly something she could have worn to a country ball. Oh I realise you know nothing of these things, Gervase, they are women's matters, but still, it is most odd. Her luggage was perhaps mislaid or stolen?"

"I know not."

"It is your business to know. I assume you gave the girl authority of your purse in your absence to replenish her wardrobe?"

He had not. He had not even thought of it.

Lady Diana was increasingly exasperated with her godson. For an intelligent and supposedly worldly man he could be frustratingly obtuse. Even Claude would have realised and remedied such a deficiency. Though Claude, his mother considered, was hardly likely to need to in his current situation. "Rather a shame Claude couldn't have married her," she mused aloud.

"Claude?" Gervase was startled.

"He must marry. For his father's sake and mine, for an heir." She waved down Gervase before he could speak. "I know about his situation, I am no greenhorn. Why you men assume that we of the fairer sex know nothing of these things, when we bear you and birth you I cannot imagine. But some suitable woman must be found. A widow, perhaps, or a plain chit without fortune. A woman past the expectation of the romance of a tawdry novelette." She gestured for him to refill their glasses. "At this late hour I'd welcome a governess or a nursery maid as daughter-in-law if he would but show some appropriate vigour."

Gervase could only laugh. Lady Diana was so supremely unruffled by conversation that would shock and scandalise any other company that he found himself admiring her.

"Anyway, you bring your bride to me and I'll make arrangements. Host a ball for you both, perhaps."

Gervase, who disliked large society gatherings, winced. It was not missed by his godmother.

"None of that, my boy. You'll suffer the necessary ceremonies and then you can both hide yourselves away in Hampshire until kingdom come, for all I care. But you will do right by that girl, Gervase, not stop at half the task. She has your name, now she needs your public presence. Dispel this silly scandal before it taints your own line."

20. The carriage

Her maid looked quite green as they travelled along a rougher stretch of road. Lily guessed it was Sarah's first time travelling so far by carriage; even a vehicle so well sprung could unsettle an unaccustomed stomach.

She had no hartshorn, but offered Sarah some Hungary water. "This may help. My mother used to apply it to her temples when she travelled."

Sarah accepted it gratefully, uncomfortably conscious that she must be neglecting her mistress's needs due to her own discomposure. She had received the news that she was to accompany the marchioness to London with a mixture of excitement and anxiety. The maid had never before been so far from her home, nor even travelled in a stagecoach before.

Now she was regretting ever having embarked on the journey. She had had no idea how the constant jolt of the vehicle could make her stomach churn, nor how endless the road would seem.

They had set off early in the morning, the Cleveland bays having been well rested overnight. The day was overcast and the air chill and damp as they journeyed. Fortunately there were warm travel rugs inside the carriage which the two passengers made use of.

The marquess had sent Duncan Ross back in the carriage the previous evening with instructions that his wife should return to

London in it the next day. Lily had been surprised to be summoned thus and wondered at the reason. She might have hoped for a letter or note but there was none.

It was only Lily's second trip to London, having once been taken to the capital by her parents as a small child. There had been no reason to go since, certainly not after they died, and her aunt and uncle had never deigned to take her.

She spoke of this to try and distract poor Sarah from her malaise. "It is many years since I went to London. I barely remember it, except for how very crowded and busy it seemed."

"I have never been, my lady."

"It will be a new experience for both of us, then." This was true of most things in both their lives since the marquess had brought his bride to Westford Park, and Sarah had received her promotion.

Sarah glanced nervously towards the carriage window. "They say they are highwaymen on these roads."

Lily, who had privately thought of this, tried to dismiss her maid's concerns. "It would be rare for them to attempt an assault in broad daylight, and George is armed with a pepperbox," she said. The numbers of highwaymen infesting the roads from London were somewhat diminished in recent years due to most coachmen now carrying guns.

She had so little jewellery, she thought, and her purse was quite empty of coin. There would be very slim pickings for any mounted robber or footpad even should they have the misfortune to encounter one.

To change the subject she asked Sarah more about her family. Sarah spoke of her brother in the army, of whom she was very proud, her older sister who had been married earlier in the year, and another who was newly betrothed.

"Your mother must be very pleased," Lily said. "But now her expectations will fall on you." She spoke with humour but her maid blushed.

"Ben - in the stables - we have an understanding," Sarah started to say. "But not while it might inconvenience you, my lady. Nothing so immediate," she added quickly.

"I hope you do not intend to delay your plans on my account," Lily said, laughing. She realised that Sarah may be reluctant to relinquish her long-awaited position. "Besides, I know of no statute that decrees a married woman may no longer continue in her previous work. Should she wish to, of course."

There was gratitude in her maid's eyes. "It's partly for my younger sister, my lady. She has... an infirmity, since her birth. It's a cause of much anxiety to my mother and to us all. We do not want her to be sent away."

Lily understood. It brought back sad memories of her own. "My father's ward came to live with us after her parents died, and she was likewise afflicted." Poor little Harriet. Edward Cosgrove had been urged to send the child to an asylum when she came into his guardianship but he had rightly refused. Instead he had taken her into his household and he and Lily had made a home for her. Harriet was a couple of years younger than Lily and had become like a little sister to her.

"What happened to her?" Sarah checked herself. "Oh I apologise my lady, I did not mean to pry."

"That is quite alright, I am happy to speak of her, though her story is a sad one. I am afraid she perished in the same typhus outbreak that claimed my father's life." Lily had lost them both within a week. It had been the bleakest week of her life: bleaker than the loss of her mother, for she had been younger then and did not remember it so well.

"Oh my lady." Sarah was genuinely distressed.

"My only consolation is that Harriet did not suffer very long. The physician had always warned us that she had a weakness of the heart, and was unlikely to live very many years."

The two girls were both silent for a while, each thinking their own thoughts. Lily was lost in the past, remembering her loved ones, while Sarah's thoughts turned to the future and to her hopes of marriage with Ben.

It was just two days since Lily's aunt and uncle had departed and she still felt faint thinking how close she had come to exposure. Never before had she felt so thankful for their dislike of her and lack of interest in her. They had made no protest when had she excused herself from their company. Nor, fortunately, had they made any compromising conversation with her when they left the next morning.

They had referred to Betsy as "your cousin" and "Elizabeth" rather than Lady Westford, so the staff perceived nothing amiss.

"Since you have wilfully chosen your own course against our guidance, we take no further responsibility for you," Sr Robert had told Lily. Pelham, standing within earshot, must have thought this strange and unfeeling on a parent's part, but it could have been interpreted as further censure for Lady Westford's supposed disgrace.

Lily had nearly slumped with relief when her uncle's carriage finally drew away. For a while, she had bought herself a little more time.

Now, each roll of the wheels brought her further away from Westford and closer to new dangers and uncertainties. In London there would surely be people who had met and remembered her cousin during the past season. She would simply have to brazen it out. Imply that they had remembered her false, or confused her with another.

But for how much longer? When would this all end?

Betsy's original purpose in this marriage deception had been to ensure that she remained free for the renewal of Tom Farrington's attentions but Lily saw no realistic prospect of this ever happening. Even less so since more of Farrington's nature had been revealed to her, partly by Nanny Noakes and also by some other things she had picked up on. From what she could establish he was thoroughly bad and selfish.

And if a large sum of money might have bought his cousin's subjugation to matrimony, surely the marquess would have attempted this before making his own offer to Betsy? Likely he had already tried and failed.

Lily noticed that Sarah had fallen asleep and felt glad for her, since she looked more peaceful. Outside the sky remained grey and seemingly more leaden than an hour ago. There was little to see in the surroundings except for fields and low hills.

Suddenly the carriage gave a fierce jolt and the two passengers were thrown against one another, Sarah immediately waking. Her eyes widened in shock as the vehicle lurched and halted, nearly falling over and resting at a sharp angle.

Lily heard the coachman mutter an oath and guessed the cause. A wheel, or its axle, had broken.

She saw that Sarah was terrified and attempted to calm her. "The carriage may need repair. We must alight." This was easier said than done with the coach at such a precarious slant. But Lily managed it, with George helping first his mistress and then her maid down onto the road.

The damage was easy to see: they would travel no further in this vehicle today. Lily's first instinct was to go to the horses, patting them and murmuring to them to ensure they were not spooked.

"I'll have to find a farm or an inn, my lady, and fetch help," George said.

This would mean leaving the two young women alone by the broken carriage. Lily looked around her. It was a lonely stretch of road, close to the edge of a thick stretch of woodland. She felt instinctively that if anywhere were unsafe for them to remain unguarded, it would be here. She might ask George to leave his pistol with her, she supposed.

"I do not like the look of this road, George."

She saw from the expression in his eyes that he feared the same.

"We have enough horses. Let us ride together to the next inn. It is some time since we passed one, so I anticipate that one must lie not far ahead."

"But, my lady, the horses are not saddled for riding."

"Then we must ride without saddles, as our ancestors did." Lily had ridden bareback a few times as a child. "Sarah, can you ride?"

White-faced, the maid shook her head.

This was a problem. To ride pillion with a saddle was one thing, but without would be far too much risk. There was only one option. "I will ride for help, George, and you may keep Sarah safely with you here."

George tried to protest. "My lady, I can't let you…"

"I will be safest on horseback, and Sarah will be safer here with you. Far safer than leaving us here alone, when dusk falls." Lily turned to Sarah. "You must wrap yourself up in the blankets to stay warm, and you will be quite well."

"Very well, my lady." George consented with some reluctance. "There's an inn some two miles from here, on the other side of the woods. The Ring O'Bells is its name." He was troubled, fearing his master's displeasure at the whole situation. Not that the coachman could be blamed for a broken axle, but maybe he should have taken more precautions. Brought along another man to safeguard the two women.

Lily selected one of the bays and George helped her mount. Lily shifted until her body was in a position that best moulded to the animal's back. There were a harness and reins at least; compared to riding with no tack this would be easy, she thought.

Reassuring Sarah once more that she would return with help as quickly as possible, and again ensuring that George's gun was ready and loaded, Lily rode off. She prayed she would reach habitation within an hour.

21. The gypsy

Lily silently thanked her father for his more unorthodox riding lessons as she journeyed along the road into the woods. She could only imagine how much it would scandalise society for the wife of a Marquess to not only be riding astride - unaccompanied on a public road - but also bareback.

This was an emergency, however, and while she shrank from further disgracing her husband she preferred to be the source of scandal than robbed or worse on the highway. She knew that despite romantic tales, many Gentlemen of the Roads were from gentlemanly in their conduct towards unprotected females. She worried as much for Sarah as for herself, but the maid would be safer with George than in her own company, Lily thought. Even though her father had also taught her to handle a pistol with reasonable confidence.

She sensed the horse was glad to be galloping free of the carriage harness, her own weight far less of a burden for it. They would reach the inn quickly.

But as she rode along she saw something at the side of the road ahead. From a distance it looked like a fallen bundle, a pile of rags. As she grew closer she saw that it was a body. Dead?

Momentarily she recoiled from the prospect but then steeled herself. She drew up the horse and as she came closer she made out the form of an a person - an old woman, she thought. Unconscious perhaps, but not seemingly dead. Lily slid down from the horse - not stopping to think how she might mount it again - and took a closer look. Gently she moved the old woman's shoulder.

"Are you hurt?"

Eyes flickered open and the woman muttered some words that Lily couldn't understand, in an unfamiliar tongue. The woman drew away from her and tried to raise herself up but seemed to lack the strength to do so.

"Let me help you." Lily extended her arm and did her best to support the ragged figure to her feet. She could feel how thin she was below the layers of clothing. The figure stumbled: she could not seem to stand unaided. She pointed to her ankle with a gnarled finger, a grimace of pain twisting her face.

Her arms seemed strong enough, gripping onto Lily so firmly it almost hurt. "If I managed to lift you, could you mount my horse?" Lily asked, pointing to the old woman and then the beast. She felt she could not leave her alone and injured by the roadside.

As she approached the horse, leaning heavily on Lily, the old woman did something strange. She reached out to the horse and stroked her finger from its forehead down its muzzle. She then made a strange gesture from side to side, as though she were drawing a sign in the air. Lily was surprised to see how still the horse stood throughout this. It was a spirited animal even after the exertion of conveying the Marquess's carriage these many miles.

The old woman turned her face, lined and weather-beaten, back to Lily, and gave a nod.

Lily had wondered if it would even be possible to lift the woman onto the bay, slight though she seemed. Yet despite having a wounded leg, the old woman sprang up with surprising ease.

Taking the rein in her hand, Lily was about to lead them further along the road when the old woman shook her head and pointed to the trees. At the same time the horse turned in the same direction and began walking into the wood. Clearly the old woman's home must be through the forest, though Lily wondered at her unusual command of the animal. She had found that the horse needed a reasonably firm hand when riding but it instinctively obeyed its elderly passenger.

They had not walked far when the trees opened out into a clearing with a campfire, wagons and other people who stood as soon as they saw them. A gypsy encampment! These wandering people had occasionally travelled through her father's estate, never staying long. Her father always ordered the gamekeeper to overlook any poaching when the Romanies passed through. "It's ill luck to cross them, and besides, we can easily spare a few rabbits," he had said.

This was the closest Lily had ever come to them. They were darker complexioned than other country folk, their clothes more patched and colourful. A slim, dark-eyed man approached them. He spoke to the old woman in their language, and Lily saw her gesture once again to her foot. He called to a youth who looked around twelve years of age, and the two of them helped their injured relation down.

The man spoke to the boy, who then spoke to Lily. "He thanks you for bringing back our grandmother. We are in your debt."

Lily dismissed this graciously. "It was no trouble on my part."

Again the man spoke to the boy, and once more then boy translated. "He asks why a fine lady is riding alone, without a saddle, and if you are in need of aid yourself?"

Lily explained about the broken wheel. "The carriage is but a mile up the road. I was riding for the Ring O'Bells inn, to seek assistance."

A discussion ensued between the boy and a couple of men. "They will ride and see what can be done about your carriage," he told Lily. "There's more of a chance they can repair it than the folk at the inn."

Looking around the camp at the well maintained wagons, Lily suspected this was so. She thanked him. As the two men gathered some tools and lumber, and rode off with their own horses, a woman approached Lily. She wore a shawl over her head and shoulders, above a faded crimson gown.

"Some tea, my lady?" Her English was clear but accented.

Lily accepted. She was thirsty and she was reluctant to refuse their hospitality, however the tea might taste brewed in these wild woods in a gypsy cauldron. She was ushered to sit on the steps of a wagon, and an earthenware cup of steaming liquid was placed in her hands. She sipped it, glad of its warmth. It had a smoky flavour and she tasted a herb but could not place it. Rosemary? Lavender? Tea leaves, unstrained, swirled at the bottom of the vessel.

No one spoke to her while she drank. Another woman nearby clucked over a baby, and some children stared at her with curious dark eyes. The woman with the shawl smiled at her encouragingly.

When Lily finished the tea, the gypsy woman held out her hand for the cup. She swirled it and frowned, and handed it to the elderly woman who had been made comfortable with some wool-stuffed cushions by the fire. The old woman took the cup, peering at it and tilting it from side to side. She exchanged some words with the younger woman.

She looked anxious as she spoke to Lily. "My lady, you have an enemy. My puridai - my grandmother - cautions you to beware. There is one who wishes you great harm."

Not believing in such superstitions as fortune telling and tea-leaf reading, Lily's instinct was to politely dismiss the warning. But seeing the genuine concern on their faces she felt a shiver run down her spine.

"Someone is watching you, my lady. Will you let my puridai read your palm?"

Lily had some idea that one was supposed to cross a gypsy's palm with silver, but she carried none with her. "I have no coins, I am afraid."

The shawled woman smiled sadly. "She does not ask for coin. You have done her more than enough service."

Feeling some reluctance at agreeing to something she had no real faith in, Lily extended her hand. The wrinkled brown fingers clasped it, tracing her palm. She was shaking her head. She looked up at Lily, her eyes troubled and sorrowful, and spoke in her own language, with her granddaughter translating.

"It is an enemy very close to you. Beware all, she says. I am very sorry we cannot offer you happier omens, my lady."

"By close... do you mean a neighbour?" Lily asked. Despite herself she couldn't prevent the image of Lavinia Leominster coming into her mind. She was not so naive as to miss the malice in that woman's demeanour towards her.

The two women exchanged words again. "My grandmother cannot say. Only that you have an enemy who observes, and is near to you."

It seemed that a shadow passed over. As foolish as she was sure it was to pay any heed to these gypsy traditions, Lily could not help but be affected. But what harm might Lady Leominster wish her? And why? She had paid her neighbourly dues with her visit and the ball, after all. She was rich and handsome, the mistress of her own estate. Lily could not think of a single reason that the widow might resent her.

Yet there it was. The warning of a nearby enemy, and a neighbour who patently disliked her.

"I thank you both for your warning," Lily said. "I will try to be careful."

22. The wait

Where were they? Gervase paced up and down the drawing room of his London home. It was already dusk and the carriage should arrived some time hence.

It was possible that they had set off late, but he was accustomed to his wife's promptness so found it hard to suspect this was the reason.

Beneath his frustration lurked a sense of concern. Daylight would not deter the most desperate and daring highwaymen. Now that darkness fell, the peril of the roads would only increase.

He should have gone himself. Or insisted that George took extra men with him.

Gervase had wished to await their arrival to dine but the hour grew late. He found he had strangely little appetite despite not eating since breakfast, since he had been out all day on business.

"There is no word?" he demanded of his servants, not for the first time.

They could only share an uneasy glance and say that there was none.

Barton, who managed the Marquess's London household, ventured to suggest an accident. "Mayhap the carriage has encountered some breakdown, my lord?"

Privately Barton feared robbers, for there had been several recent attacks on the stretch of road they were travelling on, with no one yet apprehended. However he did not want to cause alarm.

"It may be so," Gervase said. It was a fine carriage and well-maintained, of this he was certain as he trusted his men. But even the finest of vehicles might meet with accident.

Though he barely wished to admit it, he felt a flicker of fear at the image of his young bride lying in the roadside, like a fallen flower.

How absurd that such a thought should come to him! Was his mind softening with the advancing years? He reminded himself that his marriage was a transaction and not a matter of sentiment. Such fancies were out of place.

But the face of his wife, so clear and beautiful, hovered before him.

The evening grew darker.

With a noise of exasperation Gervase strode out to the hall and called for a servant.

"Have the best horse saddled forthwith. I will ride out to discover what may have befallen them."

***

"We were at first terrified to see the gypsies ride up, my lady I thought they must be highwaymen, come to rob us. But then one of them waved a white handkerchief at us, and George saw that they meant no harm," Sarah had told her mistress.

The accident and the arrival of the gypsies had both been thrilling encounters for the young maid. How shocked her family would be when she told them! Though she would refrain from mentioning the handsome young gypsy man who had made quite impudent eyes at her.

The gypsies had managed to patch up the carriage sufficiently for the horses to slowly convey it to the Ring O'Bells, but the repairs would not be sturdy enough for them make the rest of the journey to London. One of the gypsy men had ridden back to fetch Lily when the work was done, so her horse could be harnessed to the carriage once again.

They had thanked the gypsies, and George had offered coin which was refused with some politeness.

"It is a greater service that has been done for us," one of them said, with a nod to Lily.

Alone once more, the three travellers continued on their way.

The Ring O'Bells inn was an odd place, and not one George would ever have chosen to take his mistress to were it not for this emergency. As it was he feared his master's displeasure, but there was really nothing else to be done.

The landlord had the same shifty expression that George remembered from a stop some time ago, and there was a sly look in the serving girl's eye. The three travellers carried little coin, though George wondered about any jewellery that her Ladyship's might have brought with her. He might give her a word of warning, he thought. He didn't trust the locks on the doors. The keys turned too easily as though they were newly greased, and it was a certainty that the tavern-keeper kept his own copies.

"Tell your mistress to keep her valuables under her pillow," he muttered to Sarah who opened her eyes wide in alarm. "Just to be cautious," he added. "Strange folk pass through these parts and it pays to remain alert."

Sarah, who now imagined that masked robbers would burst into her room in the night and wrest her honour from her, was more than alarmed.

Lily strove to allay her fears. "We shall be quite safe," she assured the maid. "We have very little for them to steal. Can we send word to Lord Westford of our arrival here?" she asked George.

"I have asked, and they claim no stagecoach is due until the morrow," George said.

"But if another carriage passes through, we can surely prevail upon them to carry a message?" Lily said.

"By all means, if the carriage stops here." Looking around the cramped and grimy premises, George feared that this was unlikely. Nonetheless instructed the landlord to flag such a vehicle down.

The glint of a coin twisted in George's fingers caught the landlord's eye. He said he would endeavour to do what he could, his eyes following the money as George returned it to his pouch. George did not trust him. There were rumours of certain innkeepers being in league with highwayman, and if ever there was such a place that hosted such a nefarious alliance, it was the Ring O'Bells.

Shown to an upstairs room, Sarah traced her finger along a shelf as she waited for her mistress's luggage to be brought up. The dust and grime lay thick here. She saw mouse droppings hastily swept into the corner of the room, and the curtains looked moth-eaten. She had little hope for the freshness of the bedlinen, correctly anticipating that it would be damp and musty.

Sarah also knew that the Westford crest on the Marquess's carriage would signal considerable wealth and be likely to tempt opportunists. She was secretly relieved that she would be sharing a room with her mistress, for the only other room spare would be used by George.

Lily had been shown to a cramped private parlour while the rooms were hastily prepared.

"I will bring you some wine, my lady," the sly-eyed barmaid told her. It was served in a cracked goblet. Lily took a small sip but did not drink it. She had been hungry, but the odours of long-boiled cabbage and a greasy stew being served to patrons had made her lose her appetite. Instead she requested bread and cheese, even though she suspected that the cheese would be hard and the bread stale.

She ate a little from the dull pewter plate that was brought to her, hoping that George and Sarah had managed a better meal from the inn's fare. It was only one night to endure. In the morning they would procure another carriage from somewhere, and finally make their way to the capital.

***

He should have hired a Bow Street Runner. Gervase had wanted no further delay, but as he rode forth on the main highway out of London, his head cooled and he questioned the haste of his departure.

What was done was done. He rode through the late evening, glad at least of a clear sky with a bright, gibbous moon illuminating his path as night fell.

Once he had passed the outskirts of London and was on the open road, he stopped at several inns to ascertain if his carriage had passed through.

It had not.

Finally he reached a particular coaching inn where the landlord indicated two men playing dice at a corner table. "They've come from that way some hours hence."

Gervase approached them. "I am inquiring after a carriage that has been delayed, of which no news has been sent," he said. "Have you passed any accidents on your journey here?"

The leaner of the two men shook his head. "You might ask at the Ring O'Bells though, five miles to the south west. They had no rooms spare when we stopped there earlier."

It was not an inn that Gervase was familiar with, but it was on his route. He thanked the men and went on his way.

***

Despite her tiredness, Lily could not sleep. She heard Sarah breathing heavily across the room as well as the sound of George's snoring through the thin wall that divided their rooms.

After so much had happened she had expected to be overcome with fatigue and to have fallen into a deep slumber. Yet no sleep came.

Was it minutes or hours she lay there, envying her servants their oblivion? The room was too light perhaps, the moonlight streamed through. It was but a few days until the Harvest Moon, Lily thought. In London there would doubtless be heavy drapes to block out all light.

A shaft of moonlight shone through the gap in the moth-eaten curtain. It cast across the bed and onto on the door, gleaming on the handle. Lily watched it as if spellbound.

Surely she must imagine it? The handle appeared to move noiselessly, as though someone on the other side were trying to open it.

As though...

Lily sat bolt upright in the hard bed.

The key on her side of the door was slowly being turned.

Her lungs constricted and she felt her heart thump in her chest. She clutched the bedsheets.

Was it thieves? Should she close her eyes and let them take what they could find, to pretend to be asleep?

But what if they had even more ill intent?

If only she had George's gun. In the seconds of silence at the key turned, her mind raced. She grabbed a heavy candlestick and retreated to the far side of the room, where Sarah lay asleep. She tried to shake the maid awake. "Sarah!" Her voice was as loud a whisper as she dared, but her maid did not respond.

"Sarah!" Lily felt frantic. Nothing would rouse her.

She stood there alone in her nightgown, the candlestick raised.

Slowly, the door opened, and Lily recoiled in shock to see the leering countenance of the innkeeper before her. A flicker of surprise passed over his features to see her standing there, then his lips twisted in a sneering smile.

"Well, well, my lady. I did not expect to find you awake."

"What is the meaning of this?" Lily did all she could to keep her voice steady. She felt far from bold, but gathered what courage she could.

"You should have been asleep, my lady. Deeply asleep, thanks to the wine. But perhaps since you are awake, once you have kindly provided me with your jewels and gold, we may enjoy a little sport?"

Lily shuddered. His meaning was clear.

"Approach me, and you will regret it."

The innkeeper gave an unpleasant laugh. "I think not, my lady."

Afterwards it was hard to recall exactly what happened, Lily was in such a state of shock.

She remembered him lunging across the room and the feel of her hand swiping through the air, bringing the candlestick against his skull with a horrid crunch.

He fell, clutching his head.

Then suddenly the room seemed full of people. Who they were blurred into the background, because one of them, the only one that Lily perceived before she fainted, was the Marquess.

23. The journey

Gervase had managed to rouse George before dawn, but Sarah slept on, unwakeable. Whatever had been put in her ale had drugged her deeply. Lily was scared that she would never wake and wished to call a doctor, but George insisted he had seen such effects of a sleeping draught before.

"She'll come to no harm of it, my lady. See how she breathes, quite peaceful like."

Gervase had managed to procure a coach and George carried the maid into it. Lily packed her own belongings which did not take long, and George loaded them onto the vehicle.

Lily was at a loss for what to say to her husband, and he to her. She felt shame that he had discovered her in a state of undress, about to be assaulted by a common innkeeper. Even though she knew it was not her fault. But she mistook his silence as his further disapproval of her.

In fact Gervase was racked with guilt and was also uncommonly humbled with admiration for his wife. The image of her standing there, so young and slight in her nightgown, grasping the candlestick. He recalled the determined tilt of her chin as she gave the scoundrel some share of what was owed to him.

Lily had trembled afterwards, when he lifted her up and set her on the bed. The exhaustion on her face was intense. She was palest white, with violet shadows deepening her eyes. Yet her beauty remained undimmed.

Gervase had felt an instinct to keep holding her in his arms but was inhibited by not wishing to cause her any further distress.

So he had straightened, pushing the inn-keeper with his foot to ensure he was fully unconscious. Loath to leave her even for a moment he went to fetch George. Groggy from the tampered ale, the coachman had at first struggled to get up. But the news of the assault quickly set him alert.

There was nothing to be done about the landlord at that time, so they had left him there. Gervase would contact the appropriate authorities later and make his complaint. The priority was to get safely to London and procure a physician for the maid if she continued to sleep.

Lily, exhausted even more by the relief of the rescue and her own confused emotions on seeing her husband, soon slept. She had tried to hold herself carefully upright while sitting next to him, fearing his disdain if a jolt threw her against his person.

But as she drifted into a heavy sleep, her head rested against his shoulder.

For Gervase it was both touching and torture. He found himself oddly comforted by the weight of the golden head that pressed against him. If he had been of no other use or preservation to her in the danger she had faced, he might at least be a bedpost now.

He recalled his godmother's words. Yes, he must indeed offer her what was due as his wife. If that meant attending the various social affairs and assemblies he habitually shrank from, so be it. She would certainly be an ornament to display.

He convinced himself it was her physical appearance that oddly affected him. Doubtless the same charms that had affected Farrington, for his cousin to have broken his usual pattern to pursue the girl.

She was bewitching, Gervase thought. Most likely she knew it. Well, she had landed her prey hook, line and sinker so she may as well have her gowns and parties and they could both be done with it. An heir at some point, perhaps, and they could live civil but separate lives at Westford Park.

***

The Marquess's London house was exquisite. While Lily preferred the more faded, comfortable beauty of his country estate, there was no doubt that his town residence was in splendid order.

The rooms were of spacious proportion, not overly cluttered, with furnishings both elegant and discreet. It was grandeur without ostentation.

And yet there was an untouched, even neglected feel. Lily sensed that these rooms rarely bustled with people. How much time was the Marquess accustomed to spend here?

He had been nearly constantly in town since bringing her to Westford Park but she wondered whether this was his usual habit. A chill crept into her heart that he may have chosen to deliberately avoid her. This prospect made her straighten. However long their marriage might endure, she was determined to redeem her reputation with him so that when they inevitably parted, the name of Cosgrove was not wholly disgraced. She owed her father this at least.

He would be white with anger, she imagined. But she would not give him reason to fault her own conduct regarding anything other than the deception she had practiced on him. He should not also think she was wanton, or discourteous, or cowardly.

Lily hoped very much she was not cowardly. But she struggled not to quail at what lay ahead. She might be required to meet people who had made her cousin's acquaintance, and who would be astonished at finding an impostor.

The worst prospect was meeting Tom Farrington. He would surely be here in the capital and must at some point call. Could she manage to avoid him?

She had first imagined that Farrington might stay away, having heard of Betsy's supposed marriage to his cousin and not wanting the embarrassment of a confrontation. But such a meeting had to happen at some point, and the more she had heard of Farrington's character, the more she rather feared he would find malicious enjoyment in it.

Lily had ended up sleeping much of the day, as had Sarah. It was dusk when she finally ventured downstairs, having excused the wan-looking maid any duties that night. She still felt that a physician should be called for her; certainly if Sarah's pallor endured to the morrow.

If the town house servants were surprised that their mistress ordered supper on a tray to be brought to her maid, rather than the reverse, they made no remark.

This done, Lily found her way down the stairs. At least in this smaller residence she could not get lost.

Her husband was in the drawing room and rose to greet her. "Elizabeth. I trust you are well rested after your ordeal?"

"I am, my lord." She felt uncertain how to express her gratitude and relief at his rescuing them all. To acknowledge the risk that he must have exposed himself to, venturing off to find them after nightfall, might be seen as an aspersion on his courage or sense of duty. So she simply thanked him once for arriving in the nick of time.

"We were to have dined with Lady Diana Belvedere tonight, who is my godmother," Gervase told her. "Due to the circumstances this has been postponed."

Lily was troubled. "I am very sorry."

Gervase frowned. "You have no need to be. If you are fully recovered on the morrow, we will visit her in the morning."

A servant brought Lily wine and some small savouries. She sipped the drink, hoping it might ease her nerves, but struggled to eat anything. The memory of the dreadful inn, its slatternly staff and rank fare, still swirled through her senses. Her husband's presence also put her on edge, even though he seemed assiduous regarding her comfort that evening.

She had no idea how she would manage to dine with him. It would be just the two of them once more: how much easier it might have been if there had been another woman to share the table.

Lily also felt a mixed hope and fear of what might come later that night. The Marquess looked so noble and handsome as he sat before her. She shivered to remember the hard planes of his sculpted body, and his intimate caresses.

Perhaps if she could manage not to disappoint him in this regard, as she was convinced she must have done previously, his kindness to her might continue? Although she knew she deserved it, she still feared the coldness of his anger.

***

Gervase wavered over paying a visit to his wife that night. His conscience wrestled with his desire. As pale as she looked, he found himself inflamed by her. The slim curves under the muslin she had worn at dinner. The way her eyes glowed like shadowy jewels in the candlelight. The faint scent of flowers that clung about her.

He felt once more that he was seeing her for the first time. The deceptions and conflict between them were for now a thing of the past.

Most of all he longed to hold her, and this was how he justified visiting her bedchamber. She might welcome the comfort of his presence, or at least he managed to convince himself, after the ordeal of being unguarded at the inn last night.

Gervase's intentions to provide only comfort to his wife fell away the moment he saw her. She sat up in her bed startled: her hair falling like silk about her, one shoulder exposed by the loosened neckline of her gown. The ribbon had come undone: not that it would have remained tied for long after his arrival.

Yet he managed to restrain himself. He sat on the bed beside her and brushed a lock of hair back from her brow. "If you are too tired, wife..." he began, emphasising "wife" so she would understand that he sought wifely duties from her.

"I am not, my lord."

Gervase traced his fingers lightly down her neck and slipped his hand beneath her neckline and around her breast. She gasped, and he felt a surge of pride and joy to see her gaze narrow in desire rather than widen with fear.

"Do you want me?"

"Yes." It was barely a whisper.

"Tell me what you want from me."

Lily blushed to articulate it. "For you to touch me as you did before. And to...." She broke off. She wasn't even certain of what term should be properly used.

"Couple with you?"

She answered him by taking the initiative: winding her arms around his neck and bringing her lips onto his. He deepened and opened the kiss, and she found herself twisting her hands in his hair as he embraced her.

They undressed one another: Lily revelling in his warmth and strength, and the scent of the aromatic bay and rosemary that he used. Clean and masculine, intoxicating her. Was it wicked to delight in and desire a man's body so? She wasn't sure but she was too carried away to care. She also put it out of her mind whether or not their union would be properly sanctioned by the church, given the priest had been misled as to her identity.

She expected him to lay her down on the pillows, but instead he twisted around so he lay back and she was positioned over him.

Gervase saw her confusion and explained. "I can enter you like this. Then I can look upon you as we are joined."

Lily was uncertain but she trusted him. She wanted him within her, and she wanted to please him. Perhaps if she did so well enough, he would want to keep her despite everything.

Her husband guided her on to him. He seemed larger inside her than before from this position, making it almost too deep as he filled her.

His hands grasped her waist and he gazed up at her.

Although unsure what to do, by instinct she shifted around on top of him, seeking a more comfortable angle. Holding her hips he helped move her so she understood the rhythm that he wanted. Then his hands were free to roam over her body: caressing her waist, trailing up over her breasts. Lily gasped as his thumb brushed and teased her nipple.

At the same time she discovered that if she leant forward slightly, it made an intense and wonderful feeling in her own loins. This caused her to quicken her movement, longing for more of him.

"Slower, my darling, or it will be over too quickly," Gervase cautioned her.

She looked down at the sculpted angles of his face, a sheer of perspiration on his brow.

"I can only delay things so long, looking upon you like this," he told her.

Why should he want to hold back? But Lily slowed, and instead tried to make the rhythm longer and deeper. "Like this?"

"Yes, but I'm afraid it won't be much use now." He broke off and suddenly clasped her down against him, her breasts crushed against his chest. His hands cupped her rear as he took over the rhythm, thrusting violently upwards into her.

She heard him mutter an oath, muffled by his lips being against her hair. "Elizabeth… the damned sweetness of you… I lose all control."

For a few moments he relaxed and held her here, on top of him, still within her. When he finally withdrew she assumed that he was finished with her, and would leave her to sleep.

Instead he rolled her beneath him and moved swiftly down her body. He grasped her thighs, forcing them apart.

When she felt his mouth, hot over her, his tongue pressing relentlessly against the very core of her sensation, Lily was lost. Within seconds she bucked and cried out, trying to writhe away as the feeling over took her, becoming nearly too sensitive.

But Gervase gripped her firmly, continuing his ministrations until the very last wave had shuddered through her and she was still, and utterly spent.

Then he moved back alongside her, kissed her lips and then her cheek, and pulled her against him. Lily fell asleep with the warmth of his side and the weight of his arm over her. He wanted her with him, for now. It was where she wanted to be.

24. The godmother

If Sir Stephen Seton had been taken aback by the Marquess's new bride, Lady Diana Belvedere found herself infinitely more surprised.

Though she had not met the chit, having been selective with her acceptances and invitations the previous season - after all, with no daughters, nieces or wards, she felt justified in avoiding the main crushes of the marriage mart - Lady Diana did at least have her ear more closely attuned to the current than Sir Stephen.

This young woman was nothing like anything she had been prepared for. Neither in looks nor in bearing.

She was also nothing like the kind of silly young girl that Lady Diana might have expected to have been led astray by a dissipated rake such as Farrington.

It took Lady Diana less than ten seconds to form these thoughts of the new Marchioness of Westford.

"You are - or were - Elizabeth Cosgrove, I believe?" she inquired.

"Indeed, my lady," Lily told her.

"I was acquainted with your maternal grandmother many years ago, though I have not had the pleasure of meeting your parents," Lady Diana said.

Lily breathed a secret sigh of relief. She had by now apprised her husband of Sir Robert's and Lady Maud's fleeting visit to Westford Park. She had spoken of it with scant detail, and the Marquess had made but slight comment other than to trust that they were well. If he had wondered at her lack of filial feeling, or her failure to request that they should be invited for a longer stay, he did not reveal it.

"I understand that you suffered quite an atrocious ordeal on your journey to London. I was very sorry to hear of it," Lady Diana said. She had welcomed them into her morning parlour where a maid served them refreshments.

Lily reassured her hostess that all was well, and that the trouble had been brief. "We were most fortunate in Lord Westford's prompt arrival," she said.

"Rather more fortunate in your expert wielding of a candlestick," Gervase remarked.

Lady Diana raised her eyebrows. "Indeed?" She had not yet received a detailed account of the assault in the inn, only a brief note from him the previous day concerning the carriage breakdown and attempted robbery.

"I arrived to find Elizabeth fending off the villain with a brass candlestick, facing him with the courage of ten armed men," Gervase said. "I had not anticipated such bravery in my bride, when the female fashion is surely to swoon and faint."

Lily blushed at the exaggeration. But more so at his praise of her, even if said in some jest.

Lady Diana made a scornful retort at her godson's remark, that sounded not unlike "Psshaw!" There was faint disapproval on her face. "You do our sex a grave injustice, my boy. Nonetheless, I do admire your fortitude, my dear," she said, addressing Lily. She noticed the faint roses in the girl's cheeks, and her expression as she glanced at her husband.

It was not what Lady Diana had expected to see, after a marriage in such circumstances. Gratitude might be anticipated; expected, even. This was far more than that.

She was even more amazed to spy a similar look on Gervase's face. Admittedly his bride had enough beauty to win over the most jaded of rakes, and Gervase was far from that. Yet despite what Lady Diana perceived between them, the two were strangely formal with one another. If more had developed from this marriage than mere convenience, and his godmother sincerely hoped it might be so, why was there this strain between them?

There was fear, too, in the girl's eyes. Lady Diana perceived this, and wondered at it. That she might have been hesitant - ill-at-ease - on re-entering society following her disgrace was unsurprising. This was something quite else.

Whatever it was, it was not fear of her husband. The older woman knew her godson well enough to know that he would never have treated the girl severely or cruelly. At least she trusted not. Fear would also not engender the shy admiration of him that the girl failed to conceal.

He knows the worst of her, Lady Diana thought, what more could she be afraid of?

Most curious. She would get to the bottom of it all before the visit was out.

***

Lady Diana managed everything with her customary adroitness. She led the conversation at lunch, her own husband Sir Clarence muffled by his moustache and his attentions to his soup. She spoke of town affairs and relayed some of the more seemly gossip of the ton, but with an intelligent perspective and insightful comments.

Lily listened and learned. In particular she strove to hear names that Betsy might have mentioned. She must write to her cousin again soon, she thought, and get a better idea of who might recognise the true Elizabeth Cosgrove from the false.

Not that she was false, she reminded herself. She had as much right to the name as her cousin had. She was simply the wrong Elizabeth Cosgrove.

Lily was unable to contribute anything when the conversation took a political turn, and felt sorely the lack of her current education in this regard. She was not alone however: Sir Clarence said very little. Lady Diana nudged the occasional "Quite!" or "Indeed, my dear" from her husband, but it was apparent that he was not a voluble man.

Sir Clarence fled back to the peace of his study as soon as he could politely do so, and his wife dispatched her godson to town on some contrived errand. She wished a closer acquaintance with his bride and his presence hampered that. There was also the matter of her wardrobe, which Lady Diana had promised to attend to.

The girl was pleasantly attired that morning, though her muslin was on the lighter side for these cooler autumn days. Lady Diana had no idea that the gown - Betsy's old muslin - was now Lily's only acceptable outfit other than Mrs Mead's ballgown.

Lady Diana had not been entirely convinced by Gervase's account of things. At the time he had first related the story, it had seemed more likely that the girl had feigned the deficiency in her wardrobe - perhaps out of vanity or greed for finer costumes. Meeting her, Lady Diana instantly realised that this was not so.

Either way, she must be dressed as befitted a marchioness.

"The late Lady Westford was a very dear friend of mine, and I look upon Gervase almost as my own son," she told Lily as they sat in her drawing room. "As such you will forgive my lack of formality around him. As his godmother I have known him since his infancy, so we do not stand on ceremony with one another."

"I understand that his mother died very young," Lily said.

"Indeed. Which brings me onto the matter before us. Suffering a lack womanly influence in his upbringing, I fear Gervase may not have given due attention to some of the requirements of a wife. He has not yet, I understand, arranged a trousseau for you?"

Lily acknowledged that he had not. She tried to say that she was not in need of anything, but Lady Diana cut her short.

"Any woman needs a new wardrobe on her marriage, and a marchioness certainly so. I have Gervase's full permission to take care of everything. I have arranged for a dressmaker to attend us later this afternoon, who I have been assured is the very latest thing for Paris fashion."

"It is very kind of you, but…"

Once again Lady Diana overrode Lily's protestations. "Think nothing of it, my dear. Now tell me how you have found Westford. And by that I include both the estate and the man, though I suspect you will be more forthcoming on the subject of the house and grounds."

There was an amused light in her eye, and Lily found herself further warming to the older woman. She shared her impressions of Westford Park: its elegance and the beauty of its grounds. "The lake is particularly lovely. I look forward very much to seeing it in summer."

"I understand from Gervase that you are a fine rider. Even without a saddle, so I am told."

Lily blushed, surprised that her husband should have imparted this. Though it had been due to emergency, she was sure that his godmother must consider it most improper. "The horse was bridled, and the distance was not long. I was very much afraid for my maid and for George, alone on the road. And Sarah could not ride, so it seemed the only course of action."

Lady Diana smiled. "Indeed. I admire your courage quite as much as Gervase does."

Lily's eyes widened at such praise. She had been more anxious of disgracing her husband, and was surprised to learn that he had expressed the opposite sentiment to his godmother. "Thank you. I am not so certain that I could have done such, had not the greater fear of highwaymen been upon me."

A servant entered to inform them that the dressmaker had arrived. A Madame LaFleur was admitted, a Frenchwoman of a certain age, clad in a deceptively simple but beautifully tailored black gown. She brought two girls with her, who carried large bags containing fabric samples.

"It is most obliging of you to attend us at my home," Lady Diana greeted her. "You have been most highly recommended by my friend the Duchess of Kent."

"I am grateful for her ladyship's recommendation," Madame LaFleur said. She had been apprised that it would be a large commission, and for a such a customer she was prepared to travel from her salon and attend personally.

There followed a busy couple of hours where measurements were taken and materials and styles decided. It seemed to Lily an absurd amount of clothes: Betsy's wardrobe for her debut had been but a fraction of this. Lily was also nervous over the vast bill that Lady Diana must be running up. She had some idea of the cost of garments due to Lady Maud's sighs over the bills from her own dressmaker. The modiste that Lady Maud employed was also far less fashionable and far less expensive than Madame LaFleur would be.

Once or twice she tried to decline a gown: a second riding habit, or another ballgown. But Lady Diana was adamant. "If you are worried about the strain on your husband's purse, you need not be. Should you wish to have every pair of shoes studded all over with diamonds, Gervase would barely notice."

Lily hoped this was a reflection of the amplitude of her husband's wealth rather than his obliviousness to expenditure, but nonetheless tried to restrain Lady Diana from ordering the most lavish fabrics and trimmings. Not only because of their cost, but because she genuinely preferred a simpler style.

Madame LaFleur was privately impressed by the young woman's taste. Lady Westford was a highly desirable customer for her. The marchioness's beauty and graceful figure would display the dressmaker's talent to best advantage, and her high rank would ensure that the creations were seen among the best society. Lily picked out several fabrics that were exactly those that Madame LaFleur would have suggested to her. The colours frequently seemed unusual to Lady Diana, but held up against Lily she could see their rightness.

Lily and Madame LaFleur were also of the same mind when it came to the cut of the gowns: tailored lines without being stark, simple without being overly austere. A dusting of seed pearls here, a silver ribbon there, a fine border of French lace on one gown; delicate embroidery on another. It would be a discreetly expensive and stylish look. Stately enough to befit the wife of a marquess, but not an overly heavy ensemble for a young woman.

All the women were very pleased when the work was complete. Madame LaFleur vowed to have her seamstresses work night and day on the order to have it ready it as soon as possible.

Lily only had one wish: that her husband should be pleased by her appearance when he beheld her. She remembered his gaze when he had first seen her in the ballgown made by Mrs Mead. It was a look she longed for again.

25. The verdict

"I like her very much, Gervase. Westford Park has not been the setting for such a jewel for many long years." For over thirty years, Lady Diana considered. All those years ago that her dear friend - Gervase's mother - had died. Far too early, far too young. The boy still bore the scars of it, she thought with a sigh.

The boy, now the Marquess of Westford, was taken aback by his godmother's unqualified praise of his wife. He had anticipated at least some reserve if not outright disapproval.

When her reaction came, it was the reverse of what he expected.

"Of course she's far too young for you. I've never held with these winter-spring matrimonials," Lady Diana continued.

Gervase choked on his wine. "I am hardy winter, godmother."

"You are nearer forty than thirty, and she is practically a child. You ought to have found yourself someone of more suitable years, a widow, perhaps. But she is intelligent and well-bred, and I dare say wise for her years. Wiser than you at the same age, certainly."

The Marquess of Westford wondered if his godmother had taken leave of her senses. Had she forgotten the circumstances of the marriage? He started to remind her but she cut across him with some irritation.

"That concerns me not. Rather it puzzles me, in several ways. She is surely what society would deem to be a diamond of the first water. Yet she must have hidden her light under a considerable bushel, for such a reputation does not precede her." Lady Diana saw her godson wince at the mention of reputation. "I do not speak of any reputation of her conduct, Gervase, but of her not inconsiderable beauty. You cannot be so blind as to be oblivious to it." She knew full well that he was not. The way he gazed at his bride gave him away utterly, but Lady Diana was too wise to mention this.

"Indeed she is very fair, but..."

"And this brings me to my second puzzlement. From what I know of Farrington's dalliances - and do not look so scandalised, Gervase, they are common knowledge in society both polite and impolite - there is a certain type he frequents, is there not? The French girl, the Spanish chit, the chambermaid who I am told had a plump and dark-eyed look about her." She signalled for her attendant to refill her glass. "You see the pattern, do you not? All quite unalike your young bride, as fair and slender as she is."

"I am not sure what you are insinuating," Gervase said.

"I insinuate nothing, I am merely curious," Lady Diana told him. "And she is a very sensible girl, not the type to have her head easily turned, I should hazard. I have wondered if the whole thing may have been a misinterpretation, a situation that appeared compromising at first glance but was in fact nothing of the sort."

What she actually had come to wonder was whether Elizabeth Cosgrove had been any kind of willing participant at all in Tom Farrington's philanderings. That instead she may have been the recipient of quite unwanted and forced attentions. Even this would still be enough to disgrace her and bring about her ruin, such was society's injustice to the fairer sex, but it was not a matter that a right thinking person could condemn her for.

She did not mention this theory to her godson, however. He was clearly conflicted enough by the situation and his feelings for his wife. The last thing Lady Diana wanted was him calling out Farrington in some hot-headed fit of chivalry.

"Were that so, my cousin would not have seen it necessary to flee to the continent," Gervase said, referring to the idea that the disgrace was a misunderstanding.

This was true, his godmother supposed. Ah, well, there was little point speculating further. The sanctity of marriage must erase the sins of the past, and liberate the poor girl from slander and condemnation.

***

There was nothing to do but brazen it out. Lily's first social engagement would be a ball hosted by Sir Clarence and Lady Belvedere. While the plans had started small, they did not remain so. Lady Diana, as well connected as she was, had allowed the guest list to grow to many times its originally intended length.

Barely a single invitation was declined. At this time of year there was less competition from rival congregations. This was not the main reason, however, that saw the best of society rush to send their acceptances. There was feverish curiosity concerning this scandalous marriage of the reclusive Marquess of Westford. He was a figure seen far more rarely about town than his disreputable cousin, which added to his mystique.

Regarding Tom Farrington at least, there was some reprieve for Lily. He remained on the continent, perhaps deliberately keeping his distance. Whatever the reason Lily was grateful for it. The day must come when their paths would cross, but the later the better.

While they awaited the delivery of Lily's gowns and the preparations for the ball were underway, Lily enjoyed a quiet and pleasant time with her husband. She grew more confident in his company, able to converse with him on a wider range of subjects as she absorbed more about politics and society. This was largely gleaned from frequent dinners with the Belvederes, and a few select acquaintances of Gervase's.

Lily had met Claude Belvedere on several occasions and liked him very much. He had a languid wit and enjoyed gossip. Gervase professed no interest in tittle-tattle and tried to discourage Claude from indulging in it. But out of the Marquess's presence, in the company of his mother and Lily, Claude was scurrilously indiscreet.

He never tried to flirt with Lily though he paid her gallant compliments. She quickly understood that Claude was not a man who sought a wife. He was the type who preferred the intimate companionship of other men. Such things were not openly spoken of, but they were known about. Lily herself could not find anything to condemn in such a situation.

But the times she enjoyed most were those spent alone with Gervase. Once she even dared to ask him about her father, remembering to refer to him as her uncle. "I believe you served with my Uncle Edward in battle. What was he like?"

"He was no less fine a soldier than he was a man. I was greatly privileged to have served under his command." Gervase told her.

Lily's joy at this was mingled with a pang of sorrow. So many years had passed yet she still missed her father dearly. "He was popular with his men?"

"There is more than one man that owes his life to Edward Cosgrove."

Gervase himself was among them. He was silent for a while, remembering the past and his army days. The mud and the dust of battlefields. The rough camping, the days and weeks on scarce rations. The guns and bayonets, the wounded and the dead.

Throughout it all, throughout the horror and the exhaustion, he remembered that brave and noble figure. Colonel Cosgrove, without whose strategy and courage he would not be standing here today. Gervase owed his commander his life, and the only way he had been able to repay him was through saving his niece from disgrace and ostracism.

Looking upon his wife, he was reminded of other traits of Edward Cosgrove. "He was a soldier, but also a scholar. His knowledge of the Classics was immense." He took Lily's hand, his thumb caressing her palm. "A gift in the Cosgrove bloodline, which manifests also in you."

"I have not my uncle's talent, I am sure," Lily said. "But it is largely through him, and books he lent me, that such great works were revealed to me. Sir Robert - " she could not bring herself to call him 'my father' " - is not so appreciative of literature as his brother was."

"I am glad that something of your uncle lives on in you," Gervase said. "His death was a very great loss, to me and to many others."

Lily felt the welling of tears in her eyes and had to swallow before she spoke. "To us all." Though in truth she had never perceived much grief on Sir Robert's part. The brothers had not been close.

Gervase for his part found his regard growing for his wife by the day, if not by the hour. He had always assumed that after marriage, even the most affectionate of couples would resume some separation of ways.

Instead he found himself craving her company and having little wish to leave her presence for his club or any other society. He regretted all his godmother's plans for social engagements that forced other company upon him.

He wished nothing more than to take his bride back to Westford Park, and spend several months continuing her instruction in his bedchamber, where she was already an apt and willing pupil.

26. The ball

The ballgown was of pale gold, far paler than the deeper yellow that had been fashionable that year. The material shimmered with ivory embroidery and tiny pearls sewn over the bodice. The neckline was lower than Lily was used to, but not immodest.

Madame LaFleur had wished it to shine in the candlelight, with Lily as an ivory flower encased in white gold - *"comme un fleur d'ivoire"*, the modiste had described it at the time of fitting.

There were new slippers upon Lily's feet, and while she had no tiara, Sarah's clever fingers had woven pearls through her hair.

Lily contemplated herself in the mirror. She had no personal vanity, she thought only of her husband's position. Did she have the appearance and bearing of a marchioness? She hoped so.

As she sat there, knowing it would soon be time to descend and enter the carriage, there was a movement behind her. She gasped as a river of sparkling stones was wound around her neck, the metal cold against her skin.

Gervase stood behind her. "I had these retrieved from the vault earlier today. They are part of the Westford collection, now yours to wear as you please. There are other gems should you prefer them."

Lily touched the necklace. It was heavy, glittering with huge and exquisite jewels. "Diamonds?" she asked, then felt foolish for what else could they be?

"I knew not what shade you might wear, and reasoned that colourless stones would suit any raiment," Gervase said.

Colourless stones! Only a man could describe such rare and beautiful gems thus. Lily had never hungered for jewels but could not fail to appreciate ones so fine as these.

She began to thank him but was startled to feel his lips on her neck. She twisted around to receive his embrace, trying to put her arms around him. But he stood back from her.

"I had better restrain myself. The very sight of you leaves me a hair's breadth away from tearing that gown from you and telling my godmother that her ball be damned," Gervase said.

"It pleases you, then?" Lily asked him, indicating the Madame LaFleur's masterpiece.

"On the contrary. It tests me to the very limits of my self-control. There will not be a man in the room tonight who does not admire and desire you, Elizabeth."

Lily remembered her husband's reaction after Lady Leominster's ball and was flooded with shame. "I would do nothing to disgrace you, my lord. If you wish me to wear different attire…"

Gervase saw the consternation on her face and hastened to reassure her. "That is not what I meant, my dear." He took a breath. "I have long been remiss in failing to apologise for my conduct towards you following the evening at Leominster Hall. I was unjust in my accusations towards you, and even more unjust in taking this long to beg your forgiveness. What came over me I cannot say."

"There is nothing to forgive, my lord." She had assumed that she had done some wrong, and had felt no rancour towards him.

"Elizabeth." He traced the edge of her face, his gaze lingering on her. "I would that you would call me more often by my

Christian name. We are husband and wife and such formality between is unnecessary, even if we first met as strangers."

He had ordered her once before to call him by his given name and she blushed to think of that occasion. It was hard for her to use his name since she did not feel equal to him. Not due to rank, or age, or her sex, but due to the fact that she had deceived him. She felt that she had no right to be on such intimate terms with him and it remained an unspoken barrier between them.

Nonetheless she attempted it. "Gervase." Her voice was husky as she spoke.

The look in his eyes was her reward. He was pleased with her, and there was heat in his gaze. His lips came down her on hers and he parted them, tasting her and exploring her. Yet even as she felt his passion swell and his grip on her tighten, and her own body grow hot from his embrace, he managed to cease the kiss and step back, regaining his self-control.

He held out his hand to his now flushed and breathless bride. "Come. It is time for us to depart."

***

"Whoever that girl is, it is not Elizabeth Cosgrove. I am not so blind nor so addle-pated as to confuse that insipid chit pointed out to me last Season with the beauty we now behold."

The speaker was a stout woman clad in mauve satin. She prided herself on her sharp sight, and was renowned among her circle for never forgetting a face.

Her companion to the right, a thin widow with greying hair, held up her lorgnettes. "I would not know, Cecilia dear. Though I admittedly think I would have remembered one so fair as that."

The third of the trio, short and plump in faded rose, frowned as she beheld the new young wife of the Marquess of Westford. "Could it be the clothes and jewels she is wearing? A change of style can be quite transformative. And is not a style I have seen before."

The keen-sighted Cecilia disagreed. "It is a French fashion, I believe. The Countess of D'Eresby wore something with a similar line at Lord and Lady Beauchamp's on Friday last."

"It is very lovely," her rose-clad friend said. "As is she."

"A girl may blossom on marriage," the lorgnette holder commented. "Though the new marchioness is remarkably slender. She has been ill, perhaps, and lost her plumpness of cheek? A cousin of mine was barely recognisable after suffering from bilious fever for two months."

"Pah! Marriage does not alter the hair colour, nor - though I cannot quite tell from across the room, but that is the fault of the light, not of my vision - the colour of the eyes. The Cosgrove girl pointed out to me at the Aldershot ball was dark eyed like her mamma. Now that I think upon it, I remember remarking to Clara Hampshire upon the resemblance."

The little woman in rose was certain her friend must be mistaken. "News of the marriage was widely broadcast, Cecilia. And we are all acquainted with the circumstances that led to its haste."

"Mayhap the Marquess had a last minute change of heart, and took another girl to wife?" The grey-haired dowager thought this very likely, when faced with such a jewel as the new Lady Westford. Men had been known to break engagements and switch their affections for far lesser a jewel. She peered once again at Lady Westford through her lorgnettes.

Cecilia Nasebury dismissed her friend's suggestion. "I think not. There is some mystery here, some intrigue. I am determined to find it out."

"I beg you will not ask them anything, Cecilia. Only imagine how such an inquiry might be received!" The plumpest of the three women was well acquainted with her friend's inquisitive nature, but was unable to influence her against her chosen course of action. She and the other woman watched in dismay, the latter holding up her lorgnettes with trembling fingers, as Mrs Nasebury strode across the floor for an audience with the Marquess and his wife.

The newly married couple stood near Lady Belvedere, whose presence made it much easier for Cecelia to obtain an introduction. Diana Belvedere recognised instantly that Mrs Nasebury angled to be presented to the guests of honour, and was happy to oblige.

"I hope that I may congratulate you on your marriage, my lady," Cecilia addressed the Marchioness.

Lily murmured her thanks.

"You were not married in town, so I believe?" Cecilia Nasebury persisted.

It seemed an odd question, but Lily saw no danger in answering truthfully.

"No, madam, we were married at my family's home in Somerset."

"A country church wedding! Most charming." Cecilia hoped to unearth some clue to the mystery, though she knew not what.

"It was held in our family chapel, presided over by the curate from our local church," Lily told her.

"Indeed, indeed. I have often remarked to Mr Nasebury of the advantages of an intimate ceremony. Our own daughter was married at St George's and there were three other weddings performed that day!" St George's Parish Church in Mayfair was considered a fashionable venue, hosting a thousand or more weddings every year.

"Your daughter was married recently?" Lily asked.

"Oh no! Two years hence, following her first season." There was a glow of maternal pride at this successful achievement. 'It was my younger daughter, Julia, who came out this year. Perhaps you may have met her at one of the many dances for debutantes?"

Lily felt a coldness creep through her veins. "I cannot say, madam. I am afraid that with so many new people, I did not remember the names of everyone who was introduced to me. It was very remiss of me, I am sure. But perhaps I might recognise your daughter by sight?"

"She is not in town at present. She is staying with her sister in Yorkshire, who is currently *in confinement*." Cecilia Nasebury lowered her voice on this last phrase.

Lily had always found it foolish that pregnancy should be considered such an indelicate subject even between women, but such was the way of things. "It is my turn, then, to offer you and Mr Nasebury my congratulations."

"Thank you, my lady. I also attended the season, of course. There are indeed many people whom are pointed out to one, whom one is not introduced to directly." Cecelia did not quite dare to go so far as to include Lady Westford directly among these people, but her meaning was clear. Even without the keenly inquisitive look in her eye.

She knows. Lily did all she could to maintain her composure. "It is so. I am happy to finally make your acquaintance, Mrs Nasebury, and hope to also make the acquaintance of your daughters when they are next in town."

It was a polite dismissal, and both women knew it as such. Cecelia Nasebury returned to her friends with mingled emotions of triumph and continued curiosity.

"Well, Cecilia. On closer inspection is she the chit you saw at the Aldershots"?"

"She is not. Though who she is, I cannot say. I would be most interested, I confess, to view the record of that marriage in the parish register. Even in the case of a special licence the records must be entered. Still, it is not my concern, I am sure."

Cecilia was not the only guest to note the unusual appearance of the former Elizabeth Cosgrove. Most assumed their own memory must err, or that the wrong girl had been pointed out to them during the season. They certainly were not so bold as to approach the lady in question and disclose their surprise.

Just one woman, a countess who was a close intimate of Lady Belvedere and meant no harm in her inquiry, mentioned the matter to her hostess.

"She is far fairer than I recall, Diana. Whatever the reasons for the match, one cannot deny that she is quite an ornament on your godson's arm."

The women watched as Lily, who stood by her husband, was approached to dance by Claude. The two of them were at once the most handsome and graceful couple on the floor, even if Claude could not rival Gervase in looks and stature.

"Indeed she is. No less his match in wit and intelligence, either. Claude absolutely adores her."

Lady Diana was quite safe in making this comment to the countess, since Claude's proclivities were an open secret among her circle.

"Her husband also," the countess remarked. They watched as the Marquess of Westford looked upon his wife as she danced, his eyes never leaving her. There was a fierce pride in his gaze and also a defiance. He was there as her spouse and her protector, and any purveyors of gossip and snide remarks should beware.

Thus the countess saw, as Lady Diana had previously observed, just how the land lay regarding the new bridegroom's affections. They both knew that for a man of such high station to fall for a woman, the fall must be all the harder.

27. The London scene

Matrimony to a marquess, her own graces and Lady Diana's machinations saw Lily very quickly accepted among the best society. Whilst some, such as Cecilia Nasebury, continued to wonder over the situation, for the most part the ton began to move on to other matters. The Cosgrove family was not sufficiently prominent to sustain interest or inquiry.

Had Sir Robert and Lady Maud chosen to come to town during this period it might have been a different matter. But Lady Maud's dislike of travelling - her nerves had required several weeks to recover after the return journey from Buxton - had prevented her from coming again to town. She was not a prolific letter writer and nor was her daughter, so the absence of correspondence from Betsy did not cause her mother significant concern.

Lily had written to Betsy from London several times but had received only one listless reply. It held an even more despairing tone than her earlier letters.

I know not what to do. I long for any news. I am sure he cannot have forgotten me, but perhaps if he believes I am wed he will have given up hope. Oh, Lily dearest, can you not send word to him? I am sure he must come to Westford Park on your invitation, and then he will see how matters stand and he will send for me. I am not sure how much longer I can bear it here. The days pass so slowly...

It was hopeless, Lily thought. She knew not what to reply to her cousin. She herself dreaded a meeting with Tom Farrington, though she supposed it must happen eventually. But for her to invite him to Westford Park! It was unthinkable.

She found that she longed to return to the country estate, thinking fondly of its peace and beauty. She had become dangerously comfortable living there. It would not be forever, she reminded herself.

But Lady Diana was determined to parade her godson and his bride around the ton before allowing them to escape back to the country. She obtained an Almack's voucher for Lily with some ease: her rank as a Marchioness outweighing any notoriety.

Clad in a silvery creation by Madame LaFleur, Lily entered the club on her husband's arm. The rooms were crowded thick with people in their finery. As splendid as the men were, in their frock coats and close-fitting breeches, none matched the Marquess of Westford for stature and physique. Lily had observed the admiring glances of other women towards her husband - she was oblivious of the same glances directed at her - and felt all the more undeserving of her current position.

She was delighted to encounter Miss Sawthwaite there. Emma Sawthwaite was in town with her mamma, preparing her trousseau ahead of her upcoming nuptials with Sir Percival Elstone.

"You look well, Lady Westford, and what a beautiful dress!"

Lily thanked her. "Lady Belvedere took me to her modiste. I am very fortunate that she is so talented."

Miss Sawthwaite begged for the name and Lily was happy to provide it.

"Honestly there is so much to be done with all the wedding preparations. My mother bustles me here and there, and I have barely had a chance to see much of Lord Percy. Before the engagement was officially announced we seemed to meet so much more frequently than now. I fear we will be almost strangers when we wed," Miss Sawthwaite confessed. Then she looked disconcerted, remembering what she had been told of the Marchioness of Westford's own situation.

But Lily merely smiled. She was glad that whatever its origins, Miss Sawthwaite's forthcoming union looked to be a happy one. The young woman was clearly taken with her future groom.

Miss Sawthwaite asked after several people whom Lily had met at the Leominster Hall ball, but other than Sir Stephen Seton, Lily had no news to offer. "He is well, I believe. Lady Leominster also, though I have not seen her since that night."

Emma Sawthwaite paused, and then began to speak. "I must confess, though I am certain my mamma would chide me for being so indiscreet, that I fear Lady Leominster may not have harboured such warm sentiment towards all her guests as she displayed in welcoming them." She spoke these last words hurriedly, immediately regretting her outspokenness and looking anxiously at Lady Westford, who she felt sure must now condemn her.

There was a reason for her candour. She had overheard Lady Leominster saying shockingly vicious things about Lady Westford to an intimate of hers, unaware that someone else was within earshot. Naturally the slander could not be repeated to the Marchioness, but Miss Sawthwaite felt deep anxiety on Lily's behalf. Such malevolence presaged mischief, she feared.

Lily was surprised and troubled by Miss Sawthwaite's words. She was wise enough to interpret them for what they were: a warning. And indeed she could not disown that she herself had sensed an antipathy from her hostess and neighbour. "I do indeed read your meaning, Miss Sawthwaite. Your words do not come as such a surprise to me as you may have supposed."

Emma Sawthwaite was greatly relieved. "I am far too outspoken, I know. My mamma continually chides me for it."

"Not at all. I take your candour as a kindness." Forewarned is forearmed, Lily thought. She recalled the gypsy's troubling prediction and felt a thin chill down her spine.

"Are you well, Lady Westford? You look pale all of a sudden?" Emma Sawthwaite asked.

Lily recovered herself. "I am quite well, thank you. Just a foolish thing." She felt a sudden desire to share the matter. It had not been possible to speak of it to Gervase, he would think her quite cork-brained. "It is a strange tale. Some mishap befell our carriage on the way here, and gypsies encamped nearby came to our aid."

Miss Sawthwaite was fascinated. "Gypsies! To have aided you - what an adventure!"

"Indeed. But one of them gave me a strange warning, and while I know such things are nothing but fiddle faddle and moonshine, it has yet unnerved me."

"A warning!" The other young woman was rapt, though she refrained from asking its content. "How so? I am told that they divine the future with magic stones and playing cards, and I have always wanted to witness such. Though I am quite sure it is all moonshine, as you say, it must be a spectacle."

Lily was sure she had already said too much, but she continued, giving a colourful description of the encampment and the gypsy folk. "They offered me tea and divined from the leaves, and then read my palm." She felt herself blushing. "Oh! It is all so terribly foolish, I am ashamed not to have simply forgotten it all. It is only that we met with more misadventure that same night at the nearby inn, and then I recalled the gypsies' warning."

"More misadventure?"

"An attempted robbery." Lily tried to play it down, since she was sure enough scandal already surrounded her. "My husband arrived in time and we were quite safe and well. Yet it was a strange coincidence, was it not, to happen so soon after we encountered the gypsies? Such coincidences do happen, I suppose."

Emma Sawthwaite found it a thrilling tale, and said so. "Would that I could enjoy such adventures when I travel!"

Lily smiled. "It was far from enjoyable. I hope for quieter journeys in future." It occurred to her that when she returned, she would like to revisit the gypsies and thank them once again. Perhaps their warning had set her nerves on edge sufficiently to bring about the fortunate sleeplessness that had likely saved them from a worse plight. Though the encampment might have moved on, she supposed.

Despite her secret anxieties, she was delighted by Almack's. It helped that people were very polite and kind. How much of this was due to her husband's hawk-like eye upon all those who approached her, she could not say. The Marquess had taken his godmother's words to heart and stood there in the role of devoted spouse and protector. Woe betide anyone should cast a smirking glance or a snide remark.

Gervase was aided in this by the lady patronesses of Almack's. Having decided to accept the new Marchioness into their assembly, it was in their interest that former scandals were swept aside and not be permitted to sully their society. The new Lady Westford was thus embraced, with many prestigious and renowned persons introduced to her.

Lily had decided to seize the moment and take what enjoyment she could. Certainly the sand must be running rapidly through the hourglass, with discovery ever closer. She steeled herself against that prospect. It could not be worse than the fate that should have been hers earlier. If she were sent to live abroad in shame and exile, so be it.

Above all she gloried in the intensity of her husband's gaze upon her. There was ardour in his eyes as he beheld her, and she was aware of what she might anticipate in his bedchamber later that night. I am a wanton, she thought, and as such she could feel no censure towards Betsy for her folly. Had Lily herself been a debutante pursued by a man such as the Marquess of Westford, she was quite sure that she would have succumbed to any improper advances he made.

This thought made her smile, as his conduct was so proper that no such roguishness could fairly be imagined of him.

"Something amuses you?" Gervase asked her, observing her expression.

Lily was glad the room was hot or she was sure that a fiery blush would have given her away. "Merely some foolish notion," she told him.

He raised his eyebrows.

Lily could hardly tell him, given to do so would practically be to accuse him of being capable of his cousin's conduct. Yet she chose a daring course. "Merely that you are quite the most handsome man in this room, my lord."

Gervase was startled to hear such from his wife. He had little vanity and considered his eligibility to derive solely from his wealth and status. His marital union had hardly been based on any physical attraction, since he and his bride had never met before they stood at the altar. He was also aware that many men and women soon looked for attractions elsewhere following a marriage.

Standing there, he looked upon the young woman that every man in the room must surely most admire. That she should look upon him, Gervase, with genuine desire, quite took him aback. She had no need to dissemble or seduce him, let alone in public, given she already had his hand and his name.

But there was a playful fire in her eyes, silvery in the light, and Gervase had to grit his teeth against a sudden impulse to carry her off to a private room then and there, were such a thing even possible. He had never struggled with self-control, but now he had the rest of this damned evening and these people to endure, and a carriage ride, before he could be alone with her.

28. The warning

As the horses made their way through the trees, Lily smelt wood smoke and glimpsed the painted wagons of the gypsy camp. She found herself unaccountably relieved that the Romany folk were still there. Some days the encounter seemed so fantastical that she wondered if she had imagined it.

Gervase had been amused by his wife's request to revisit the gypsy people. But he was in very good humour following the stay in London, which had been successful both in public and private, and time was not of the essence. Thus he was happy to oblige.

Sarah was once again left in the care of George as Gervase unshackled two horses and accompanied his wife through the forest. They had not yet had the opportunity to ride together and he was impressed by her seat and handling of her mount. He looked forward to riding out with her around Westford Park on future days.

The late autumnal scents filled Lily's nostrils. Damp and decaying leaves, wet earth, the fragrant blue smoke from the gypsies' fire. She felt a sudden wild envy of their lives, which seemed so simple and free. Were she banished, she wondered what it might be like to join them and live life on the road, as far from disapproving society as possible.

Common sense overcame her brief romanticism as she considered the reality of the outdoors: the harsh grip of winter, foraging for food from the frozen, barren wintry fields. Bitter rain like needles driving through the patched rags they wore. Being shunned and chased off the land. A colourful life it might appear to outsiders, but it was surely not an easy one.

Distracted by her thoughts, Lily did not think to wait for her husband to help her dismount. She slid off her horse and was only caught just at the end by Gervase. She apologised but he was amused rather than affronted by her independence. "You had a highly competent riding instructor, I can see," he observed.

Lily could not disclose that her riding instructor had been her father, the man Gervase supposed to be her uncle. "I was very fortunate, my lord. Though some may be of the opinion that I was unfortunate, since I was taught to ride more like a man than a woman."

The Marquess laughed. "If it means we may ride together without my horse forced to traipse along at the speed of a snail to keep pace with you, all to the better," he told her. Against all his expectations he was starting to enjoy married life. His wife continued to surprise him and his enjoyment of her surprised him.

Lily walked slightly ahead of her husband as she entered the clearing. The gypsies fell silent at the sight of the visitors, but the woman who had read her palm approached her. She wore the same crimson gown as before.

"I came to thank you again for your help," Lily said. "I trust your grandmother is well?"

"Her injury is very nearly healed," the woman said.

Lily hesitated. "I also wished to thank you for your warning. That same night we were accosted by robbers, and thanks to your caution I had anticipated trouble. We managed to escape unscathed."

The young woman frowned. She turned and said something in her language to another of her people, who nodded and went inside one of the caravans. A few moments later the old gypsy woman emerged, hobbling on a stick and helped along by her kinsman. The younger woman went to exchange words with her, and returned looking even more anxious.

"My lady, it was not robbers my puridai and I saw in the lines of Fate." Her eyes flicked to the Marquess and back, she clearly felt restricted from speaking freely before him.

Lily turned to Gervase. "I must go to reassure the old woman that I am well," she said, hoping the excuse would suffice. Leaving him with the horses, she went with the woman to the gypsy elder, out of her husband's earshot.

The woman in red lowered her voice. She spoke in pieces, translating from the strange words uttered by her grandmother.

"It is a closer and more dangerous enemy than robbers which we saw. It is someone near to you, someone who has moved within your home. They threaten a great evil to you. My puridai regrets that she cannot see whom this enemy is, but the future is not yet woven clearly. As the hour approaches, so the threads will tighten."

The old woman was murmuring what sounded like an incantation. Lily did not know if the younger gypsy was translating all her words precisely or giving a mere sense of things.

"Beware all. Trust no one. Avoid being alone in a room unlocked by key. I wish we could offer you gladder tidings, my lady, but the Fates reveal only this."

***

Lily dared not meet Gervase's eyes as they rode back. In part because she feared he might think her foolish. But also because she wrestled with herself over the fears the gypsies' warning had aroused in her. They had not seemed mischievous or cruel, she considered, for their warning to have been nothing but a trick. She felt that they sincerely believed it.

But should she believe it? Their superstitions contradicted all the things she had been properly taught and educated in. She could well imagine what her father or the family curate would make of them. Despite wishing to dismiss them, a sense of unease seeped deep into her bones. Nagging at the back of her mind was a fear she could not quite bear to think upon. She did what she could to suppress it, but remained troubled for the rest of the journey.

It was nightfall when they arrived at Westford Park. Lily felt a strange surge of joy and relief in her breast at being home. Guilt quickly replaced it, for this was not truly nor honestly her home.

The Marquess saw that his wife looked pale and tired from the journey, and resolved to make no demands on her that night. It would take some self-control, for he had become accustomed to the joys of her body each night. He was aware that her mood had changed since the visit to the gypsies. He wondered what they had said. Some silly superstition, no doubt. He reminded himself how young she was, and that a maiden's head might easily be filled with such moonshine.

Then he checked himself, for it did his wife an injustice to condemn her sense due to her age. Despite her years he was daily impressed with her learning and her quiet wisdom. Whatever the Romanies had said to her must remain a mystery for now. He regarded Lily, feeling an impulse to put his arms around her but not wishing to disturb her reverie.

They had married as strangers, he thought, and a great part of her was a stranger to him still. He resolved to know his wife better. All he had learnt so far of her had brought him nothing but delight.

"Have the horses seen to but leave the carriage until the morrow," he told George as they alighted. Gervase did not require his men to work unnecessarily late. He would not need the carriage in the morning thus there was no sense in George and Ben attending to it that night.

Lily longed for only two things as her husband escorted her into the house. For the cool fresh sheets of a comfortable bed, with downy pillows, and the warm strength of her husband's body beside her.

She was glad to see Mrs Hollis waiting for her, though she regretted that the housekeeper had had to stay up so late. She made the simplest of demands for refreshment: just a tisane to be brought to her room, no supper. Mrs Hollis eyed her mistress anxiously.

"You are unwell, my lady?"

"Simply tired from the journey. I am sure I will be well recovered by the morning."

Sarah had endured the journey as well and appeared even more exhausted. Despite her protestations Lily dismissed her, saying that she could manage by herself tonight. Sarah cast her gaze from Lily to the Marquess, then hid a blush as she realised her mistress might well have other assistance to untie her stays.

"Thank you, my lady. I will be with you in the morning."

"We are all tired, Sarah. I shall not rise early, and you must take the sleep that you need," Lily told her, and the maid departed gratefully.

Gervase had not attended this exchange, since he had been in conversation with his steward. As such he was surprised when Lily informed him that she required his assistance.

"Where is Sarah?"

"I have sent her to bed. I thought, my lord, that you..."

He saw the soft flame in her eyes and hoped that he read her meaning correctly. "You do not wish to be undisturbed?" he asked her.

Lily, despite her tiredness, wished very much to be disturbed.

With the rest of the household eventually dismissed, the Marquess stood alone with his wife in her bedchamber. The fire that had been lit in the grate still burned bright and illuminated the curve of her neck and shoulders as he unfastened her gown for her. He ran his fingers over her skin and she trembled.

He knew she was tired so he was gentle with her, making love to her in smooth, firm strokes that eased the tension that had built in his loins throughout the day. Finding his body needed her - nay, craved her - was a new and unsettling discovery. Had she preferred solitude that night he suspected he would have found sleep difficult.

How he had gone without this comfort for all these years, for he was not a frequenter of bawdy houses nor had he sought out mistresses, he could scarce comprehend. Gervase recalled the one former occasion he had pursued matrimony, a plan that had not come to fruition. It had seemed a bitter disappointment and humiliation at the time.

Knowing what he had discovered of that lady in the years since he now felt nothing but gladness. And from what he was getting to know about his new wife, he was all the more glad.

29. The meeting

Gervase steeled himself. He had ridden out at dawn with the express purpose of encountering his friend and neighbour, to whom he owed a sincere apology. His wife still slept deeply and he had not wished to disturb her. This was a meeting he needed to carry out alone.

The ground was crisp with frost that morning and Orion snorted plumes of vapour into the chilly air. As expected, Gervase soon sighted his target along the crest of the dividing hill.

He approached him and began to speak, but Sir Stephen raised a hand. "I did not accept your previous imputation, Westford, thus I have no need of your apology."

"It is more than generous of you to say such, Seton, but I know what I said. It was grossly unjustified. I am sorely troubled to have insulted you so gravely."

Sir Stephen again demurred. "No insult was taken. When a man is overtaken by a derangement, his words cannot be held to contain anything of significance."

"You consider me deranged?" Gervase asked, taken aback.

"You do not consider yourself so?" His neighbour smiled. "They call it a kind of madness, when it comes upon a person at any age. But perhaps at our stage of life, when wisdom and sobriety should be the greater, their collapse is all the more severe."

A madness. Was that was it was? "I had not expected to be overtaken in such a way. The strain of dealing with my cousin, the rushed marriage…"

This time Sir Stephen laughed. "If you wish to attribute it to such. In my view there is a far more obvious cause for your derangement. Whether you choose to admit it to yourself is your own business." He grew serious. "Let me speak with candour, Westford, for we are old friends."

This took Gervase somewhat by surprise, for he was accustomed to Seton's reserve. His neighbour had already spoken more candidly than was his wont. What more could he divulge? "I beg you to speak freely."

Sir Stephen turned in his saddle to face Gervase more directly. "The follies of a man, nay crimes even, that are so easily dismissed on his behalf, are a thousandfold the wrong that he does to a woman. Dozens of incidents we tolerate from him, but one slip from her and she is eternally condemned. And to what end?"

He did not mention Farrington but his meaning was clear.

"These young chits, newly thrown into the lion's den of the Season, they are as innocent as lambs. You cannot imagine that the things which a young man learns from an early age are taught to them. Show an infant a burning candle for the first time without warning, and it will reach for the flame. Had I a daughter I would prefer she knew how to avoid getting burnt, and why."

Gervase was startled. Seton had always been a mild mannered fellow but he spoke with force on this subject.

"It is not something I had thought of," Gervase admitted.

"I hope then that you will think upon it." Sir Stephen's gaze grew distant. "Life is so brief, Westford. Accident, war or fever may sever loved ones in an instant. I sometimes wonder we do not admire those who grasp the day. Those with the courage to disregard convention and take their joys while they may."

Gervase knew that Seton was thinking of his own lost love, but could not see how this applied to Farrington's dalliances. "If there is some pressing reason for haste, perhaps, but otherwise I see no purpose in defying custom and outraging society."

"I have lived long enough alone to wonder if love can ever be an outrage?" Sir Stephen said. "But we do not honour the dead with melancholy. Let us celebrate the present, and your own most fortunate union. To that end I hope that you are able to dine with me, you and Lady Westford, at the end of the week if convenient. I trust you will both be well rested by then. It seems too long since you were last at Grantlings."

Gervase, still disconcerted by Seton's revelations, thanked him. He accepted the invitation on his wife's behalf. "I look forward to it."

He had much to think about as he rode off. Had he become deranged over his young wife? He certainly felt passions that he had not imagined were possible. Even the long ago girl who had jilted him for another had not aroused such intense feelings: either of the heart or of the loins.

A fortunate union? His friend echoed his godmother in this opinion. For Gervase, who considered himself to have been the one bestowing fortune on a ruined girl, it was a difficult inversion to contemplate. Galling, even, to see this different perspective through others' eyes.

Yet the more he considered it, and the more he thought upon his young and beautiful bride, the more some small doubt crept in as to whether he was indeed as worthy of her as he had assumed.

***

Lily awoke late in the morning, alone. The absence of her husband's form beside her gave her a pang, but she reasoned that he must have plenty of estate business awaiting him following their extended stay in London. Doubtless he had risen early to attend to it.

As for her, she could think of no task that lay before her. In London there had been preparations to make, people to receive, places to go. She had frequently been occupied with the various items of correspondence demanded by polite society.

The Marquess had expressed a desire to ride with her, so Lily decided to wait for his invitation. Instead she would read some of the books she had shamefully neglected over the past fortnight. She might also pay a visit to Nanny Noakes who might be glad of news from town.

She rose and dressed, not calling Sarah. Lily was now in possession of what seemed an obscene amount of new gowns, more than she had ever owned throughout all her years combined. Yet Lady Belvedere had already mentioned recalling Madame LaFleur to refresh her wardrobe the following spring It was a distant and unlikely prospect, Lily considered.

Choosing a silvery grey morning gown that was cleverly cut to require no corset, she made her way down the corridor intending to head towards the library. In the hall she encountered Mrs Hollis.

"Good morning, my lady. I trust that you slept well?" The housekeeper frowned. "But you have not breakfasted? Sarah has not taken your orders to the kitchen, to my knowledge."

"I slept very well, thank you," Lily told her. "I did not wake Sarah, for I fear we were all very tired following the journey, and our busy time in London."

"If you will forgive me, you seem paler than your custom, my lady. If you would like me to send for a tonic, I have one that is very effective for sound sleep."

Lily, suspecting it contained laudanum which her father had always cautioned her to avoid, assured her that it would not be necessary. "Thank you, but I am quite well." Although she had no appetite that morning she sensed it would relieve the housekeeper if she requested breakfast. "I will take some tea in the library, if you would be so good as to have Mary bring it."

This satisfied Mrs Hollis, who nodded. "Certainly, it will be brought at once."

Lily spent a happy and peaceful morning in the library, buried in verses by poets of two thousand years ago. It was a connection with her father, for he had loved these odes. She was grateful that he had thought her worthy of instruction in the Classics, for many parents only provided such tuition for sons, not daughters. But Edward Cosgrove had taught his daughter everything that he might have taught a son.

Despite the fire the cold greyness of the day seeped through the house and Lily decided to fetch a shawl. She could have summoned Sarah to bring one but preferred to go herself. Without the exercise of her morning ride she already felt slothful.

She fetched a red cashmere shawl that had been Lady Diana's choice, though Lily had to admit it brightened the gown in a becoming way. Reaching the landing, she stopped to see a crooked figure standing at the top of the stairs: Nanny Noakes.

Lily greeted her warmly. "I had hoped to pay you a visit today. We arrived back late from town last night. I hope that you have been keeping well?"

Nanny Noakes's eyes were as beady as ever. "Very well. I was just returning to my room. The girl is bringing tea, she can fetch an extra cup."

Interpreting this for the invitation that it was, Lily followed the old servant to her chamber. Over the next hour she related various events to Nanny Noakes, whose information about society was far more current than Lily might have expected. With the Belvederes she was of course well acquainted, for they were old family friends of the Westfords.

"A smart lady, that Diana. Always knew what she wanted. But she's been thwarted in her ambitions regarding Master Claude, make no mistake. Clear as the nose on his face before he was even breeched, that one. You can always tell. Not that he was in my nursery but I saw enough of him in his younger days to be quite certain about that. Not Master Tom though, oh no. Of a very different stock, that young man. From the time he was walking he was the most determined little fellow..."

She had drifted off into her habitual reminiscences of former times, when the various men and women that Lily had become acquainted with were still in frocks. Once again Lily was keener to hear of the Marquess's boyhood, but she supposed that Tom Farrington's boyhood was a few years more recent and thus clearer in his old nanny's memory.

When their conversation came to an end and she rose to leave, Nanny Noakes fixed her with a sharp glare. "Ailing, are you? You've a pallor about you. A dose of castor oil is what I always gave my young ones to restore their spirits."

Lily laughed. "I'm not sure that I'm in need of castor oil. Mrs Hollis has offered a tonic, but truly, I am quite well. The journey last night was more tiring than expected, and I am certain I shall be quite well on the morrow."

Later that evening when Sarah was helping Lily undress for bed, Lily noticed a bottle on the tray that Mary had brought up earlier. Mrs Hollis and her confounded tonic! "Should I pour you some?" Sarah asked.

"No thank you, Sarah, it's very kind of Mrs Hollis but I don't plan to take any." She saw that her maid looked doubtful, and sought to reassure her. "If I find I am unable to sleep later on, perhaps I will try a dose. But I feel so weary now that I am sure slumber must come very easily."

Sarah nodded, and dismissed, left for her own quarters.

Lily awaited the Marquess. She felt the usual shiver of anticipation for his masterful yet tender attentions.

30. The visitor

Fascinating yet infuriating news had reached Lavinia Leominster during the time that her neighbours were in town. She was greatly irritated to discover that the new Marchioness of Westford had not only been received by the haut ton - "embraced" was the word her correspondent used! - but had made something of a sensation. A voucher for Almack's, no less! For a no-name chit who had utterly disgraced herself.

Lady Leominster half wished she had ventured to town herself, though it was not her usual custom at this time of year. She was fortunate to have a friend who wrote frequently and fervently, and while Lady Leominster might wince at the style and tone of this friend's letters, she pored over every mote and detail.

"...just think, Lavinia dear, the Nasebury woman claims the new Marchioness is not the chit she saw during the season. Quite a different girl! She is convinced of it. Of course I said she may have remembered the wrong girl, or that the wrong girl had been pointed out to her, but she will not have a bit of it. I am sure if there is anything to know that you must discover it, Lavinia, being such a frequent guest and neighbour of Westford Park..."

Lavinia Leominster knew of Cecilia Nasebury but did not include her among her intimates. She considered the woman vulgar and beneath her in every regard, yet her nose for scandal had its uses. For Lady Leominster, gossip was not a diversion but a useful source of information and subsequent leverage.

But it was the subsequent lines that her correspondent sent that caused her the greatest fury.

"Only think though, that he is quite smitten with her! One would imagine him to behave quite coldly towards her, given the circumstances of the marriage, and to barely wish to be seen in public with her. But at Almack's they waltzed together - actually waltzed, would you believe! - and he was said to look at her quite 'violent with desire'! That was the very phrase used, Lavinia dear. And he escorted her all over London quite as though they were a courting couple, one might think it was almost unseemly, but for his being a Marquess and they may conduct themselves as they wish, of course. I suspect she must be very practiced in her wiles to have so thoroughly snared the affections of both cousins. Though of course she is all gentility and graces when you meet her."

Lavinia Leominster would have loved nothing more than to have considered Lady Westford as devious and wily. But even she could not convince herself that it was so. Damn the girl! To have thwarted her own ambitions so utterly. So humiliatingly too, for several of her intimates had guessed her design upon her neighbour, and she feared she could not trust them not to gossip.

Who was this confounded girl, who so greatly differed from the description of the foolish chit that Tom Farrington seduced? If there were some mystery here, then Lavinia Leominster knew it was in her interests to sniff it out. As much as she loathed the very thought and sight of Elizabeth Westford - even the name stuck in her throat - she would have to cultivate some familiarity with her to dig it out.

***

It had rained that morning and Lily had forgone her usual ride with the Marquess. He had some tenants to see, for which Duncan Ross would accompany him. He would be gone most of the day. Lily was disappointed but given the heavy downpour, saw the sense in staying indoors. Over the past few days she had delighted in riding with him. He had shown her many aspects of the estate and she had learnt much more about the history and operations of Westford Park.

The drumming of water against the window panes, incessant since lunch, distracted her from the volume of Theocritus. She gazed out at the leaden skies. It was nearly evening and the world felt heavy as though the dusk was literally falling and weighing it down.

She found herself glad to be interrupted by Mary. "Excuse me, my lady, but Mrs Hollis said to inform you that a visitor is here."

It was apparent from Mary's tone that the visitor was unexpected by all. Certainly Lily was not expecting anyone, let alone at this hour. Were it Lady Leominster or another neighbour or friend, they would have been announced.

"Did he provide his name?"

"No, my lady." Mary looked awkward. "It is not a man, it is a woman."

Lily sensed some calamity. "I will come at once."

She rose and went through to the hall, with the maid following her. Mrs Hollis, who was just leaving the morning room, greeted her. "Lady Westford, there is a visitor for you whom I have shown into the morning room. It is a young lady. She has not given her name."

Lily knew so few young women that she supposed for a moment it might be Miss Emma Sawthwaite. Entering the room she stopped and caught her breath.

There, looking shockingly changed, was Betsy. Thin and pale, her eyes reddened from weeping and her clothes dishevelled from travel, she looked quite ill. Lily saw instantly that Betsy was on the verge of tears again so she dismissed Mrs Hollis and Mary, who was hovering behind her with curiosity. "Mrs Hollis, this is my cousin... if you could please bring us some refreshments." Lily nearly provided the name, then remembered that Betsy might need to use the guise of a different name. It may have been too much to even let slip their relationship.

Mrs Hollis glanced from one girl to the other and nodding to Betsy, politely took her leave with Mary in tow. The housekeeper had the tact to pull the door closed behind her rather than leaving it ajar.

Before Lily could speak, Betsy put her hands over her face and burst into a flood of weeping. Lily put her arm around her cousin's shoulders in comfort, and was taken aback by how slight and frail Betsy felt. The material of her gown, so fitting before, now hung loose about her form.

"O Betsy, what has become of you, dearest? What is wrong? Are you ill?"

Betsy recovered herself and looked up at Lily, her countenance wet with tears. Her features had bloomed with a pleasing plumpness before, but now her eyes were shadowed and her cheeks hollow.

"I am not ill, save for my heart is sick, or even broken, Lily dear. I could not bear it a moment longer. Weeks and weeks of living so far away with no news. I have barely been able to eat or sleep. Anne Carter wished to call the physician but there is no remedy he could prescribe that would be of any use." Betsy said.

Lily's thoughts were in turmoil. For Betsy to be here meant certain discovery for them both. What could they do? She had already disclosed that Betsy was her cousin. It would be perilous for the Marquess to discover the existence of another Elizabeth Cosgrove.

"Betsy, we will speak of this at length but Mrs Hollis will return soon. When she does it seems safest to introduce you as Miss Anne Cosgrove, lest the coincidence of our names be remarked upon."

Despite her discomposure, Betsy understood. "Of course." She covered her face again and began another fit of sobbing, and Lily scarce knew what to do.

She must contrive some reason for her cousin's distress. She shrank from yet more untruths but what other course was there? "For now, let us say that you have brought news of the death of Aunt Frances whom you are grieving very bitterly." Aunt Frances was their distant relation in the Highlands. She was some form of cousin rather than an aunt, but it mattered not.

"But we have never met Aunt Frances!" Betsy replied.

Lily felt exasperation. "I know that we have not, but who else here is to know that? Let us suppose that she was very dear to you, and is now the cause of your great distress, and also the reason for your unannounced visit." Betsy, absorbed by her grief, did not seem to have comprehended how her impromptu visit might be received by the household. Not to mention by the Marquess. Lily did not think she could face the two of them meeting tonight and the explanations that must ensue. "Let us also say that you are unwell" - which was little embellishment on the truth, for Betsy looked on the point of collapse - "and that you have taken to your bed. We can talk more privately there."

Betsy readily consented to the plan for she was exhausted from her journey. When Mrs Hollis returned Lily requested that a room be prepared, only to discover that that efficient woman had already arranged such. "Given the hour and the inclement weather, I had taken the liberty to presume that your cousin would be our guest tonight, my lady. I have sent Mary to make ready the rose room. Mr Pelham will have the lady's articles taken up there."

The rose room! Pink had always been Betsy's preferred colour, but few roses bloomed in her cheeks at present.

"That will do very well, Mrs Hollis, thank you for your consideration." Betsy being out of the way would be some small relief. Her cousin could recover her composure - a good night's sleep in a comfortable bed would be solace to her strained nerves - and they could talk more tomorrow about what they should do. Lily hoped that some inspiration would reach her by the morrow, since at the present time their prospects seemed bleak.

Right now her thoughts were in disarray. She had to dine with Gervase within the hour and somehow explain her cousin's presence in the house. Meanwhile she was frantic with worry and guilt over Betsy's situation. She was not sure how she would endure it all.

***

Gervase saw that something was amiss with his wife when he joined her for dinner. He had arrived back later than planned from his estate business with Duncan Ross, and had gone straight to bathe. The rain and the mud and the horses would not, he felt, make him the choicest of dining companions. Nor a companion in a more intimate setting.

He thought, half grim and half amused, how he had expected and even been quite determined to remain unaltered by any change in his matrimonial circumstances. Yet his wife had altered his conduct in far more ways than anticipated. Gervase had also become painfully conscious of his years when seeing the admiring glances of young bucks towards her.

If Seton was right and he was deranged, so be it. All he knew was that for the first time in many years, he felt a joy in his heart that he had not known since his boyhood.

"My lord, we - I - have a visitor. My cousin Anne," Lily began, wincing inwardly at the false name. "She arrived earlier this evening, and rests upstairs."

Gervase's brow furrowed. "I take it that her visit was unexpected? Or did a letter go astray?"

"Yes, and no." Lily paused. She could not quite bring herself to state that Aunt Frances was dead. "She came bearing sad tidings of a relative of ours. She is most distressed and I thought it best if she rested until the morrow."

Gervase studied his wife's face. "You also suffer considerable distress yourself, I imagine. Should you wish to be with your cousin…"

Lily spoke rapidly. "Indeed I find I am more distressed for my cousin," she said, in all truthfulness. "She enjoyed a much closer acquaintance with our relative and her loss is the greater." Had she been speaking these words of Tom Farrington, they would have been no lie. For the real reason for her cousin's distress was the loss of a man who was now Lily's relative, and it was also a distress that Lily did not share. While she hoped for anything that might ease Betsy's heartache, she could not in all conscience wish for Tom Farrington's return. Not given what she now knew of that man.

If only she were able to offer Betsy more recent news of him. He was of course one topic that could not be broached with her husband: his name had not once been mentioned between them. But if she had been able to apprise Betsy of Tom Farrington's most recent mischiefs, it might begin to lance the boil of misplaced affection.

"I regret that I was not able to inform you of her visit earlier," she told Gervase, "since I knew of it not."

Her husband smiled. "Albeit preferably in happier circumstances, I am extremely glad for you to have the company of your family." He knew that marriage to him had severed Lily from her home and her kin. He had planned to suggest they paid a visit to Lord and Lady Cosgrove in the spring.

He little imagined the utter dread with which his wife would greet such a prospect.

31. The discussion

Lily slept poorly that night despite the comfort and presence of her husband, and rose early. She dressed with haste, not calling for Sarah, and hurried to see her cousin.

Betsy was still asleep but woke at the sound of Lily entering her room. Lily guessed that she had wept in the night but nonetheless her cousin looked better than she had done the previous evening.

"I have not called for breakfast but I will do so now," Lily greeted Betsy. "You have become so thin, dearest. It worries me."

"I am sure you are also more slender than you were," Betsy told her.

It was true: Lily had grown thinner with anxiety in her first weeks at Westford Park. But since the visit to Westford Park she was sure she had more than recovered her appetite and health.

"It has been a trying time for both of us," Lily said.

When breakfast was brought, Lily poured tea for Betsy. A selection of different dishes had been provided, but Betsy could do no more than to nibble on a slice of dry toast. However this and the tea revived her spirits a little and she managed a weak smile as she beheld her cousin.

"It is so good to see you, Lily dear. I have longed for your company and your counsel."

"My counsel? If only I could offer such to either of us. I fear I do not know how any of this must end," Lily said, indicating herself and the room.

Betsy's face showed alarm. "End? Lily, you cannot possibly mean that you would end your situation here. We would both be quite exposed."

Lily sought to assuage her fears. "I do not mean such at all, I only fear that it cannot endure indefinitely. Should you once again encounter Mr Farrington" - she shrank from even suggesting this possibility since it now seemed to her so utterly unlikely and undesirable - "then of course our deception must be exposed. What is to become of me then I care not, truly, so long as you are made happier than you are now." Her sentiment as she spoke was genuine, for she had been horrified by her cousin's appearance and distraught manner. Better that she were banished to the Highlands or abroad than Betsy should continue to suffer as she had been.

Lily set down her tea cup. "I feel great guilt, Betsy, that I have been so comfortable and fortunately placed while you have been forced to endure a lonely wait. Indeed on your behalf I deeply regret our plot. The Marquess has turned out to be a man of great kindness and generosity, and I am certain that to have married him would have been most advantageous to you."

Betsy put up a hand. "Stop! I can scarce bear it, you sound like that horrid letter which my parents wrote to me, ordering me into marriage with him. I could not bring myself to consider marrying another, let alone some repulsive old man, when my heart is given to another."

"But he is not at all old, Betsy," Lily protested. "He is not much past thirty or thereabouts. And indeed his form is not at all repulsive, quite the reverse. I do not say this out of gratitude or courtesy to him, but I am sure that he would be considered most handsome among any company. He is also a man of learning and intelligence, greatly respected by everyone in his household."

She stopped, realising that she may already have said too much, for Betsy was now eyeing her with suspicion.

"Do not tell me that you have developed an affection for him, Lily, surely not?"

Lily could not respond for she had not liked to articulate such a thought to herself. She felt a blush flood through her.

Betsy gasped, her own woes momentarily forgotten. "You are in love with him, are you not? What an amazing thing! To think that you had never even met him and now you find yourself in love with him. A man of twice your age, Lily!"

"He is not quite twice my age," was all Lily could bring herself to say. "Or at least I do not think that he is." She supposed he might be, for she had not inquired as to the year of his birth. It mattered little, since he was at any rate far from the quavering and ancient creature that they had conjured up from Tom Farrington's disparaging description.

Betsy sat back, for a moment having the appearance of her old self. "This is quite a revelation. I did not think such a thing would be possible, and now my own consternation at having urged you to take my place is lessened. You must never think that I do not feel daily gratitude in my heart for the sacrifice that you made, Lily. It is only that my ongoing anguish over Tom and the distance between us quite eclipses everything else. Only do tell me what you have heard of him, for you said so little in your letters, and I am sure that more must have been spoken of him."

Lily was at a loss for words. "Truly very little has been said by anyone here, the reasons for which as you can imagine are quite obvious."

Betsy sighed. "But he must pay a visit here at some point, surely? Can you not suggest to the Marquess that he be invited here, in some gesture of reconciliation?"

The idea was so foolish and so appalling that Lily barely knew how to respond. "Surely you can see, Betsy, that for me to do so would be quite unthinkable? If my husband wishes his cousin to visit, he will invite him of his own accord. We did not see him in London, remember, though I heard some suggestion that he was on the continent."

"Perhaps he does not invite him because he fears your distress. But of course you will not be distressed, Lily, so it will matter not if he comes."

Lily decided that Betsy had lost all sense of propriety if not her entire reason, and sought to change the course of conversation. She looked out of the window onto the grey, wet morning. "Since we are to be kept inside this morning by the rain, let us occupy ourselves with adjusting your clothes. We may talk further on this as we do so. For now, you shall wear one of my gowns since I am sure that yours must all gape as your travelling dress does."

It was an astute move to get Betsy onto the subject of her wardrobe. Her cousin had always been more concerned with her appearance than Lily had been with hers. Now that there was more of a chance, however remote, that Tom Farrington might arrive here, Betsy would not wish to be dressed in an unbecoming fashion.

The gowns that Lily displayed before her served to distract Betsy from her wild thoughts and plans. "But there are so many!" she exclaimed. "And such fine silk and lace! I am comforted that your husband's ample purse must have helped assuage the discomfort of your matrimony with him."

Lily restrained herself from the response she wished to make to this. After all, her cousin had not yet been introduced to her husband. She was sure that Betsy could not fail to be impressed by other more worthy aspects of his person once she encountered him. "His character is such that I believe any woman with sense would have married him were he a pauper," she told Betsy.

"Then you know how I feel about my beloved Tom," Betsy countered.

Lily was losing patience with her cousin's wilful blindness, though she tried to feel compassion. Betsy's nerves were so fragile and her constitution so diminished that any blow might shatter her. She bit her tongue. Her cousin must learn of Mr Farrington's true nature, and soon. But for the present time her spirits and health needed to be restored.

***

They were interrupted by Mrs Hollis who arrived at the open door, looking distraught.

"My lady, forgive me, but I must make an urgent request of you. It is Sarah. Word has been sent that her mother is dangerously ill and the very worst is feared. I beg your leave to allow me to send her home. I will make whatever arrangement I can for your needs in her absence."

Lily was unconcerned about her own need. "Please tell her to go at once, and to take the carriage."

"It is not far, my lady, it will be as quick on foot. I thank you greatly," Mrs Hollis said.

"And a doctor," Lily said. "We must send for a physician."

Mrs Hollis's fingers twisted the fabric of her gown. "I am afraid that their circumstances are not..."

Lily felt exasperation. "My lord will bear all expense. Have Mr Pelham arrange it. Please accompany Sarah yourself or send Mary with her. We can manage quite well here."

There were tears in Mrs Hollis's eyes. "You are most compassionate, my lady."

Lily spoke gently. "I have lost my own mother, Mrs Hollis, and my father. If Sarah can be spared such a bereavement, let us do all we can for her."

The housekeeper left, too overcome for more words. Lily looked outside. The morning was grey and drizzling. She said a silent prayer for Sarah and her mother. There was the little invalid sister too. Something must be done for her, should the worst happen. But Lily hoped it would not come to that.

Betsy spoke. 'It still seems strange to see you in such a position, Lily, managing a household. How quickly you have learnt!"

"I am very fortunate. There is but little for me to do, they are all so efficient," Lily said.

"I should be terrified, a house of this size."

Lily, still worried for Sarah, managed to smile. "I confess I was so at the start. Doubly so, due to the deception I am also practising. But I scarce imagined that a man could have inspired such respect and duty in his staff as Lord Westford has." Then she realised the obvious comparison to Sir Robert, who did not inspire any such affection in his own staff, and began to apologise.

Betsy interrupted her. "Do not apologise, dearest. I am aware that my father has his share of shortcomings." She smoothed the edge of her shawl between her fingers, sighing. "While I know I erred in my eagerness and haste to be with Tom, yet their conduct towards me showed little understanding nor the possibility of forgiveness. Mayhap I did not deserve such, but you showed it to me, Lily. And Anne Carter too, though she chided me for my folly, was still kind."

Lily could find little of comfort to say to Betsy. What she said was true. While her offence may have be considered grave, there was still the possibility of parental love, however stern. None had been shown to her. Sir Robert and Lady Maud had preferred to marry Betsy off to a complete stranger than pay any regard to her own wishes.

Yet Betsy might have been very happy wedded to the Marquess. His kindness would surely have won her, and in time her affections would have switched from Tom Farrington to Gervase Dainard. Alas, what was done was done and it was too late for that now.

What would become of either she or Betsy, Lily knew not. But if their fate was to live abroad, exiled as the fallen women they were not supposed to even know about, they would make the best of it.

32. The cousin

Gervase was not especially taken with Betsy, though he considered Lily's "Cousin Anne" to be pleasant enough. He perceived her general air of dejection, which he attributed to the fictitious bereavement, and took pains therefore to be courteous to her. She was dear to his wife, and this inclined him to act kindly towards her.

He had tactfully pretended to be occupied with estate business so the two cousins might enjoy one another's companionship during the day. Though in truth he had time to spare, that he would have preferred to have spent with his young wife. At least Lily was his each night. He revelled in her and kept her in his bed with him until morning, or stayed with her in hers. It was something he would never have dreamt of a few months ago.

Gervase had invited Duncan Ross to dine with them, thinking that this might create a balance and evenness at the dinner table. Before his marriage he had not infrequently dined with his estate manager, though had rarely done so afterwards. This was largely because he preferred to dine alone with his wife, valuing the time he had with her.

Unfortunately Mr Ross's naturally dour demeanour and his lack of any common ground with Betsy did not make for merry conversation.

"Mr Ross is from Scotland," Lily prompted when Betsy yet again fell silent.

"I believe your late aunt resided in the Scottish highlands," Mr Ross said. "Whereabouts was her home?"

Betsy had no idea and Lily only remembered because it was burned into her mind as the intended place of her banishment. "It is near Inverness, a village called Kirkhill," she told Mr Ross.

The Scotsman brightened. "I know it well," he said. "Relations of mine had a farm near there."

Lily caught Betsy's eye, her heart sinking. God forbid Mr Ross or his relatives were also acquainted with the far-from-late Aunt Frances. "What a coincidence! I am afraid we have not been there," Lily said.

"Ah, well. You would find it a bonny part of the land, were you to visit," he told them. He began to talk of the many charms of the village that had come so close to being Lily's fate. She was spared that forever now, for Aunt Frances would hardly countenance a divorced or deserted woman residing with her as companion.

Betsy had started out quite terrified of the Marquess, due to her preconceptions and the lies that Tom Farrington had told her of his cruel and authoritarian cousin.

But she saw from his tenderness to Lily, and the affectionate way he treated her cousin, that he was not fully the tyrant she had imagined. Since she could not entirely disbelieve Tom's words, she thought that perhaps the Marquess had made an exception for her cousin, or was gentler to women than men. Certainly his servants respected him and he had no harsh words for any of them.

It made his cruelty and meanness to Tom Farrington all the more contemptible and unreasonable, Betsy thought. She was still determined to resent and dislike him, though his continued courtesy towards her made this increasingly hard.

Betsy had also been surprised by the Marquess's appearance. While she still regarded him as older, viewing a man of Tom's age as ideal since Tom was perfect to her in every way, he was not the stooping geriatric she had imagined. And she could not dispute Lily's description of him as handsome. He was exceptionally handsome, Betsy was forced to admit.

Still she did not envy Lily her position, for all its wealth and status, fixated as she was on her first love.

Yet it would not be remarkable for some small doubts to begin to gnaw at her. Though presently they were too deep and confusing for her to acknowledge.

***

After they had breakfasted, with Betsy now clad in a far more becoming gown of Lily's, Lily suggested they take a walk around the gardens. Just as they were about to step outdoors they were thwarted in this plan by the arrival of Lady Leominster, come to pay a visit.

Lily's heart sank, for she disliked their neighbour at the best of times. And these were far closer to the worst of times.

She greeted Lady Leominster with all politeness and introduced her to Betsy.

"My cousin Miss Cosgrove, Lady Leominster. Anne, this is Lady Leominster, our neighbour." Lily remembered the ruse to explain Betsy's hasty arrival. "I am afraid my cousin arrived to bring sad tidings of the death of our aunt. It is not in the happiest spirits that you will find us today." She hoped greatly that this would be sufficient encouragement for their visitor to take her leave, but Lavinia Leominster intended to do nothing of the sort.

A previously unmentioned cousin, of a similar age! Lady Leominster was immediately interested. She did not for a moment suspect a switch, but the notion that society may have confused the pair began to form in her mind.

She eyed Betsy closely. Yes, this girl far better fitted the description she had been given of the chit that had sullied herself with Tom Farrington. But the name was not the same. There was something here, but she knew not what.

"I beg your forgiveness to have intruded at such a time," Lavinia Leominster said. She did not say: "Of course I will depart" but instead stood her ground, so Lily was forced to grant her hospitality and offer her refreshments.

The three women sat in the morning room, the two cousins both feeling ill at ease. It had suddenly struck Lily that neither she nor Betsy were in mourning clothes.

"You must forgive our attire," she said to Lady Leominster. "With the suddenness of the news we have not yet arranged mourning clothes."

Lavinia Leominster gave a dismissive wave of her hand. "It is not a custom I hold fast to, buried so deep in the countryside as we are." Indeed she had only worn black when absolutely necessary following the death of her husband. Her half-mourning gowns had been barely distinguishable from her usual wardrobe, choosing violet and lavender as she had, rather than the sombre greys and browns that might indicate a deeper grief.

Although it was unacceptable for a widow to attend social functions during mourning, receiving calls was permitted, and Lady Leominster had ensured that she received a good many. So the other women's lack of mourning dress was easy to dismiss. "I should not even trouble to notice it," she assured them.

"You are kind to say so," Lily said.

"You are recently returned from town, are you not?"

"Indeed. But three days ago," Lily told her, offering her the dish of sweetmeats that had been brought.

Lady Leominster declined them. "It is not a habit of mine to be in London during this month. Though you may have met friends of mine, perchance?"

"I met very many people, it was quite a whirl of activity," Lily said.

Her neighbour mentioned a few names that she was quite sure Lily would not have met. Then she sharpened her dagger. "And a Mrs Nasebury, perhaps you were introduced to her?"

She got the reaction she wanted. Alarm flickered in Lily's eyes and Betsy started.

Lily spoke quickly, trying to move past the subject. "I was introduced to her at Lady Belvedere's ball." She did not elaborate.

Lady Leominster was satisfied. She began to plot: somehow she must get Cecilia Nasebury down here, odious woman though she was. She would be able to confirm whether or not this Anne Cosgrove was the disgraced girl.

Aware she could glean nothing further at this stage, she changed the subject. "I wonder if you enjoy music, Lady Westford."

"Very much, but I am afraid I am no player. My cousin Anne has a talent for the spinet."

Lady Leominster regarded Betsy with feigned interest. "Is that so? We have a fine spinet at Leominster Hall. We must arrange a musical soirée. When you are out of mourning, of course."

Lily could think of few greater ordeals than an evening spent in the hospitality of her neighbour. Nonetheless she replied with gratitude. "That would be delightful, I am sure. Would it not, Anne?"

Betsy was at that moment toying with a thin slice of bread and butter.

"Anne, dear." Lily spoke more firmly since Betsy was slow to respond, unused to the other name.

Betsy looked round in surprise and bewilderment.

Lily attempted to excuse her. "I fear that you are quite distracted in your grief, dearest. Lady Leominster mentions inviting you to try her spinet."

"O! I am sure it is most kind of her," Betsy mumbled.

Lady Leominster did not extend her torture of the two cousins, preferring to return home and plot her next move. Her current musings were that the ton were simply mistaken in their idea that the Marquess had offered for the disgraced Cosgrove girl. Or that he had done so, but been more taken with her cousin. Despite her loathing for the girl, Lavinia Leominster could see why she might have been preferred to the other one.

It was time to write a few letters.

***

Lily had been hesitant to take Betsy to visit Nanny Noakes. She feared that the old woman's reminiscences about Tom Farrington would disturb her cousin.

But it rained that afternoon and Lily felt a pang of conscience for neglecting the old servant. So, having arranged for tea to be brought up, she took Betsy to meet her. "She is the old nursemaid of both Lord Westford and his cousin after him," Lily had explained to Betsy. "She has few visitors and suffers badly from rheumatism."

"Has she no family that wished her to return to them?" Betsy asked.

"I believe not. Those from her own generation may well have passed on, and she has not mentioned nieces or nephews. It is really very sad, but she is a spirited old person."

Nanny Noakes fixed Betsy with her usual beady eye when Lily introduced them. "Well, well. And there's another of them," she said. "It's many years since we had young women at Westford Park, and now there are two of them."

"It has been a very small household since the death of the Dowager Lady Westford, Lord Westford's mother," Lily explained.

Betsy noticed the small portrait of a woman, set in dark oval frame. "Is that the lady you speak of?" she asked.

"She's from very long ago," Nanny Noakes said. She gave a cackle. "She met a far from merry end, that one. Took poison, or so they say. Some say it was her husband that did it. Thought she'd played him foul, and had her done away with. Hemlock, as the story has it."

Lily shuddered, not so much at the terrible story but at Nanny Noakes' glee in re-telling it.

Betsy shared her sentiment. "How awful! I am sure it cannot be true."

"Many's the man who's wished himself rid of a barren or faithless wife," Nanny Noakes said.

"I am sure most don't resort to poison," Lily said.

The old servant narrowed her eyes as she gave a gloating smile. "More than you might think, my lady. I know what I've seen in my time, and what I'll take to my grave."

Lily steered the conversation onto more pleasant topics, or at least ones less macabre. She asked after Nanny Noakes' rheumatism, and then spoke of Mrs Hollis's daughter, who had recently had her first child.

Nanny Noakes was counting the months on her gnarled fingers. "Came early, did it?" Her implication was clear.

Lily disregarded this. "He is a fine young fellow, Mrs Hollis says, and is to be named Henry after his grandfather, her late husband."

This led Nanny Noakes back to her nursery reminiscences about a former charge of hers, also christened Henry. She had tended to the "little Master" as she called him, before her time with the Dainard family. "Married a woman from Spain after killing her husband in a duel. An heiress, she was."

Lily was glad that she did not directly refer to Tom Farrington since she feared Betsy's reaction. She let the old servant rattle on about the long-ago Henry, who sounded equally as spoiled and unpleasant as Tom Farrington. The type of boy that Nanny Noakes relished was not the type of child that Lily admired.

"What an awful old woman!" Betsy said as they left. "I do not know how you can bear her."

"I feel sorry for her. There is little to amuse her these days, and I sense she gets enjoyment from her fanciful stories."

Betsy disagreed. "Fanciful! She was positively malevolent. She addresses you with no respect at all, Lily. You might have been a scullery maid, the way she spoke to you and the scandalous things she said. And do not blame it on her advanced age, dearest, for there is nothing addled about her brain. I would judge her to be sharper than either of us, the old witch."

Lily laughed. "She is at least entertaining, is she not?"

"It is a strange way to be entertained," Betsy said. "I almost feared she was warning you, at one point."

33. The dinner party

Lily tried a different approach with Betsy. Her cousin's nerves were as yet too delicate for Lily to impart any of the terrible things she had learnt about Tom Farrington. Betsy must be convinced through different means that a marriage to him was unlikely if not impossible.

She decided to raise a delicate point with her cousin. "This marriage I have entered, Betsy, were there to be issue, do you not see the consequences to Mr Farrington? Of how materially it may affect his prospects?"

Betsy had not. "I see that it makes no difference."

"But it may make every difference. Should I - should there be - a certain event, Betsy, it may mean the end of Mr Farrington's expectations."

Betsy, who was working on a very indifferent piece of embroidery, frowned. "What event do you mean?"

"I mean if I conceive a child. Even if our marriage is annulled or dissolved, as it must be when our deception is exposed, such a child may yet remain the legal heir of Westford."

"Oh! Children. I had never thought…"

Lily interrupted her. "But I have thought, Betsy, and I see that it would be of the utmost disadvantage to him. To you both, were he ever to renew his suit."

"He has never withdrawn his suit," Betsy insisted. She was silent for a while. "Even so, it matters not. I do not marry for money, only for love."

Lily felt frustration. "But he - Mr Farrington - his circumstances may require him to consider such. Your father's estate is entailed, Betsy." This was on a distant relation who was long married with children of his own. "Your own fortune may not be so considerable as to tempt him."

She regretted her choice of words as soon as she had spoken them, for Betsy became indignant. "Tempt him! As if he would care about my money. It is love that binds us together, Lily. I am only sorry that you have no understanding of such things yourself. Though that is my fault, I suppose, begging you to enter an arranged union."

It was useless. There was nothing that Lily could say to shake Betsy's resolute belief in Tom Farrington's affection for her. That he had deserted her, that he had made no attempt to contact her for many months, none of this swayed her faith in him. She was too fragile, perhaps, to face the truth.

But it must be realised eventually.

Betsy pricked her finger, causing a drop of blood to fall onto her embroidery, and cried out. "Oh! Confound this silly thing. It is quite ruined." She set it down.

Lily retrieved it. "You might embroider over the stain, but I am sure Sarah can remove it. She is very clever at that."

"Where is she?" Betsy asked. The maid had been away the past two days.

"I am afraid she tends to her mother still. The poor woman has been very gravely ill, I am informed. She came close to death, so the doctor said."

Betsy had been musing upon an earlier subject. "Should you wish to have a child, Lily?"

"It is not something I have given much thought to."

"It would mean having to subject yourself to certain attentions," Betsy said.

"Subject myself?" Lily was startled.

"To those things which husbands wish for, necessary to beget a child."

"A wife may also wish for those things, Betsy." Lily wished for them very much. A mere expression in her husband's eye could send her longing for the bedchamber, as wanton as she was sure this must be.

"Mamma said they are to be endured with forbearance. I do not think a woman could welcome such," Betsy said.

This was bewildering! "But Betsy, surely you and Mr Farrington, I had thought that it was why…" Lily trailed off. She hardly knew what she was asking.

"Indeed I welcomed his attentions and it was most wrong of me. His kisses and caresses quite made my head whirl. But when it came to the final uncomfortable thing, no one could like that, Lily. I am quite certain. Indeed I was shocked by it. But he said he could not restrain himself, since I had aroused his passions."

"Oh Betsy!" Lily knew not what to say. It was a more candid conversation than either had been used to. She recalled Betsy's reticence on the subject on the night the Marquess came to claim his bride.

"When you are with someone you love, you won't mind anything" Betsy had said. It struck Lily that Betsy may have deliberately avoided more explicit details so as not to frighten Lily from agreeing to the marriage.

If so, it mattered not now. What was done was done, and water long flowed under the bridges.

But to think that Betsy had suffered only discomfort from the very act that had ruined her and brought about her disgrace, it was too cruel! Lily felt the most violent surge of anger against Tom Farrington that she had yet experienced.

***

The Marquess and Marchioness of Westford had been invited to dine at Grantlings that evening. When Sir Stephen Seton heard that Lily had a relative staying, the invitation was naturally extended to Betsy.

"It will do you good, Betsy dear," Lily told her. "You have been too long out of company."

"Perhaps."

"Sir Stephen is a kind man and an old friend of Lord Westford. I am sure he will be a pleasant host." It would be Lily's first visit to Grantlings as well, for there had not been opportunity before, what with the trip to London.

The two girls finished their toilet together, arranging one another's hair as they had done so many times in their younger days. Lily had not thought it necessary to replace Sarah while she was away. She and Betsy could manage perfectly well for now.

Sarah had earlier done beautiful work taking in Betsy's gowns and repairing them, far better than Betsy's own efforts had been. Betsy had never had the aptitude nor skill with a needle that Lily had had to have, through necessity.

With her hair arranged, and renewed bloom in her cheeks from a brisk walk with Lily earlier that day, Betsy had regained something of her former prettiness. She was certainly far removed from the distraught, tear-stained creature who had arrived earlier that week.

Lily felt a swell of gladness and relief in her heart from seeing her cousin's restored appearance. "You are quite beautiful tonight, dearest." She regretted that there would be only the Marquess and Sir Stephen to behold her, unless Sir Stephen had invited other guests. Lily felt that the attention of other young men might help begin the cure for Betsy's broken heart. At least for Betsy to consider another future, rather than her hopeless dream of Tom Farrington, would be a start.

Gervase's hand clasped hers in the carriage, and she knew from the pressure and the movement of his thumb against her palm that he had plans for her later that night. Much as she loved Betsy, Lily wished for a wild moment that her cousin and all the staff might vanish for a night and a day, so she could lie with Gervase undisturbed by people or duties for endless hours.

What am I becoming? She chided herself. But catching her husband's eyes, piercing her own, she knew that he felt likewise.

She must make the most of the time she had with him. If that made her greedy and wanton, so be it. The rest of her life might well be a loveless and chaste exile once she was found out.

She managed to banish these wild thoughts when she was greeted by Sir Stephen. He appeared genuinely glad to welcome his guests and neighbours, and was very courteous to Betsy, giving her his arm and leading her through. Betsy looked nervous but accepted his hospitality.

It was a very enjoyable evening. Sir Stephen's cook was skilled and the food was excellent. Though by nature their host was a quiet man, he was skilled in leading conversation that might interest all present.

For Sir Stephen's part he was gratified to see that things stood well between his old friend and the young woman he had married. Westford had clearly managed to get his head together after his confused outburst and contrite apology. Sir Stephen enjoyed a private chuckle just thinking about it. He had been unable to take offence, so absurd had the accusation been.

Instead he was greatly amused and pleased by the changes that had come over his friend. For so proud a man to enter such a marriage, and then have his resolve and reserve entirely swept away... Sir Stephen raised a silent toast to the god of love. Yet how could any man fail to resist a young woman of the Marchioness's beauty and grace? A warm beauty too, not a cold reserve. Sir Stephen could tell from the way that Lady Westford looked at her husband, her eyes dancing, that she had flourished through his passion.

The quieter little cousin intrigued him. Even had he not been forewarned of her bereavement, he would have recognised one who, like himself, had suffered and still suffered from some loss. She was unhappy and wary, and it seemed to Sir Stephen that this was a longer and deeper unhappiness than the loss of an elderly aunt. However dear that aunt may have been to her.

He did what he could to bring Betsy out, regretting that he did not have a tuned instrument for her to play when he learned of her aptitude for the spinet. In the drawing room he was happy to show both young women the portrait of his lost love, her dark hair and eyes immortalised by the brushstrokes of Sir Thomas Lawrence.

"She is so beautiful, and the expression in her eyes so wise and kind!" Lily said. Sir Stephen was moved to see that the Marchioness's own eyes brimmed with tears on viewing the painting.

"It was many years ago now, and there are those who say I should set her memory to rest and hang her painting in a more private location. But my grief has long since been transformed to a happy appreciation of the time we were blessed to have spent together. I am glad to look upon her and remember her. I have mourned for what might have been, and now I choose to be grateful for the short time we did have."

To their surprise Betsy spoke quite fiercely. "One can never cast one's love aside," she said.

Lily was startled and feared that Betsy might give herself away. "I am sure that cannot be what Sir Stephen's friends recommended to him," she said.

"For the most part, no." Sir Stephen agreed. "And yet there are people who are discomfited by deep emotions in others, and seek to downplay them."

"Such people have not human hearts," Betsy said.

"I prefer to consider that their own hearts have not yet been opened," Sir Stephen said. "And that it is to their greater tragedy if they never are." He smiled at her and Betsy blushed, suddenly embarrassed for her outburst.

"Forgive me, sir. I spoke too strongly," she said.

"There is nothing to forgive," her host told her, and led her with Lily to a comfortable sofa, where he ordered wine and port to be served. He had already announced that since their party was so small and he wished to better make their acquaintance, they would dispense with the usual custom of the gentlemen retiring.

"For I am also aware that there are ladies who prefer port to Madeira, and as such should not be deprived of their first choice," Sir Stephen had said.

Lily drank little but was glad to accept a small glass of port rather than the sweet Madeira. Too much wine made her head swim. Betsy also accepted a glass, sipping it with some hesitation.

Sir Stephen looked at Gervase and burst out laughing. "I fear I have served wine to those that would prefer water at this hour, or even tea."

Gervase was suddenly struck by how young the two girls were compared to himself and Seton. Were it not for his marriage to one of them, such a gathering would outrage society. Two young maids, no chaperones, two older bachelors. But for these vows spoken late at night in a small chapel, they would be quite ruined. It reminded him of the fragility of a woman's state, and the lack of compassion with which society treated one who might lapse in the merest way.

His opinion had grown increasingly close to Seton's on the matter in recent weeks, and he was not altogether sure that he did not now share it completely.

Regardless, seeing the candlelight shining on Lily's soft hair and watching her face light up with laughter at something said by Seton, he was profoundly glad and relieved to have married her. He felt no further jealousy towards his friend for he was fast learning the difference in the way that Lily looked at him, her husband, compared to other men. Now he could perceive the desire in her eyes for him, he saw that it was not in her expression as she regarded others.

Yet something within him strived for more. To capture an even deeper emotion from her, something more secure. He felt a need to own more than her body and her fidelity.

34. The illness

Just as Sarah returned from her mother's house, that woman happily now fast recovering, Betsy fell seriously ill.

It was two days after their dinner at Grantlings. Had it not been for Sarah, who had woken in the night and heard a strange disturbance from Betsy's room, the young woman might well have died. Not knowing what to do, the maid ran for the housekeeper and banged upon her door. "Mrs Hollis, oh do come quick! Something is wrong with Miss Cosgrove."

Mrs Hollis appeared, wrapping her robe around herself. Taking a candle they went to together to try the door of the guest.

Inside, what a sight met their eyes! Betsy was in terrible distress, heaving and writhing, crying out in agony. Sarah began crying in fear. "Oh! It is like my poor mother, what shall we do?"

"We must waken her Ladyship," Mrs Hollis said, and went to knock on that chamber door. There was no answer, thus she tried the Marquess's door.

Lily did not waste a moment when the news was imparted to her. Not even thinking to dress, she hurried in her nightgown to visit her cousin. Betsy was unable to communicate, she seemed to lapse in and out of consciousness. Only her pain and sickness were all too apparent.

Gervase joined her and instantly had a doctor summoned, the same physician that had attended Sarah's mother. He was brought to Westford Park within the hour.

The doctor's expression was grave as he studied the patient. Betsy was wracked with pain and so sick that the doctor asked if purgatives had been given.

They had not. The doctor then suspected an ailment of the digestive system, but Betsy had shown no signs of sickness earlier that day.

"There was no misadventure in the preparation of the food served earlier?"

Both Lily and the Marquess and Mr Ross had dined at the same table, and were unaffected.

It remained a mystery. The doctor remained at Betsy's bedside with Lily insisting on remaining in attendance. "I cannot sleep, while my cousin suffers so," she told Gervase, who understood.

He did not rest himself, but sat up at his desk, awaiting news. He had a selfish fear lest this be some transmissible ailment that his wife might also be stricken with.

Sarah refused to sleep but remained in attendance, as did Mrs Hollis. They were all sorely troubled.

It was a long and harrowing night. There were several moments when death was feared for Betsy and Lily did all she could to assist the doctor, praying desperately for her cousin.

Then, as the darkness of the sky began to dispel as the thin grey of dawn crept from the east, the worst danger was past.

Betsy remained unconscious. Her face was ashen pale, but the paroxysms had ceased and her breathing was even.

"When will she wake, do you know?" Lily asked the doctor.

"I cannot say. Let her sleep for now. I will not prescribe any tonics as yet, for we do not know what substances may irritate her stomach further. Give her small sips of water for hydration, and anticipate that she may purge again. No food as yet, nor even broth."

The doctor went to speak with the Marquess, who arranged that he should call again towards the middle of the day. He then went to the patient's bedside, his arm clasped around his wife.

"I do not know what I should do if she died," Lily said. She had held tears at bay all night but now she turned to him, her face against his chest, unable to stop crying.

Gervase stroked her hair, and felt how young and vulnerable she was. She had all the grace and wisdom of a woman of many years older, and yet she was not so. In this moment she was but a frightened girl, quite broken with the strain of the past night.

"All will be well, my dear," he said, feeling hopelessly inadequate.

Lily tried to recover herself, feeling embarrassment for leaning on her husband this way. She turned back to the bed. "She is so very pale," she said.

"You are nearly as pale yourself, you must take some breakfast." I cannot lose you, Gervase thought. He could not look at Betsy without imagining Lily in her place, and the picture chilled him.

Lily was reluctant to leave Betsy but she found her husband surprisingly firm. "Sarah will stay with her, and then she must rest. I know I will fail to persuade you to do likewise, so we will have a quilt brought and you may sit and sleep in the chair beside your cousin. But not until after I am satisfied that you have eaten enough to restore your own strength."

He rarely commanded her to do anything, which made Lily realise the extent of his concern for her. She acquiesced and orders were sent to the kitchen to prepare food. Gervase joined her at the table but Lily found it difficult to eat, she was so anxious.

As she left to return to Betsy, she turned in the doorway.

"Thank you for your great kindness to my cousin."

Gervase's features, stern with anxiety, softened. "It is the very least I could do for anyone. Let alone one so dear to you." Lily smiled in gratitude, which made Gervase's heart constrict. Then he was left alone while she went again to her cousin, wishing he could be of more comfort to her.

***

It was not until evening that Betsy awoke, just as the sun was going down. The cool twilight filtered into the room and everything was very calm and restful.

Betsy's eyes flickered and she saw Lily at her bedside. She tried to speak but was too weak.

"Say nothing, dearest. You have been very ill but the doctor has been and assures us that you will make a full recovery," Lily told her.

A twinge of pain crossed Betsy's brow.

"You may sip a little of this water, but you must rest for some time yet." Lily sponged a few drops onto Betsy's mouth. The patient closed her eyes again but Lily was much more encouraged now she had woken.

Betsy whispered something, it sounded like "such pain!" but then slept again.

Later that night Gervase entered to find both girls asleep, with Lily looking wretchedly exhausted in the chair. Not stopping to consider it, he went straight over to his wife, picked her up as she slept, and carried her to her own chamber. He undressed and lay beside her the whole night, holding her in his arms.

In the morning when she awoke he quelled any questions with a kiss. "Your cousin is much better, and Mrs Hollis has been attending to her."

"What time is it?" Lily asked.

"It is still early. I feared to rouse you, lest you become ill yourself."

Her thanks was in the embrace she returned him.

Lily dressed and went at once to Betsy. The patient remained pale but did not have the ashen look of the day before. Blood flowed in her veins at least. "What can have happened to me?" she asked. Her voice was barely a whisper.

"We are not sure. You have been gravely ill, we fear it may be the same ailment as Sarah's mother suffered. God forbid there is some strange sickness afflicting the people hereabouts. The doctor is concerned."

Sarah was over in the corner of the room, having brought fresh linens. She looked troubled but did not speak. Having completed her task, she hurried off again. Lily thought there appeared something odd in the maid's manner, but perhaps she was distressed to remember her mother's suffering.

"The pain, Lily, it was more than I have ever known. It overtook my whole body, and then I do not remember much at all. How many days have passed?" Betsy asked.

"Only one. You fell ill the night before last."

"I remember waking yesterday, but I was so tired," Betsy said. She still looked as though she could sleep for a hundred years.

"Rest longer, dearest," Lily urged her. She gave her cousin some more sips of water. Great was her relief to see Betsy so much recovered compared to the previous night.

The doctor came again and was likewise pleased with Betsy's progress. He gave instructions to Mrs Hollis for dishes that might be served to the invalid, which the housekeeper made careful notes of. But he confirmed that the main danger was past.

Lily agonised over whether she should have sent for Sir Robert and Lady Maud. What if Betsy had died? But she had not, so Lily might be spared any such regrets.

Time was running out. Lily sensed that the deception could not be maintained for much longer.

35. The soirée

If her cousin's illness had any silver lining, it was in providing an excuse for Betsy to decline Lavinia Leominster's invitation to what was described as a "musical soirée". Lady Leominster wrote to inform them that she had had her spinet repaired, and that she would be most delighted if Miss Ann Cosgrove would play before her guests, some of whom were lately arrived from London.

Lily interpreted this as the threat it was. It was inconceivable that both she and Betsy could be there. Were Betsy recognised, and should something be said, disaster would befall.

Betsy had been slow to recuperate, staying in her room for more than a week while she gradually regained her strength. The weather was chill and the doctor had not yet recommended a turn outdoors.

Sir Stephen Seton had been very neighbourly, sending flowers and a basket of fruit from his forcing house. He had dined several times with Lily and Gervase, and Lily found she greatly enjoyed his company.

Not solely because he was a man of culture and intelligence, for so was her husband. But Lily liked the interaction between the two men. Gervase, naturally reserved, was jostled into conversation by his good natured friend. Sir Stephen frequently encouraged Gervase to express opinions and discuss topics about which he would otherwise have been more guarded.

"But what of the scandal in Parliament regarding the Duke of York? There are rumours the lady in question intends to publish a memoir," Sir Stephen said.

"You know that I do not occupy myself with tittle-tattle, Seton," Gervase replied.

"It is a government crisis, not mere tittle-tattle, Westford. The word is that he may be forced to resign."

Another time Sir Stephen referred to a book that was causing a sensation. Gervase initially declined to comment, beyond stating that it would be unlikely to find a place in his own library.

Whereupon Sir Stephen chided him for his narrow devotion to authors such as Herodotus, Plato and Cicero. "It behoves all men to broaden their diet of literature, Seton. And women too," he said, acknowledging Lily with a courteous nod. "I will have my copy sent over to you first thing tomorrow morning. You may both read it, and provide me with your opinions on it."

Lily hid a smile. The novel in question was one that she hardly imagined Gervase would countenance her reading, and would likely forbear to peruse himself.

"I fear you will be waiting a very long time for any such opinion from me," Gervase informed him.

Sir Stephen merely laughed and moved the conversation on to a subject with which his friend was more comfortable.

Despite his convictions, Gervase was sometimes left uneasy by these exchanges. He was aware that younger people were freer in their talk on matters such as scandal, and in the books that they read. If Seton, a man of his own years, should manage to find interest in such topics, should he, Gervase, reconsider them? He had a high regard for Seton's intelligence and discernment.

What Gervase also felt, though he shrank from acknowledging it, was a fear that his wife, so much younger than he and with a quick and lively intelligence, might find him dull even as she found Seton entertaining. He no longer had any fears that either of them might betray him. He was growing more assured of Lily's affection for him every day.

But still, he wished to engage and amuse her as much as Seton was able to. As much as that damned Claude Belvedere had, though Gervase would never stoop to his level of scandalous tattle. So when the dreaded volume arrived from Grantlings, he surprised his wife by suggesting that she try it. "I will trust your judgement, Elizabeth, as to whether I should follow your and Seton's example in reading the thing. Should both of you find merit in it, I will acquiesce to your opinion."

Lily was surprised but secretly pleased. She surprised her husband by spontaneously putting her arms around his neck and embracing him. They were in the hall and any of the servants might have walked past. Gervase might have chided her for the indiscretion. But he was more than distracted by the feel of her body against his and carried her straight up the stairs, spending the rest of the afternoon in bed with her.

He quite forgot, or he forgot to care, that he had arranged to meet Duncan Ross to go over some estate business. Mr Ross was due to make his annual visit to his home for several weeks, and Gervase wanted to get certain affairs concluded beforehand.

***

Then came the event that Lily had dreaded: the soirée at Leominster Hall. She wore the silver gown that she had first worn at Almack's, and had not worn since. She remembered the appreciation in Gervase's eyes when she had worn it, and hoped to inspire the same response again.

As much as it pleased her husband, it thoroughly displeased Lady Leominster. She had worn what she considered to be a striking and alluring crimson gown. But she saw at once that it was no match for the radiant youth and beauty of Lady Westford, softly illuminated by the pale shine of silvery lace and silk.

Lavinia Leominster also wished to curse aloud when she realised the absence of the cousin. Thwarted! She did not for a moment believe any report of illness. The devious little chits had cooked up such a tale to avoid discovery. For Lady Leominster was increasingly certain that she was correct in her suspicions.

"I believe you have already made the acquaintance of Lady Westford," she said to Cecilia Nasebury, leading Lily over to her. "I am afraid she informs us that her cousin, Miss Cosgrove, who was to have delighted us on the spinet, has been taken unwell." The falsely-sweet tone of her voice failed to mask the acid beneath.

Lily felt deep unease at encountering Mrs Nasebury again. It was a much smaller gathering, and thus it would be harder to evade her scrutiny and insinuations than at Lady Belvedere's ball. She recalled that Mrs Nasebury had daughters, newly married or soon to be married, she could not exactly recall.

"I trust your daughters are well?" Lily inquired. "I remember that you spoke of them to me at Belvedere House."

"Indeed they are, my lady. I am disappointed to learn that we will not meet your cousin tonight."

"I regret she was forced to stay behind," Lily said. "She has been gravely ill, and is as yet recuperating."

There was a strange light of suspicion in Cecilia Nasebury's eyes. "Let us wish her a swift recovery," she said.

Lavinia Leominster had not directly disclosed to Cecilia Nasebury the reason for her presence here. Having been the recipient of a snub from her current hostess on more than one occasion, Cecilia Nasebury had been both gratified and curious to receive an invitation to Leominster Hall. She was herself wily enough to recognise that some purpose other than hospitality lay behind it.

When Lady Leominster had mentioned that a cousin of Lady Westford would be among her guests, light began to dawn. She wishes me to take a look at this cousin, Cecilia Nasebury had thought to herself. Yet they were to be thwarted, if that lady had chosen to stay away.

"I believe your cousin may have been introduced to me last Season," Mrs Nasebury said. "Would that be so?"

"I cannot say, I am afraid," Lily said.

"It was at a ball given by the Aldershots."

Lily knew that the woman was digging. "It was not an event I attended, though I will mention your name to my cousin."

"I may be mistaken, of course," Cecilia Nasebury said. "For I am quite sure that I did not have the pleasure of meeting two Miss Cosgroves last Season."

Her slight emphasis on "two" was enough to make Lily grow pale, though she kept her composure. "We did not attend all the same events," was all she managed to say.

Sir Stephen Seton, who was also among the guests, overheard this last line and saw Lady Westford's reaction.

He wondered at it. Many things about this evening had seemed strange to him, the odd selection of guests for one. The stout woman in purple did not seem to him to be typical of the usual crowd who frequented Leominster Hall.

It was also not customary for his neighbour to hold such an event at this time of year, so Sir Stephen's curiosity was already aroused when receiving her invitation. Lavinia Leominster was not a woman he admired or liked. Beyond the very minimum that courtesy required, he did not solicit her company.

He had been uncomfortably aware of the widow's designs on his friend. Fortunately Gervase had remained indifferent or oblivious to them, saving himself much trouble. Sir Stephen had feared that Lavinia Leominster might have tried to entrap Westford through compromising them both in some scheme, but the Marquess's marriage now represented a welcome defence against any such machinations.

Sir Stephen had seen how his hostess regarded Lady Westford, and it was not with any kindness or liking. On the contrary, he had once or twice observed jealousy and a keen dislike in her gaze. He was confident that Lady Westford was astute enough to realise her hostess's antipathy.

The line "two Miss Cosgroves" struck him. The seeds of an idea germinated in his mind. The more he had become acquainted with Lady Westford, the harder he had found it to believe that she had fallen for the wiles of Tom Farrington. His first theory was that she had been discredited against her will, that Farrington had seized and violated her through some trickery. Not that she would be considered any less ruined from this than if she had consented to his advances.

Now he wondered. Could it be possible that instead, it was Miss Ann Cosgrove who had compromised herself, and Lady Westford who had chosen to take the blame upon herself? He had found his sympathies aroused by Miss Cosgrove when she had dined at Grantlings. She was clearly a young woman who had suffered some distress or disappointment in her life. She also seemed to Sir Stephen to be a far likelier type to have been hoodwinked by a rake.

But no! It was too fantastic. Had the former Elizabeth Cosgrove been innocent of all condemnation against her, she would surely not have felt compelled to accept matrimony to restore her reputation. Nor then to suffer Westford's earlier harsh judgement of her. No one could make such a sacrifice, surely?

Troubled by these thoughts, he came to Lady Westford's rescue by interrupting the conversation. "Lady Westford, it is good to see you. Though I do not believe I have had the pleasure of making your companion's acquaintance?"

"Forgive me," Lily said, secretly overwhelmed with relief at his appearance. She made the appropriate introductions.

Cecilia Nasebury was not glad of the introduction for she believed she was close to some discovery. But she was forced to be gracious, and enter a conversation about the surrounding countryside and the recent weather.

Sir Stephen caught Lily's eye. He knows something, she thought. But his demeanour was friendly and he had clearly come to her rescue.

Across the room, Lavinia Leominster eyed the three guests. She trusted the Nasebury women to delve as far as propriety allowed. The Marquess stood near her, and remembering his earlier discomposure at seeing his wife with Seton, Lady Leominster sought to goad him.

"How delightful that Sir Stephen and Lady Westford enjoy such pleasant conversation. It must be gratifying for you to have your closest friend and wife on such cordial terms, given the propinquity of Grantlings. I imagine it makes for many a merry evening," she commented to him.

It did, but not in the improper way that Lady Leominster was implying. Gervase gritted his teeth, wishing he had not gone against his better judgement so as to accept this invitation. He had never greatly liked Leominster's wife, now widow. The contrast of his own wife's graceful conduct and conversation with Lavinia Leominster's archness and insinuations only served to condemn that lady further in his opinion.

Distracted by his thoughts, he barely paid attention to Mrs Nasebury's conversation, when she later approached him without waiting for an introduction.

"I was most sorry to hear of Lady Westford's cousin's illness. I am certain that I met Miss Cosgrove during the season last year," Cecilia Nasebury was saying.

"You met my wife?" Gervase asked.

"Indeed I did not. It was her cousin, Miss Ann Cosgrove, who was introduced to me. However my memory must deceive me, for I am certain that she was introduced to me as a Miss Elizabeth Cosgrove. Perhaps our mutual acquaintance erred?" Mrs Nasebury said.

Gervase had not the faintest idea of what the woman was implying. He simply wished to be rid of her so he could rejoin his wife. Lily looked pale and he was concerned for her.

Lily was suffering an absolute ordeal. She dreaded to imagine what Cecilia Nasebury was saying to the Marquess. What if Mrs Nasebury had guessed, and planned to expose her? Lily's hand trembled as she held the glass that Sir Stephen had handed to her.

Sir Stephen noticed her anxiety. "You are unwell, I think," he said. "I shall fetch Westford so he can escort you home."

"I am quite fine, thank you," Lily managed to say. But the quaver in her voice betrayed her.

Gervase was wracked with anxiety when he joined her side. "Seton fears for your health, my dear. Looking at you, I share his concern. We shall return home forthwith."

"Thank you." The relief she felt at escaping Lady Leominster and her scrutiny made Lily feel fainter still. Gervase took charge of everything. He had the carriage summoned, he escorted her to it, he lifted her inside with him. She had never felt so protected, nor so painfully conscious that her husband was protecting her from her own wrongs.

Lady Leominster was mildly gratified when Cecilia Nasebury related the conversation to her later. So the chit was rattled, was she? Damn Seton for intervening at such a point.

There was one thing left to do.

Later that night, when her guests had departed or retired to bed, she sat by candlelight at her writing desk. Dipping her quill in the inkpot, she wrote a brief note.

"My Dear Mr Farrington,

"I advise you to return forthwith to Westford Park. I believe that what you will discover there may be of some considerable surprise to you, and even to your advantage.

"A friend."

Lavinia Leominster did not sign her name. She must not be formally connected to any meddling. If for some reason the chit was not who she claimed to be, Farrington was the one person who could expose her. And even if she were the intended Elizabeth Cosgrove, the presence of Farrington might be enough to foment discord between husband and wife.

Either way, she remained hopeful that marriage might yet be annulled. This would leave the field happily clear for her own marital machinations.

36. The revelation

A few days passed, and Betsy had finally been permitted outside. Though the weather was cold, she and Lily wrapped up warmly and went for a walk around the lake. Lily had told her about Lady Leominster's soirée, and the presence of Cecilia Nasebury.

"I feel sure that she had some mischief in mind, for Mrs Nasebury does not strike me as the kind of woman to be an intimate friend of Lady Leominster," Lily said. "It seemed too much of a coincidence, that she should have spoken to me as she did at Lady Belvedere's ball, and then appear at Leominster Hall and make such strange insinuations. Though I would never have wished you to suffer so, your illness may have saved us from exposure."

"Indeed." Betsy fell silent. "Lily, Sarah asked me a strange question the other day. Or rather I found her manner strange."

"She has seemed out of character these past weeks. Yet she has not disclosed what troubles her, though I have asked her if anything is the matter," Lily said. "What was her question?"

"She asked if I had taken any of your tonic. Are you taking tonic, Lily? I have not seen any in your room."

Lily was mystified. "I am not. I wonder why she should ask such a thing?"

"She referred to the night that I fell ill. But I drank no such thing that night, nor do I recall seeing any. All I remember is drinking the wine they brought to you room, for you did not want it."

Lily remembered this. "I do not usually like wine before bed. I have told Mrs Hollis this, but she perhaps forgot. She did once provide me with a tonic, even though I had declined it. It was some time ago, when she feared I was unwell."

"Did you take it?" Betsy asked.

"I did not like to. My father always warned me against taking certain remedies, and I did not know what was in this one."

They walked along in silence again, Lily lost in thought. She was troubled but she could not establish why. She recalled the bottle of tonic that Mrs Hollis had sent her, which she had discarded. Since then she had not been presented with any more.

Back inside, she sent for Sarah. The maid was clearly suffering some anxiety. She looked very nervous as she approached Lily.

"Sarah, do not be troubled," Lily said. "It is only that I am puzzled by something that you said to Miss Cosgrove."

"Yes, my lady." Sarah's eyes were downcast and she clutched her apron in her fingers, twisting the white linen.

"You mentioned tonic. I wondered why you might have thought she had taken my tonic, for I had not provided her with any, nor do I have any."

"O! My lady!" Sarah burst into tears, burying her face in her hands.

Lily was perplexed and anxious for her. "Please do not distress yourself, Sarah. You are not in trouble. We are simply keen to understand why you had thought such a thing."

Sarah, sniffing and red-eyed, regarded her mistress. "I did a most foolish and terrible thing, my lady. I am sure that you must dismiss me once you hear of it, but I will tell you."

"Go on." Lily was sure the maid's supposed transgression was far slighter than Sarah thought, for she was generally a good and honest girl.

"If you remember, my lady, there was that evening where you had appeared unwell, and some tonic had been provided to you. I saw that you did not take it, for I found it in the basket when I came to clear your things. My mother was also ill at the time, and we could not afford to have the doctor. I thought that no one should miss the tonic if I took it. So I did so, though I know it was very wrong to have taken it without asking."

Lily's heart bled for Sarah and her family. To suffer such poverty that they could not seek help when they were ill! "You must know, Sarah, that the Marquess would never allow any of his tenants to suffer. He would happily bear the expense of any physician or remedies to spare you or your family from pain," she told the girl.

Sarah hung her head. "It is more than kind of him," she said. "But I did not know, so I gave my mother the tonic and she took a dose. It was shortly afterwards that she became so violently ill, and nearly died. Since then I have blamed myself sorely. I feared the tonic must have disagreed with her, but I was too ashamed to speak of it to anyone."

The maid took a handkerchief that Lily offered to dry her eyes and blow her nose. She continued. "Then, when I saw Miss Cosgrove with such a similar fit of sickness, I wondered if she might also have taken such a tonic. For it does not seem to be an illness that passes from person to person, my lady. You have remained quite well, despite nursing your cousin. Myself as well, and my brothers and sisters."

Lily smiled. "You can reassure yourself, Sarah, that it was no tonic that brought harm to my cousin. The only draught she took that evening before bed was some wine."

Even as she said it, her heart stilled. Her wine. Betsy had taken her wine, for she had not wanted it. Nor had she ordered it. The tonic brought to her, unsolicited, may have made Sarah's mother deadly ill. And now Betsy had fallen sick after imbibing a cup of wine, that Lily had also not requested.

It was mere coincidence, surely?

Someone near to you, someone within your home, threatens a great evil to you...

A chill ran down her spine as the gypsy's words came back to her. Lily sought to get a grip of herself. She needed to speak with Mrs Hollis, urgently.

***

The housekeeper was arranging items in the linen cupboard when Lily found her. "Mrs Hollis, I need to ask you some questions," she began, feeling awkward.

"Of course." Mrs Hollis put down the neatly folded linens.

"Some time ago you had a tonic sent to my room. I wondered if you knew what its ingredients were."

The housekeeper drew her brows together, puzzled. "A tonic, my lady? I have never dispensed such to you."

"It was shortly after we returned from London. You mentioned it to me, as an aid to sleep, and sent it to me on the tray that Mary brought," Lily said.

Mrs Hollis was bewildered. "I have a notion I mentioned such to you, but that you declined it. So of course I did not wish to force it upon you."

"But a bottle was brought to my room. I did not take any, yet Sarah now reveals that she administered some of it to her mother, shortly before she fell so ill."

There was shock on the housekeeper's face. "I am sure that Sarah would know better than to help herself from the stillroom without asking. What can she have been thinking? I had not noticed that the bottle was disturbed."

"It is still there, then?" Lily was confused now. Sarah had admitted to taking the entire bottle, and had not mentioned returning it.

"You may see for yourself, my lady, if you would be so good as to accompany me to the stillroom."

Lily went with Mrs Hollis to the room where various items for the household were prepared. Soaps, tonics and other decoctions were all neatly labelled and arranged in the cupboards and on the shelves. The housekeeper opened one of the cupboards and brought down a bottle. "Here you are. As you can see it is labelled. Barley water, lavender and vervain."

She opened the bottle and smelt the contents before handing it to Lily. "It does not appear to have spoilt. It is a very mild remedy, but I have found it most effective myself."

Lily took the bottle and also inhaled the pleasant aroma of flowers and herbs. "But this is not the bottle that was brought to me, Mrs Hollis. I remember clearly that there was no label, which made me hesitant to try it, not knowing what its ingredients might be. It was also a different shape and size."

"This is the only such remedy I have for sleep." The housekeeper opened the cupboard door wider, to display the full collection of bottles. "Did it resemble any of these?"

It did not. Lily thought it best to summon Sarah, who also verified that that none of the bottles resembled the one she had taken for her mother.

Lily handed the sleep tonic to Sarah. "Does this resemble the draught your mother took?"

Sarah sniffed it gingerly, as though expecting a strong aroma. "No, my lady, this is quite pleasant. The tonic I took for my mother had a strong and bitter aroma, though I did not taste it myself."

The next step was to interview Mary. She could not remember whether a bottle had been on the tray or not, but she certainly had not put it there herself. "Mrs Hollis would never wish me to meddle with anything in the stillroom without being told to," she said.

Knowing both Sarah and Mary to be truthful girls, Lily was satisfied that they had nothing to do with this mystery. Then she recalled the wine.

"Some wine was brought to my room a few nights ago." She refrained from mentioning the precise date. "I had not requested it, and though it was a kind consideration, as I have mentioned, I prefer only water before bed." Lily was aware it was a strange thing to say, particularly to all three of them, but she wished to see their reaction.

All three were nonplussed. "I have not instructed any such thing to be brought your room, my lady, not since you made your preferences clear," Mrs Hollis said.

Sarah and Mary likewise denied any knowledge of it.

Lily felt faint. "I did not drink the wine, but Miss Cosgrove did. It was the same night she fell so direly ill."

Sarah gasped in shock and Mary looked wide-eyed and fearful. The housekeeper's face went white. "This is a strange and terrible thing. I hope you cannot think that we - but no, if there has been some wicked mischief, I fear we must all lie under suspicion."

Lily sought to reassure her. "I do not think such of you at all. I am still hopeful that some dreadful mistake or coincidence has taken place."

Mrs Hollis pressed her lips together. She clearly thought the worst, but said nothing.

Lily dismissed them then and returned to the morning room, for she needed some time to think. She could not quite bear to think that there had been any deliberate crime.

Particularly as if it were so, she must be the intended victim. But who would want her dead? And why?

37. The revenant

Thoughts swirled around Lily's head. She dared not frighten Betsy with her suspicions of a deliberate poisoning. As for telling the Marquess: she shrank from the very notion. He would think that she had lost her wits.

She made her way downstairs, where Pelham met in her the hall. He had an uncomfortable expression on his face.

"My lady, there is a guest arrived. The cousin of his Lordship. He is in the morning room."

Tom Farrington had finally appeared.

Lily felt such a coldness sweep through her body that she felt faint.

The man who had ruined her cousin's happiness, and could now be her own undoing.

Her first instinct was to return upstairs and avoid him. But what good would that do? Both she and Betsy would have to feign some indisposition to avoid him. He might reside here for days. They could not hide away indefinitely.

What should she do?

Masking her turmoil as best she could from the steward, Lily decided that the only course of action was to face the man. Perhaps he had some shred of good nature she could appeal to.

From everything she had heard of him, her hope of this was slim, but a confrontation was inevitable.

"Thank you, Pelham. I will go there now."

Lily walked to the morning room as if in a daze. Inside stood a young man. He was tall and of slim build, though not so tall as the Marquess. His appearance was not far from what Lily had imagined. Somewhat handsome, as Betsy had described, but in Lily's view marred by dissipation. He had a supercilious look in his eye as he initially regarded her, which swiftly transformed into a blatant appreciation of what he saw.

"I did not know my cousin had guests at present," he said. "Whose acquaintance do I have the very great delight of making?" He spoke in a drawl, his emphasis insultingly explicit as he spoke of delight.

Lily avoided giving her name. "I am afraid we were not expecting visitors," she said.

"I would hardly call myself a visitor, this being my family home. I am Tom Farrington, cousin and current heir to Lord Westford," he said.

"I had guessed as such, sir."

His lips twisted in a lascivious smile. "My guess is that you are some friend or relation of my cousin's new wife?"

Tom Farrington wondered if this strange girl had anything to do with the mysterious letter he had received. It had been in a woman's hand, though none that he recognised.

His cousin's marriage had greatly annoyed him. Gervase had previously shown no intention of matrimony, leaving Tom's own hopes comfortably secure. The Marquess had even censured his cousin many times with reference to the title that he might one day need to be deserving of.

When Tom had heard the news that his cousin had taken it upon himself to marry the Cosgrove girl, Tom had been astounded and enraged. That the chit he had toyed with might bring forth a usurper of his inheritance was more than could be borne.

Before Lily could answer his question, Mrs Hollis entered. She greeted the visitor with the requisite politeness but there was clearly no liking between the housekeeper and Tom Farrington. "I shall have your usual room prepared, sir."

She turned to Lily. "My lady, Pelham informs me that his Lordship is not yet back from the estate. I did not know if there might be any changes to the arrangements for dinner?" The housekeeper looked at Lily with the same awkwardness that Pelham had. There was also sympathy in her gaze.

She knows, Lily thought. They all know. It was humiliating and infuriating: for of course she needed no sympathy from them. The man that stood before her was nothing to her.

"I should be glad if you will inform my cousin of our guest. There is no need for her to disturb herself if she is resting," she told Mrs Hollis. Betsy still reclined most afternoons, her strength not yet fully recovered.

"I will do so forthwith, my lady."

Mrs Hollis departed and Tom Farrington regarded Lily with a glint of curiosity. "My lady?" His gaze fell to her hand and the ring she wore. "So you are married. I wonder if that is a pity or whether it offers the chance of even greater pleasure in your company?"

Tom found himself attracted to the young woman who stood before him. She was not his usual type. But her beauty and form were such that any man might be tempted. Married women were frequently far more sporting, Tom found. This chit was looking at him with barely disguised outrage but this only amused him and spurred him on. Corrupting a young wife would be just as amusing as seducing a maiden.

Her presence would certainly make his stay here more pleasant. He wondered who her husband was and if he were about.

Deliberately he ran his eyes up and down her body, hoping to discomfort her. There was a question in his gaze as he returned to her face. "Who might your husband be, I wonder? For you have still not provided me with your name."

Lily swallowed but kept her countenance composed. "My husband is the Marquess of Westford, sir."

Tom frowned, then gave her an incredulous smile. "I do not think that it can be, my dear. For it is well known that my cousin was recently wed to a Miss Cosgrove, with whom I am personally gratified to be very intimately acquainted. And you are certainly not she."

Lily refrained from reacting to the insult to her cousin. His meaning of "intimately" was clear from his tone.

"Nonetheless, sir, I am the wife of the Marquess of Westford."

This was bewildering. Tom briefly wondered if some trick were being played on him. "But you are not Miss Cosgrove."

"I am no longer. My name before my marriage was Cosgrove." The girl had every sincerity on her face as she spoke.

"You are not Miss Elizabeth Cosgrove, though," Tom said.

"Until my marriage, I was Miss Elizabeth Cosgrove."

Tom laughed in disbelief. "There cannot be two of you. Or if there are, he wed the wrong one." He spoke in jest, then saw the look that passed over Lily's face. "Good God. Could it be so...? You, such a delectable thing, married to my cousin?"

He lent in towards her, bringing his face closer to hers. Lily tried to move back but the sofa was behind her, blocking escape. Tom gave an unpleasantly suggestive sneer. "It is no wonder that he changed his mind..."

Before he could finish speaking, the door opened and the Marquess entered.

***

Gervase, in his blur of rage at his cousin's unannounced arrival, saw only two things when he came into the room.

His damned cousin's mocking glance at him, and Lily ashen pale, with two bright spots of crimson in her cheeks.

So this was how it stood?

All this time and she still blushed and swooned for Farrington? Who appeared to have been on the point of embracing her?

Gervase's gut was wrenched with the harshest pain he had ever known. Just as he was growing to believe that his young bride had conceived an affection for him, he was faced with this.

She and Farrington alone together. Discomfort and a guilty fear all over her face as he, her husband, interrupted their little tête-à-tête.

Gervase had never imagined that seeing the pair of them together would disturb him so. He had known it must happen at some stage, though he had pushed it out of his mind.

But the reality brought everything rushing back to him. It utterly eclipsed any brief and foolish jealousy he had felt toward Seton or any other young buck who had ogled Lily in London.

For this was a man with whom his wife had been intimate. A man for whom she had cared so much for that she had ruined her reputation.

Gervase's expression turned to steel. He gave them both a curt nod. "Farrington. My lady."

Then he turned on his heel and strode out.

Not knowing what he was doing or where was going, he found himself heading in the direction of the stables.

There, he saddled Orion, mounted the horse, and rode off.

***

Lily was horrified by the accusatory look on her husband's face

"My lord..." she called after him but he was gone instantly. She froze for a moment, not looking at Tom Farrington, then followed after Gervase.

But he was already through the front door which he slammed behind himself, not even looking back.

Lily despaired. She guessed what he may have thought, finding her alone with Farrington. She had to get to Betsy, urgently, to inform her of Tom Farrington's presence. She dreaded how Betsy might react.

Lily turned back to her unwelcome guest with a mix of distress and fear.

"I regret to say that I am occupied elsewhere, sir, and must take my leave of you," Lily said.

Tom meanwhile had been intrigued by his cousin's reaction. There had been sheer fury on the Marquess's face. Granted, Gervase had caught him in close communion with this woman who purported to be his wife. And given the various peccadilloes that Gervase had dealt with on his behalf, Tom figured it was fair to assume that his cousin did not wholly trust him around women.

But not to stand his ground? To storm off in such a fashion, without waiting for a moment's explanation? After all, Gervase must know that the two of them had met only moments before. There could be no prior intrigue to arouse his suspicions.

Something was afoot.

"Wait," Tom commanded Lily. "I am curious to know how my cousin's change of plans came about. How come he married you, and not the other? For based on what you claim, there must surely be two Miss Cosgroves." It struck him that his Miss Cosgrove, Betsy, was likely some relation of this strange and tantalisingly beautiful girl. He himself had dallied with the wrong one, if so. No wonder that Gervase had doubtless changed his mind and switched his intentions on seeing this girl.

"I do not know what you speak of," Lily said.

An unpleasant smile drew across Tom's face. "Come, now. You must be aware that his plans were to marry quite a different Miss Cosgrove."

Lily tried to brazen it out but knew she trembled as she spoke. Her nails dugs into her palms in an effort to maintain her composure. "What my husband's plans were or were not before our marriage, I cannot say."

She knows, Tom thought. What strange pretence was this? "Perhaps my cousin will be better able to inform me on the matter."

He spoke mainly in jest, but he saw fear come over her. A notion so absurd, so shocking then came to him that it was more as a joke that he said: "I assume he is aware he married the wrong Miss Cosgrove?"

Her face told him everything.

Tom took a breath. "Surely it cannot be that he *does not know*?"

"Sir, I beg you..." Lily did not even know what she was asking him. She saw from the cruel and calculating gleam in the man's eye that he would do her no favours.

"Let me establish the facts," Tom said. "My cousin was to have married an Elizabeth Cosgrove - doubtless some relation of yours, if you speak the truth about sharing her name - and some substitution took place? Without Gervase's knowledge?"

"It is not as it seems, sir."

Tom laughed, mercilessly. "I am quite sure it is not as it seems." What a tale this was! His stiff stick of a cousin, entrapped into marriage with entirely the wrong bride.

Lily fought a desire to throw herself on his mercy. To beg him not to tell Gervase. But she knew from looking at him that it would be of no use. He would have a price higher than she could pay. And ultimately, he would expose her. For it was in his interests to do so.

What she needed now was time. Time to find Gervase and tell him herself. Because she could not bear that the man she loved should suffer the double humiliation of learning of his betrayal from a third party. Let alone from his loathsome cousin. He should hear it first from her.

"I beg for your discretion, sir," Lily asked Tom Farrington. She hoped to buy herself a few hours through some bargain.

This aroused an amused contempt. "You expect me to keep news such as this from my cousin? That is a very large favour to ask. But I am not wholly unreasonable. I am sure that you would be prepared to extend a favour of similar magnitude to me, would you not?"

Tom ran his finger down the exposed flesh above the neck of Lily's gown. In truth he had little desire to squander such leverage as this on a forced dalliance with the girl. He derived far more enjoyment when they came willingly, even against their own better judgement. Any fool with two arms could take a maiden by force. It was a greater victory to make them the authors of their own ruin.

But seduction was not his ultimate goal here. For assuming this marriage was lawful, the girl stood in his way. She was young, she might well beget a serious obstacle to his expectations, at least if Gervase had it in him. His cousin's involvement with women over the years had been so slight - Gervase did not even keep a mistress, at least that Tom knew of - that Tom had never had much to fear when it came to his future inheritance.

Now, all that was changed. He needed some time to think about the best way to go about this business. For now, he would enjoy a little terrorisation of the new, but hopefully temporary, marchioness.

"What are your terms?" Lily asked. She made an attempt to look resigned and defeated, but in reality she had no intention to be the victim of blackmail. Her father had once told her that nothing was worth such a price. A man he had known, facing exposure over some stolen letters, had taken his own life to escape the shame.

"It was never worth it, Lily," her father had said. "He left a widow, three children, a babe unborn that would never know its father. All would have been content with a quiet life away from town if it meant having both their parents with them. As it was they faced disgrace and penury." Edward Cosgrove had done what he could for the family, though it could not replace the loss of a husband and father.

But the lesson remained with Lily. Never give in to blackmail.

Fortunately Tom had not yet formulated his demands, buying Lily some precious time.

"I may need some time to consider my terms," Tom Farrington told her. "As I am sure you will appreciate time to consider your willingness to pay them. We shall discuss this business again tomorrow. For now, let us be at leisure. I shall take great pleasure in dining tonight with you and your... husband."

38. The decision

"He is here? O, Lily, is he truly here?"

Lily had hoped desperately that Betsy would not be agitated to such excitement at the news that Mrs Hollis had brought. "Yes, dear, Mr Farrington is below. But I fear I must tell you that he did not come for you."

"He did not? But he suspects I am here surely? He does not know that it is you who married his cousin, rather than me?"

Lily's head was already pounding with the worry of it all. "I am afraid he does. And I am also afraid that he plans to blackmail us."

Betsy was incredulous at this. They were sitting in her room, where a fire had been lit due to the coldness of the season. "It cannot be, Lily dear! He could not do such a thing. I will speak with him."

It was impossible, Lily thought. Betsy could not see reason, so blind were the hopes she clung to.

"You must listen, Betsy, for there are things I have not told you." It was time to stop protecting Betsy from the truth. As briefly as possible Lily recounted everything she had ever heard of Tom Farrington. The rumours she had gleaned during her time here. The bare facts as they stood. And the conversation she had just had with the man, as near word-for-word as Lily could relate it.

Betsy was silent for a while. "Lily, why did you tell me none of this before?"

"I feared you would not accept any of it, and I feared to make you even more unhappy."

Betsy's forehead puckered. She did not look at her cousin but gazed down at her hands as she twisted and pleated the fabric of her skirt between her fingers. "I know that you would not lie to me, for what would your motive be? And yet none of it accords with what I have known of Tom's character."

"Only think, Betsy dear, of his conduct. You were discovered and he fled abroad. He made no attempt to contact you, either through direct or covert means. He left no message with anyone here. He simply vanished, knowing the trouble you would be in. Although it pains me to tell you, I also believe that he created further trouble with some other woman, though no one has told me so directly. Lord Westford was forced to go to town very suddenly. Then there are rumours I overheard at Almack's as well as Lord and Lady Belvedere's ball."

"I can only imagine that perhaps he is in some dire situation, and this is why he may seek favour from you, Lily." Betsy still tried to think the best of her former lover. But her confidence in him was shaken by her cousin's words.

Lily took Betsy's hands, fearing she would ruin the fine material of her gown if she kept twisting it. "I am not worldly. And yet the little exposure I have had to society has made me aware that the rowdy behaviour of young men is not universally condemned. There are even those who express admiration for such behaviour, albeit privately. Yet the comments made regarding Mr Farrington have no such suggestion of tolerance or warmth. It is hard for me to convince you, I know. Only consider what he told you of Lord Westford, compared with the reality of the Marquess's character and bearing that we have both been able to discover."

"Did Tom not even mention me? Or ask after me?"

"Only to insist, at first, that Lord Westford had married you. After that he did not ask me one thing about you. Not how you were, or where you were. Or even why we had made such an exchange."

Even Betsy must concede now that the situation was bleak. "And what of Lord Westford? Where was he during your conversation?"

Lily's face clouded over. "He saw us talking and I fear he suspected the very worst. Which one cannot blame him for, given what he believes of my former acquaintance with Mr Farrington." She did not tell Betsy of the way that Tom Farrington had leant towards her and touched her.

"What did Lord Westford do?"

"I do not know. He went out," Lily said.

"I cannot imagine what dinner will be like with the four of us," Betsy said.

Neither could Lily. It was a dreadful prospect. Even the dour company of Mr Ross might have steadied the troubled waters, but he was presently in the Scottish Highlands visiting family.

***

Gervase did not come back that evening nor that night. Lily established from Ben in the stables that the Marquess had taken Orion, but had ordered no coach or carriage to be prepared.

"He rode off in some great haste. Over the hills, towards the London road."

There was a shortcut that could be taken by horseback by not by carriage. Lily hoped desperately that Gervase had not gone to London. She must talk with him before Farrington did.

She and Betsy excused themselves from dinner. There was a gleam of approval in Mrs Hollis's eye when they requested a supper tray instead. "I quite understand, my lady."

Betsy was quite desperate to see Tom Farrington but Lily managed to delay this encounter. "He will be here tomorrow. Let us wait until then, at least. When Lord Westford is here, there will be more propriety in such a meeting."

It took some persuasion but eventually Betsy acquiesced. A reminder that her complexion would be all the fresher after a good night's sleep did much to finally convince her.

There was no comforting sleep for Lily. She lay awake until the early hours, hoping to hear the sound of Gervase returning to his adjacent chamber. But he did not return. She agonised over the situation in her mind.

Even if Mr Farrington's silence could be bought, could her secret be kept forever?

She recalled Lady Leominster's soirée and the awful Nasebury woman. Mrs Nasebury clearly suspected. Then there were Sir Robert and Lady Maud, who could not be kept at bay forever.

Most of all, Lily found she could not bear to continue deceiving the man she now loved and respected above all others. She would rather lose Gervase than keep him under false pretences. She had enjoyed her stolen pleasures, but they were not truly hers.

Even without the shadow of Tom Farrington's blackmail, the deception needed to end.

Lily managed to sleep for a couple of hours just as a grey dawn crept across the sky. But her slumber was troubled.

When she eventually rose, feeling as unrested as the night before, she went at once to Betsy.

"I have an idea that I should ride to Grantlings. It may be that Sir Stephen knows where Lord Westford has gone. It is imperative I speak to Lord Westford before Mr Farrington does, Betsy."

Betsy gaped. "You cannot mean to tell him? Surely Tom can be prevailed upon to keep our secret? I am sure that if I spoke to him, I could persuade him so."

Lily rejected the idea. "Even if you could, we cannot maintain this charade much longer. There are others who are close to discovery. I cannot avoid London forever, and you cannot spend the rest of your days hiding away. We have done what we have done, and we must face the consequences."

Betsy cried at this, and Lily sought to comfort her. "Have courage, dear. I will tell Lord Westford that it was all my idea. After all, I was the one that stood before him at the altar, and spoke vows to a man who believed me to be someone else."

Betsy still did not agree. In her mind if she were to be reunited with Tom he would be once again enraptured by her. And then everything would be as it should be. Lily and Lord Westford, and she and Tom.

But Lily insisted. "Whatever may come of this, you and I have one another. Have courage, dearest. For your own wrong, if it can even be called such, is only to have avoided a marriage that you did not seek. Whereas I entered matrimony with lies and deceit."

**

Gervase was still absent by noon. Both Lily and Betsy grew more anxious and strained. Betsy fidgeted but did not manage to continue any of her embroidery. She was increasingly anxious to see Tom, and Lily knew that her powers of keeping Betsy away from him were waning.

"There is nothing else for it. I will ride to Grantlings and see if Sir Stephen knows anything of Lord Westford's possible whereabouts," Lily said.

"And if he does not?" Betsy asked.

"Then I do not know. Then we can only wait, I suppose."

Neither had much of an appetite for lunch, despite the delicacies that Mrs Hollis had arranged for them. The housekeeper was conscious that both women were avoiding the unexpected guest below, and had some idea as to why.

Shortly after they had eaten, Lily slipped out to the stables, managing to avoid Tom Farrington. He would have to be faced again at some point, but the later the better.

Lily was uneasy at leaving Betsy alone in the house with Farrington. But she could think of no other course of action. Except to ride to London, but to make such a journey herself would be both dangerous and scandalous. She would have to command the carriage and take Betsy and George with her. It was a great deal of disruption for what might be a wild goose chase.

It was better that she ventured forth alone first, to see their neighbour. Ben was absent when Lily arrived but knowing her daily habits, had already saddled Dido for her. The horse gave a soft whinny of greeting and Lily stroked her velvet nose. "You have been a dear companion. I shall miss you when I am cast out of here," she told the horse.

She mounted Dido and rode off up the hill towards Grantlings. What she would say to their neighbour she had no idea. Sir Stephen would doubtless find the reason for her visit to be very odd. Lily struggled to imagine how the conversation might go but she had hope of Sir Stephen's understanding. He would of course find out the deception as well soon enough, and she regretted the inevitable loss of regard in his eyes.

But it was Gervase who concerned her most. He must know first.

A heavy pewter sky hung above her. Lily felt the weight of it, and the dampness. Rain threatened; she must quicken her pace.

Dido broke into a canter as they reached the top of the ridge. They rode past the abandoned shepherd's cot, which Gervase planned to have repaired in the spring. Finally, just as she sighted Grantlings at the foot of the valley, Lily found herself slipping.

For a moment she was confused, then realised she was falling.

She clung on in panic but the saddle slid around. What was happening? Was it not fastened correctly?

Bareback she might have clung on but she slipped along with the saddle. Her attempt to grasp the horse startled it, and the animal bucked and bolted.

There was no time to slow Dido before Lily was flung, violently, from the horse.

She struck her head as she fell, and lying on the hillside, knew no more.

39. The attempt

From the window of his room, Tom Farrington watched his cousin's wife ride out towards the hills. A small smile played at the corner of his lips. He was not a man to remain idle when a task needed to be carried out.

With the girl and Gervase absent, the house was his to command. He barely gave a thought to anyone else. Such was his fixation on the marriage that the mention of a cousin upstairs had slipped his mind. The possibility that it was the Elizabeth Cosgrove that he had known quite escaped him.

Had he even considered so, he would have considered it far too brazen a situation. Both the hussy and the impostor to have resided together under the same roof? It was unthinkable.

So he stood there, unaware of the turmoil his presence caused to the young woman in another wing of Westford Park.

As the hours passed and no one returned to the house, Tom grew satisfied with the course of action he had taken.

Resolving to avail himself of his cousin's wine cellar in celebration, he descended to the library. Knowing it was Gervase's favourite chamber made his own invasion of it all the more gratifying.

Tom summoned Pelham. "A bottle of brandy, if you will. But not that swill you served me at dinner last night. I recall a 1789 cognac that my cousin laid down some years ago. Bring that, if any remains."

The order left Pelham in consternation. Sir Thomas was his master's guest and close relation, who must be granted due hospitality. Yet he was sure his master would not choose to offer the "young pup", as Pelham thought of him, his finest vintage.

"I will attempt to do so, sir, if any of it remains."

Pelham departed for the cellar. He was torn between two courses of action. To dissemble and claim that none of the 1789 bottles remained, when he knew there were several. Or to decant a cheaper vintage and serve it as the 1789 cognac.

Deciding on this latter course, which if necessary he could later claim as an error on his own part, he selected an inferior bottle. He set about decanting it into a crystal flask. He hoped that he was not taking too much of a liberty.

***

Betsy grew increasingly anxious and distressed. The confinement to her room for a second day was affecting her nerves.

Where was Lily, and why was she taking so long to return from Grantlings?

It had been hours now and the light would soon fail. Betsy was sure that Lily would not intend her to remain alone at Westford Park for an extended time, with Tom Farrington downstairs. Sir Stephen's house was but minutes away by horseback.

Had something happened to Lord Westford? Was there some emergency or crisis?

Betsy could sit there frantic and ignorant for no longer. She could also put off seeing Tom no longer.

During the night, some of the sense of Lily's words and warning had begun to dawn upon her. Betsy was now increasingly uncertain as to her former convictions about her lover. It was true that Tom's conduct had not been such that she might have expected. She had to admit it was hard to justify his prolonged lack of correspondence and his current reaction.

Even if he were shocked by what he had discovered, should he not have rejoiced to learn that she, Betsy, was not now trapped in matrimony? Yet according to Lily he had not even asked after her. And Betsy knew that Lily would not lie to her.

"But where is Miss Cosgrove? Can it be that she remains free for me to renew my suit? Lead me to her at once!"

These were the words that Betsy had imagined Tom might say. But he had not.

Suddenly she could bear it all no longer. She had to see him.

Checking her appearance in the glass, smoothing her hair and willing some bloom into her still-wan cheeks, Betsy suppressed her nerves. She went to find the man for whom she had disrupted both her own and her cousin's lives.

In the hall she encountered the steward. "Mr Pelham, do you know if Lady Westford is yet returned?" Betsy asked.

"No, madam. Neither her Ladyship nor his Lordship," Pelham told her.

"And Mr Farrington?" It was hard to keep a tremble from her voice as she spoke his name.

"He is in the library, madam."

For a moment Betsy's courage failed her. "Perhaps he does not wish to be disturbed."

"He has not given any such instructions," Pelham said.

Digging her fingernails into damp palms, Betsy walked to the library door, knocked lightly, and pushed it open.

There stood Tom.

All the months she had waited, and wondered, and agonised. And now the object of her ordeal stood before her.

For one moment Betsy was flooded with the same emotions she had felt the previous Season. Her heart leapt and her whole body felt giddy to be in his presence.

Yet this was swiftly replaced by confusion and a growing sense of injustice. Somehow she had imagined her lover to have been overcome with the same grief at separation she had. She had imaged his handsome face hollowed by sleeplessness, a sad and melancholy expression in his eye. For had he not looked such at her, many times, on parting from her at the various balls and soirées?

He was still handsome, yet the only emotion she perceived was a mild surprise and even amusement at her presence.

"Miss Cosgrove. Of course, I should have guessed it must be you that the new Marchioness of Westford referred to." He put an odd emphasis on Lily's title.

"Tom." Betsy found her voice was faint, she could barely speak.

"Quite a fascinating little scheme the pair of you have devised. My cousin is apparently totally in the dark."

Where were the loving looks? The expressions of longing, of gladness and relief at being reunited with her after so long?

"I did it for you, Tom. So that I might remain free for us to be together."

Surprise turned to derision on his face. He laughed, as Betsy felt her heart grow to a heavy stone.

"What an immensely foolish notion that was, my dear. You might have been a Marchioness. As insufferable a straight-laced old bore my cousin is, his ample purse must surely have sweetened the pill."

Betsy was horrified. "But all the things you said. The promises we made to one another!"

Tom could barely remember what he had said, but presumed it was much the same as he had said to a dozen or more bits of muslin both before and after this one. "We had a dalliance, my dear. Such things are things one says in the heat of the moment.

You can't surely have supposed anything was meant by it, can you?"

"I did think so." The world was spinning. It was as if a stranger stood before her.

"How very unfortunate." He was mocking her. Not even a fragment of compassion showed.

"I had thought that you loved me." Betsy said, in one last desperate appeal to his conscience.

But Tom's smile was cold. "With no fortune and little else to recommend you? Hardly so."

With this the last hope and emotion died in Betsy. Instead of grief she felt a strange, numbing calm. Summoning the last of her courage and her dignity, she replied. "You are cruel, sir. I will not remain to hear more of it. Only I would ask you if you have seen my cousin, Lady Westford, or know of her whereabouts?"

"I have not."

"She went out riding some hours ago. It now grows dark and she has not returned, and I am anxious for her," Betsy said.

Tom shrugged. "It is not my concern."

"I am sure that it would displease your cousin, should anything happen to her and no attempt is made to aid her."

Betsy saw from a gleam in his eye that she had touched the right nerve. Dependent on the Marquess's continued tolerance, Tom could not risk angering him. Duped or not, Gervase apparently had developed some form of affection for his wife.

And while Tom himself was fairly sure what might have happened to Lady Westford, it was wiser to be certain.

"Very well, I will see what can be done. In which direction did she ride?"

"Towards Grantlings," Betsy told her. She left, hoping that he might at least do this one thing for her. At least if it could be established that her cousin was at Sir Stephen's house, she could rest easy.

Betsy was not sure why, but a small fear nagged at her. Something was not right.

***

It was dusk; the light fading fast but still sufficient to ride by. Tom saddled a horse and rode swiftly in the direction of Grantlings. He had planned to venture after his cousin's wife anyway, if only to be sure of the success of his scheme.

While a broken bone might be enough, there remained a chance she might survive a cold night on the hillside. Better to break her neck, and if falling from the horse hadn't done that, Tom might need to expend a little more effort himself.

There was the chance she had clung on and made it to Grantlings. But he doubted this. The surprise of the sabotaged harness should be enough to throw most riders. It was a trick Tom had employed before. He knew exactly the amount to cut through the leather such that it would not fall apart immediately.

Expecting to find her on the hillside, he felt a minor sense of alarm when there was no one to be seen. He looked about him, wondering how far she had got. At the top he passed a stone building, then saw something slumped in the grass.

A crumpled shape, unmoving.

Inwardly Tom rejoiced. She looked dead.

But it paid to check so he dismounted and went for a closer look. He pushed the figure with his foot. She was limp but she breathed, regretfully there was none of the cold, white slackness of death.

The easiest thing would be to finish her off himself, though he wondered if he might do so without trace. Also, the Cosgrove chit knew he had ridden out here. If there were suspicion, it might well fall on him.

He could pretend to have missed her, he supposed. But she lay clear on the path, so unless he moved her...

This gave Tom an idea. The wind was whipping up, carrying cold dashes of rain with it. In a hour it would be a full rainstorm. He would drag the body to the cottage, and burn it down. The wood inside should be dry enough for it to go up like tinder. To anyone finding the burnt remains, it would seem as though she had lit a fire to keep warm but passed out and been overcome by smoke.

Tom would, of course, help insinuate this notion.

He dragged the unconscious Lily over the ground and onto the stone flags. There was little left inside, save for a wooden stool, an old bedstead, and a pot over the empty fireplace. But there was tinder in a nook by the mantelpiece and Tom made good use of it.

It caught alight quickly, and he used a stub of tallow candle to help spread the blaze.

He could only hope that the fire would burn hot and fast enough to do its work before the rains came. He himself could not afford to spend any more time here. He would ride to Grantlings, ascertain that Lady Westford was not there, and return to Westford Park.

There, he could await Gervase's return, to the joint discovery that not only was his wife dead, but she was not even the woman he had intended to marry.

This latter would cause Tom some considerable amusement. It more than served Gervase right for trying to cut Tom out of his inheritance. His cousin would be so humiliated and bitter that the prospect of any future nuptials would be out of the question.

40. The crisis

Betsy's unease did not leave her even after Tom Farrington had gone.

She returned to her room and sat there for a while, wondering how long it would all take. She tried to read but could not concentrate. She turned her hand to some needlework but could not still her thoughts. There was no one to write a letter to, save for Anne Carter, and what could she write to her?

Betsy felt so ashamed and forlorn about her folly over her former lover that she could not bring herself to share any news about herself.

Eventually she rose. Perhaps if she went to Lily's room, which looked over the front of the house and had a view of the hillside, she might see her cousin riding back.

She walked along the corridor, taking a candle with her since it was already a gloomy hour. The house felt echoing and empty, despite all the servants below.

Betsy pushed Lily's door and entered. Then she stopped, startled.

A black-clad figure stood at the window, looking out, dimly silhouetted by the fading twilight. Betsy's heart stopped in her chest.

Then the figure turned, and Betsy felt a rush of relief at seeing that it was only Nanny Noakes. Before she could ask the old woman what she was doing in Lily's room, Nanny Noakes spoke. Her thin lips drew back from teeth which looked sharp and crooked in the flickering light of Betsy's candle.

"The bride has gone, then."

Her eyes were as beady as ever, but in the candlelight, they seemed to have a malevolent gleam.

"I beg your pardon?" Betsy found herself recoiling. Nanny Noakes looked quite deranged. She was gloating and smiling, straggles of grey hair escaping her cap like cobwebs.

"Gone from Westford Park. I knew my young master would settle what I could not." The elderly servant sounded a note of triumph in her voice.

Betsy thought that she must be mad. "Whatever do you mean?"

But Nanny Noakes was musing to herself. "Such a tricky thing, she was. Wouldn't take the tea. Gave the tonic to her maid. Then the wine as well. That was you who drank that, wasn't it dear? A nasty time for you. If only I had been more careful with my dosing it would have been much easier for you. All over, nice and quickly."

It was very hard for Betsy to keep her voice steady. "Do you mean to confess that you were you trying to poison us? That you deliberately put something in the tonic and the other drinks?"

There was a cackle of laughter at this. "I, confess? Mad old Nanny Noakes rambles about all sorts of things. No one pays attention to addled old Nanny Noakes." She cackled some more. "Oh no, dearie, it's only your word and your fancy."

Betsy was sure she must be in a dream. Or rather a nightmare.

"Why would you do this?"

Nanny Noakes's laughter twisted into a fierce and savage sneer. "How dare she come and usurp his place? A fallen woman, too. To blacken Westford Park so. Don't think I don't hear and see many things. My ears are long and my eyes are sharp." She glared at Betsy. "It was promised him from boyhood. He was to have Westford, once his fool cousin was out of the picture. And he was content to wait, my young master. But then this hussy came to steal it all from him, first casting her soiled wares at him and then inveigling his cousin into matrimony."

She took a step towards Betsy. "And now she pays the price for her meddling and all her soft wiles."

"What have you done? Where is my cousin, where is Lady Westford?" Betsy's terror was growing.

The elderly servant began singing in a cracked, tuneless voice. "Ride a cock horse to Banbury Cross. And she shall ride till she can ride no more."

"Stop it!" Betsy couldn't bear to listen to the mad old woman any more. "Just tell me where she is!"

But Nanny Noakes kept creaking out her sinister song. "Ride and ride and ride until she rides no more."

Betsy fled.

***

She must find Mrs Hollis and seek her help. She would surely know what to do. As Betsy headed towards the passage that led to the stillroom and the kitchens, she heard the clanging of the front door.

She felt relief and fear. Could it be Lily, returned? Or the Marquess?

Or worse tidings?

Tom Farrington strode through, brushing damp from his hair. "It's turning to a foul night," he said. He entered alone; there was no one with him.

Betsy's heart sank as fear rose in her. "Where is Lily? Lady Westford, did you find her? Is she with Sir Stephen Seton? Where is Lord Westford?"

Tom deliberately paused before answering. He saw how frantic Betsy was, and it amused him to prolong her anxiety.

"I found no sign of any of them."

"None at all? Sir Stephen had heard no word?" Betsy could not think where Lily had got to. It was but a short ride to Grantlings and her plan had been to head straight there. How had Tom not come across her?

"I am afraid not. We will simply have to await their return, won't we?" He gave a smile edged with malice and took himself off to the drawing room, pointedly closing the door behind him and not even inviting Betsy to join him. The snub and the lack of courtesy were clear.

Betsy distrusted him. A ghastly thought struck her. Might Tom Farrington even be in league with Nanny Noakes? When the old woman had spoken of him "settling what she could not", what had she meant? Could Tom himself have wished Lily ill?

Her terror grew. The mad old woman upstairs, this hostile man downstairs. She could not yet bring herself to seriously consider them murderous, but Lord and Lady Westford were both disappeared.

What should she do?

Betsy hurried towards the kitchen where she found Mary, busy with some task. "Do you know where Mrs Hollis is?" she asked the maid.

"She is not here, madam. His lordship gave her leave to visit a niece of hers who is recently out of confinement."

James Pelham, then. "And Mr Pelham?"

"It is Mr Pelham's half day, madam."

For both the head servants to be away was inconvenient and troubling. Even the man Duncan Ross was absent. Betsy could hardly confide her anxieties in Mary or any of the other lower-ranked staff.

Betsy felt desperately isolated. She was fearful to remain in the house herself. What might that wicked, mad old woman do? Or even Tom Farrington himself?

There was only one course of action open to her. As terrified as she was of horses, she must summon her courage and ride to Grantlings herself. She would seek the counsel of Sir Stephen. He would surely know what to do.

Betsy quickly dressed herself in a riding habit and made for the stables, the rain pelting down. Ben, who was still tending to the horse that Tom had returned on, was startled to see her.

"There is no news of Lord or Lady Westford?" Betsy asked. "Their horses are not returned, I see?"

"No, madam."

"May I take that horse, Ben? I must ride urgently to Grantlings."

Ben was aware that Miss Cosgrove was no rider. "I can take a message for you, madam."

But Betsy could not stand to wait behind while yet another person rode off. She also needed to seek help in person: how could such a message be transmitted through a stable hand? It was not as though anyone was sick or injured, or there was any known emergency. There were simply the strange absences of Lily and the Marquess, and her own terrible sense of foreboding.

"I must see him myself, Ben."

Ben was reluctant to saddle the horse for an uncertain rider on a foul night. But there was a horse in foal and he could not leave. He chose the gentlest mare and helped Betsy to mount. As he watched her ride off, clinging on with obvious fear, he was uneasy to have let her go.

41. The rescue

Once again, Gervase found that the pounding rhythm of Orion's hooves helped drum out the maelstrom of emotion in his breast.

The sight of his wife and his cousin together had wrenched him to the very core. Fear, rage, jealousy and a deep, sad pain wracked him. The two of them had been so close as to have been in an embrace. Perhaps they had been so.

Until the moment he saw them together, Gervase had not realised the depth of his affection for his wife. Or how he had come to believe that she returned it.

Now, all seemed to be a lie.

He had no clear plans of where he was going, other than to distance himself from Westford Park. He headed for the London road, but the night was pitch dark and he carried no lantern.

Gervase had ridden for a couple of hours when he caught sight of a dim light in the distance. Approaching nearer, he realised it was the door of an inn. It might be wiser to turn in early for the night. Even if highwaymen did not intimidate him, it would be an idea to drown his sorrows with some rustic ale. Sleep might soothe his turmoil.

He spent an unsettled night. The musty, unfamiliar bed offered little comfort and he longed for the soft form of his wife beside him. Images of her coupling with Farrington tormented him.

Conflicting desires came over him. One moment Gervase imagined nobly releasing his wife so that she could be with Farrington, and even settling a dowry on her. The next he had wild fantasies of demanding satisfaction of his cousin and ordering his wife back to the marital bed. Albeit the prospect of a duel was absurd.

He had also heard a troubling rumour of Tom fighting a duel somewhere in Normandy. An account of Farrington turning too early, some said deliberately. But his opponent had survived and it had been hushed up.

No, a duel was not the way.

The cheap tavern drink further confounded Gervase's thoughts. It took a restless slumber of twisted dreams until he awoke, calmer and more collected, in the cool light of morning.

He had to go back, he knew that. He could not hide away from the situation in London indefinitely.

But it was not until nearly evening that Gervase felt he could face matters. Dusk was gathering as he rode back, retracing his earlier route. This took him back through the shortcut, along the crest of the hill that divided his lands from Seton's.

Drizzle was turning to rain and a leaden dusk sky darkening to pitch as Orion approached the summit. Gervase was surprised to see lights ahead. His surprise turned to consternation as he realised it came from the disused sheepcote. Had it been put to use again?

The aroma of smoke grew stronger as he approached, and to his horror he saw that there were uncontrolled flames licking at one of the pane-less windows. Only the falling rain was arresting their progress.

Orion disliked fire, so Gervase dismounted some distance away and made his way towards the old building on foot. Covering his face against the heat and fumes, he peered inside.

A body lay there, the flames nearly reaching it. The smoke was so thick it was hard to see clearly. He first thought the figure might be some vagabond or poacher, taking shelter from the storm. To sleep through this blaze, though, why wouldn't the rascal wake?

Or did he lie there in a more eternal state than sleep?

Gervase could not take the risk of a man burning alive, so breathing the clear night air deep into his lungs, he held his breath and rushed in. He had intended to drag the figure however he may, by its feet if that were easiest.

But as he did so the hood fell back.

The pale, lifeless face of his wife lay before his eyes.

***

Betsy had never been more terrified than when she mounted the mare that Ben saddled for her, and rode off alone towards Grantlings. She did not tell the groom so, but it was the first time she had even ridden alone.

It was also night, and raining, with the wind whipping strands of her hair across her eyes. She prayed the horse might know the direction better than she did. She took the longer route which skirted the hill and did not pass the ruined sheepcote, for she feared to ride up the steep slopes.

The back of her riding habit was soaked when she finally drew near to Grantlings. She was so relieved to have reached her destination that it overwhelmed any nervousness or sense of embarrassment at her unannounced presence and dishevelled clothing.

Sir Stephen agreed to see Miss Cosgrove immediately, and knew at once from her appearance that something was terribly wrong. It added to the mystery of the evening.

Only a couple of hours earlier he had had a similarly unexpected visit from Farrington. This had surprised him, for he had not known that the man had returned to Westford Park. The nature and brevity of his visit also left Sir Stephen puzzled as to the man's intentions.

He had fancied a devious look in the man's eye, though in Sir Stephen's view, Tom Farrington's face rarely showed much honesty or virtue. Farrington had mentioned he was "passing that way".

"I apologise for any interruption to you and your guests," he had said.

"I dine alone this evening, and it is no interruption," Sir Stephen had replied. Such was his courtesy that he had even offered Farrington food and wine, but Farrington had declined.

"I must return, the hour grows late."

Then why had he come?

Perhaps Miss Cosgrove might solve that mystery. Sir Stephen suspected some row between Westford and Farrington. Perhaps Westford had finally cast his cousin out, and Farrington had briefly thought to avail of shelter at Grantlings, before changing his mind.

"Sir, I am most sorry to disturb you at this hour and in such a manner," Betsy began. "It is just that I wondered if either Lord or Lady Westford might be here, or if they had passed by. Or if you had seen them at all, or if you knew where either of them might be."

She was trembling and Sir Stephen was alarmed.

"My dear Miss Cosgrove, pray be seated near the fire and take some wine. I am afraid I have seen neither Lord Westford nor your cousin, this night or this day," he told her.

There was despair and fear on Betsy's face. "Oh! I am so very greatly afraid," she said, and then could speak no more for she was trying to suppress tears. It would not do to embarrass Sir Stephen by weeping.

His voice was calm and gentle. "Only tell me what is wrong, and what I can do to help."

Betsy tried to get the story out, but it was jumbled and confused. She could not reveal the reason that the Marquess had stormed off.

"Mr Farrington arrived a couple of days ago. Lord Westford had to make an urgent journey, whither I do not know, but he did not return as expected. We were anxious, and Lady Westford rode out to see if he was here. But then she did not return either. It grew darker, and so Mr Farrington rode out to find them both, but they are not here, are they?"

Sir Stephen was astute enough to realise that this was only a fraction of the story. He was certain there had been a row, and regretted to find himself suspecting it was something to do with Farrington and Lady Westford. But surely such a wise young woman as the Marchioness, who looked upon her husband with such adoration, could not have had her head turned again by that rake?

"Mr Farrington indeed passed by here some time ago. Has he not returned to Westford Park? He is missing as well?"

A flicker that Sir Stephen could not interpret passed over Betsy's face. "He has."

The obvious question was why Miss Cosgrove had later decided to make her own visit, if Farrington had reported his to be fruitless. Why the need for a second inquiry?

Sir Stephen was also worried by the absences, all the more so given that Lady Westford had apparently ventured out alone. Had she pursued her husband towards London, perhaps? He would send a man down the London road immediately to make inquiries along the route.

"I perceive that there is some trouble at Westford Park," he said. "Lord Westford and I are old friends and neighbours, and I am not unaware of tensions between him and his cousin. If you are able to take me more fully into your confidence, I may be better positioned to assist you."

Betsy's anxiety was eroding any sense of impropriety. "There was indeed a row, sir, but I beg you not to ask me the cause. But that is not the only thing that troubles me. There was something else very strange, that made me dreadfully afraid to remain at Westford Park. Though as I tell it now, I am sure that you will think it very foolish of me." For after all, Nanny Noakes was but an old, foolish woman. Half mad and full of fancies.

She told Sir Stephen about her encounter with the old servant, expecting derision. She omitted the part about Tom Farrington, for she feared it sounded absurd. Much as Betsy's feelings had now turned against him, she struggled to believe that he had been in league with the elderly servant. Thus she contained her revelations to those pertaining to the poisonings.

Sir Stephen did not dismiss her concerns regarding these. Instead his face grew grave. "I shall return with you to Westford Park. We will take the carriage, for it is too foul a night for horseback."

***

All thought of anger and condemnation were gone the instant Gervase's eyes beheld Lily, lying there immobile. In that moment, he was flooded with love and despair for the limp form that he lifted into his arms.

He staggered out and carried her a safe distance away from the burning building. He laid her on the damp grass, gently, as though putting a child to bed.

Then he knelt over her and wept.

He did not even wonder how she had come to be there, only that he had lost her.

Some instinct made him run his fingers over the top of her chest, and he perceived that her skin was not as cold as it could be. The nearby flames had warmed her, most likely.

Then, though at first he thought he imagined it, he felt her chest rise under his fingers. His hands trembling, he explored for a pulse, and felt one.

She lived!

He cradled her to him, kissing her forehead and her eyelids.

She lived, and all was not yet lost. In an instant Gervase knew that he was going to fight for her. Whatever it took, he was going to win her from Farrington and keep her as his forever. Willingly, in body and soul.

Lifting her once more, he took her to Orion. Somehow he managed to haul them both up upon the great horse.

Holding his wife before him, lifeless as she seemed was, he cantered down the hillside towards Westford Park.

42. The discovery

Gervase arrived back at Westford Park with Lily just moments before Sir Stephen and Betsy arrived by carriage. In the rain and darkness all was confusion, though Gervase had but one focus: the unconscious form of his wife and his desperate desire to save her.

Sir Stephen at once saw there had been some terrible accident. "I will ride forthwith for the physician, Westford." Before he left he laid a hand on Betsy's arm. "All will be well."

The kindness in his eyes calmed Betsy's terror and gave her courage. Lily appeared to be dying or even dead, and Betsy had felt near to hysterics at the sight of her. Collecting herself, she followed Gervase and a footman upstairs, as they conveyed Lily to her bedchamber.

Arriving there, as servants rushed to administer what aid they could in the form of water and poultices, Betsy felt of little help. The Marquess was barely aware of her presence. His eyes never left his wife, watching for every faint rise of her chest, lest there should not be another one.

Betsy felt as though she were an intruder.

She away slipped to her own room and sat there, wondering what she should do. There was a glass by her bed and it reminded her of the what the crazed old servant had said. Its contents, apparently water, did not appear to have been adulterated. But

Betsy was no longer taking any chances and she tipped it out. She would not consume any substances in this house until that mad old woman was gone.

She must warn Lord Westford though. What if Nanny Noakes attempted to switch some draught that the doctor brought?

But she wavered, not wanting to add to his current consternation.

If only Sir Stephen could return quickly with the doctor. Betsy felt the time tick by as the danger for Lily increased.

***

None of them thought of Tom Farrington at that time. That man, lurking in the library, heard the arrivals. Surely the chit could not have survived the fall and the fire? But the snatches of conversation he had heard suggested that Lady Westford still clung to life.

Tom cursed. He had been idiotic not have simply put his foot on her neck. The chances were that the tread of his boot upon her skin would not have been remarked upon. It was folly to have attempted something more elaborate, to have trusted to fire and to fate.

No one would know, at least. She would have no memory of any of it.

The cousin though, the silly bit of stuff that he had once enjoyed toying with. Might she suspect? She should surely have no reason to. After all, he had played it all so carefully. He had even called at Grantlings to establish that Lady Westford had not passed by. His actions were surely unblemished.

Tom did not know that the elderly servant's lips had begun to loosen.

He drained his glass of Gervase's brandy, which was not so fine as he recalled. He eyed the crystal and cast a look over the other ornaments and comforts of the room. All this should be his. It had been promised to him.

His gaze fell upon the poker by the fire. He was tempted to grasp it and make good use of it.

But no. It was too much risk.

He still had his information, that his cousin had married the wrong Miss Cosgrove. That alone must sunder this damned union that threatened to deny him his birth right. The only thing that restrained Tom from sharing it now was that Gervase had apparently developed some mawkish sentiment for his swapped bride.

At such a time as this it would be rash to reveal the truth. Faced with the prospect of her death, his cousin might not look with favour on the bearer of more bad news.

With luck, she would die. This was Tom's earnest hope.

***

No other thing mattered to Gervase save that the pale young woman next to him should waken. His self-recriminations were bitter. Had he not been caught up in his fit of rage and jealousy, she might not be lying here now.

The doctor had done all he could. "Her pulse is steady. For as long as it does not weaken, there is hope for her."

He had suggested that Miss Cosgrove or one of the female servants could remain with Lady Westford throughout the night, but Gervase would not hear of it. No one but him should stay by her side.

Given the lateness of the hour, the doctor was given a bed for the night.

The next day brought no change. Lily remained there, alabaster pale. The doctor was satisfied that her pulse was no weaker, though this was all the good tidings he could offer.

The rest of the household went about their business with sombre faces, speaking only in hushed tones. Betsy was wretched with worry for her cousin. She blamed herself as much as the Marquess blamed himself. Tom Farrington kept apart, feigning polite concern, but inwardly gloating that the situation was so serious.

Sir Stephen Seton called later in the morning and his presence was of great comfort. Betsy longed to confide in him about Tom Farrington but she dared not. He had already advised her not to trouble the Marquess on the subject of Nanny Noakes for the present.

"As like as not it is an addled old woman's fancy. And if the worst, Lady Westford is currently attended to all times by her husband, and has not woken to take tea or tonic. There is no opportunity for mischief. But we can both remain vigilant," he said.

Because of this, Betsy had initially decided not the mention anything to Mrs Hollis either. The housekeeper was already distressed that she had been absent at such a time. Betsy did not wish to add to her self-recrimination, albeit misplaced.

While Sir Stephen did not know the full story, he had noticed a flicker of fear and distrust in Betsy's eyes on the one occasion that Tom Farrington had joined them. He remained curious as to what had taken place at Westford Park between them all.

Betsy was all the more glad of Sir Stephen's presence when they received a visit from Lady Leominster.

"News was brought to me of poor dear Lady Westford. I wished to offer my sympathies." There was little sympathy in the widow's sharp gaze that flicked from Betsy to Sir Stephen. Lavinia Leominster suspected some drama in the household, and was infuriated that neither of them would reveal it. She was sure the Cosgrove chit must know more than she let on.

"That is very kind of you," Betsy said, knowing it was nothing of the sort. She was aware the neighbour hated Lily.

Lady Leominster herself had only recently returned from visiting friends, and had been intrigued to learn that Tom

Farrington had returned to Westford Park. "It must be some comfort to Lord Westford, having his cousin returned home," she said, once again eyeing the pair of them for a reaction. Except for a faint colour that appeared in Miss Cosgrove's cheeks, she received none.

Tom Farrington himself did not put in an appearance then, much to Lady Leominster's vexation. She had toyed with the notion of beguiling him rather than his cousin, should it ever appear likely that he would be in line to inherit. If only the Marchioness would die quickly, this might be so.

She did not linger long, disliking the whole business of sickbeds and invalids. Both Betsy and Sir Stephen privately rejoiced to see her leave.

Wishing to do something practical, Sir Stephen had sent some of his own men to look for the missing horse. Likely the beast had been spooked by the storm or the fire, and wandered somewhere in the hills.

"Ask around the inns and cottages too, lest someone has been seen with a mare of her description, or been trying to sell one," he instructed them. There were plenty of shady folk who might steal a lost horse, and Sir Stephen considered this the most probable scenario. Most likely they would ride her far off to some market, where no one might know of her origins. If so, there would be little chance of her recovery.

He turned to Betsy. "Word should be sent to the family of Lady Westford, that she has suffered a grave accident."

Betsy shrank from this suggestion, unable to conceal her horror. "I beg you not to trouble them, Sir. My... aunt suffers from nerves, and such news might affect her health." She could only imagine the impact on her mother's nerves to learn that her niece was married to the Marquess, and not her daughter. Her father's reaction was not even to be imagined.

Sir Stephen frowned. "Even so, I doubt they would wish that such a serious event be withheld from them."

"Please, you do not know my aunt. Send tidings when my cousin is recovered."

They both knew that recovery was not a thing of certainty. But Sir Stephen detected fear in Betsy's eyes. Anxiety or concern for her aunt might be expected, but there was terror here.

He was unsure how to proceed. He knew that Sir Robert and Lady Maud had paid but one, brief visit to the Westford Park, which might suggest some estrangement. Unless Lady Maud's nervous condition made travel difficult for her.

Sir Stephen sensed there was some other trouble that lay between them all, Miss Cosgrove included. The pleading in her soft brown eyes moved him. She suffered already from her distress and anxiety over her cousin. Even if her aunt and uncle were informed, if the worst happened it was likely to be soon, and they would not arrive there in time. Justifying his decision with this final thought. Sir Stephen agreed that word could be delayed until Lady Cosgrove's condition was better known.

But he remained puzzled, and troubled. What was this mystery, this secret that was being concealed? Was Westford aware of it?

43. The confession

A day passed, and while Lily still breathed steadily and her heart still beat, Gervase was losing hope. He reached and stroked her hair back from her brow.

As he did so, she stirred.

He froze. The breath caught in his throat as he saw her eyes flicker, and - miracle of miracles - open!

"Gervase." Her voice was no more than a whisper.

"Elizabeth, my darling." He brought water to her, encouraging her to sip a few drops.

She looked at him, her face grave.

"Are you in pain, my dear? The doctor is at hand."

"I am not," Lily managed to say. Something troubled her, Gervase saw. "What has happened?" she asked.

"You have lain here for two days. We brought you back from the old keeper's cottage. You do not remember?"

Lily remembered nothing. Her head ached and she felt terribly weak.

"There was a fire," Gervase continued. "Perhaps you sheltered there in the storm, and a fire you had lit grew beyond control?"

She could not recall lighting any fire. "I was riding Dido." She closed her eyes, trying to summon her last memory. "It was dark. I sought you. Then I remember nothing."

"You sought me?" If Gervase had blamed himself before, his regret was even more bitter now. To hear that he was the reason she had ridden out alone, and nearly lost her life. If only he had been more measured, more rational. Even if she did care for Farrington, it was no reason for him to have ridden off like a spurned fool.

Lily swallowed with difficultly, since her throat was dry. She could not bear any more of this deception. Wherever Farrington was and whatever he intended, Gervase would hear this from her first.

"My lord, I must tell you something."

Gervase saw the strain on her features. "There is no need to trouble yourself. Rest more, my dear. I will fetch the doctor." Dismissing her protests, he went to seek the physician.

***

It was Ben who found the missing animal. The stable hand rode to the crest of the hill on Orion, and thereafter let the horse lead where it would. The two horses were stablemates, and Ben trusted that Orion might detect some trace of his companion.

Orion led him to the edge of the woods, but would venture in no further. It was unlike Dido to have entered woodland, Ben thought, but the fire may well have spooked her. He tethered Orion to a tree and ventured in. The undergrowth was thick in parts, but there were clearings and gaps that could be ridden through.

He had walked perhaps half a mile when he saw her, and his heart lifted to see the mare standing and apparently uninjured. He called her name, and she recognised him. Slowly he approached, and though he found her uncharacteristically nervous, he was able to calm her with soft words in her ear. Grasping her reins, Ben led her out to the edge of the wood.

Mounting Orion again and leading Dido beside them, it was not until Ben returned to the stables to untack the horses that he noticed the broken leather strap. His first thought was that it must have worn through, though this surprised him as he maintained all the tack in good order.

He inspected it more closely and his face set in a grim line. He knew tampering when he saw it. No natural wear had led to this break. It had been cut with a knife.

But who had done this? Had one of the village lads thought to prank the lord and lady? Ben would give the culprit the hiding of his life if he found out who it was.

And if it were not some foolish rascal...

This was a horrid prospect. Ben could not readily believe that the master might wish rid of his wife, and given his swift exit two days previously, when would he have had the time? Who else might wish harm upon Lady Westford?

Ben wondered if he should say something, or if he should make his own investigations. He was reluctant to trouble the Marquess at such a time as this. The whole household was in a state of enough worry over the Marchioness's condition.

He might talk it over with Sarah, he considered. Those servant girls gossiped enough and listened where they should not. He had chided her about it on more than one occasion. "You keep your ears covered and your lips closed, or your mistress will send you packing, my girl."

Now it might all come in useful, if she had heard something.

Ben took the sabotaged tack and hid it under some bales of hay in the loft. He was not entirely sure why he did this, it was merely an instinct. If anyone asked where it was he would tell them it was with the saddler.

***

When the doctor had gone, Lily sipped a small amount of the broth he had ordered. She felt it restore her strength, if only a little.

It was enough to tell Gervase what she needed to tell him. When they were alone again, she resumed. "I have to speak with you. There is something that you must know."

The urgency in her tone startled Gervase. He feared a confession of her continued feelings for Farrington, and did not think he could bear to hear such. But he waited for her to continue.

Lily was determined to speak. He must not remain in the dark any longer. She spoke again, her voice calmer. "I am afraid that a gross deception has been practiced upon you. Though it is not what I fear you suspect it is."

"I am well aware that you wish me to release you for Farrington." Gervase's voice was emotionless.

"My lord, it is not that. Though it is something that Mr Farrington is aware of, and I wish to be the one to tell you. I have wanted to confess this to you for a very long time and I bitterly regret that I lacked the probity to do so." Lily saw the consternation that the mention of Tom Farrington caused to Gervase. She was silent for a few moments. In her mind she had rehearsed endless ways to break the truth to him but all the phrases seemed hollow now. Starting from the very beginning seemed the only course of action.

"When you came to the house of Sir Robert and Lady Cosgrove offering marriage to their daughter, you were wed to a woman who gave her name as Elizabeth Cosgrove."

Gervase felt some confusion. Where was this going? "Such is or was their daughter's name, was it not?"

Lily continued. "It is. However the woman whom you took as wife was not their daughter."

Gervase frowned. "I do not understand."

"My cousin, whom you know as Miss Ann Cosgrove - another deception which I am sorely sorry for - is by birth Elizabeth Ann Cosgrove. She is the daughter of Sir Robert and Lady Cosgrove."

It took Gervase several seconds to comprehend this. "Then you are not she? You are not Elizabeth Cosgrove?"

"I am also Elizabeth Cosgrove. Elizabeth Ann Cosgrove. We were both named for our paternal grandmother. I am Edward Cosgrove's daughter," Lily explained. The name - her former name - was ringing in her head, she seemed to be repeating it so many times.

Gervase's eyes narrowed. "Edward's daughter is dead."

"No, my lord, she lies here before you." Lily had dreaded this moment for so many months and now all she felt was a strange sense of calm. A feeling of relief that the burden of deceit was finally lifted from her shoulders. Nothing that happened to her now could be as torturous as the weight of the lies had been.

"'He is dead, and the poor little girl with him'." Gervase's tone held a light mockery. "That was the news imparted to me."

Lily felt a momentary confusion, then realised the horrible truth. "Harriet." Poor, poor little Harriet. Her eyes blurred and her throat felt constricted. Even at this awful time, after so many years, the horror of their deaths was suddenly vivid in her mind. She could not speak.

"Harriet?"

"My father's ward." Lily's voice was barely a whisper. "She was two years younger than me. She died but a few days after him, of the same sickness. By some miracle I was spared the evil that took them both."

At the time it had seemed far from a miracle. She had wept and raged, had longed to follow her father and her playmate. They had been dark days, and darker still when she was torn from her home and sent to her father's brother and his wife. They had shown her little sympathy, believing that a child could and should recover from such a loss quickly. Not "indulge herself in grief" as Lady Maud had called it.

It seemed that the world stood still for hours. They were both silent: Lily lost in the past and Gervase's head spinning from her revelations.

The young woman who lay before him claimed to be someone other than he had thought she was. What could all this mean?

44. The revelations

Gervase regarded his wife. He saw the set of her jaw, and was reminded of his old commander. He briefly remembered a miniature that Colonel Cosgrove had kept with him of his wife. As soon as the realisation dawned it seemed almost absurd that he had not noticed the likeness before.

"You are Edward's daughter." His words were slow, weary. It was a statement more than a question.

"I am. Since his death I have lived with my aunt and uncle. My cousin has been my closest friend and companion. You know already the sad story of her disgrace. It is hard to describe how terrible a time it was for us all. Then when your offer came, we were overcome with gratitude."

"Gratitude?" The very term, considering how Gervase had begun to feel for this girl, struck him to the core. "And yet…?"

"And yet my cousin felt unable to accept your kind offer. Her affections were elsewhere engaged, very deeply engaged, but my aunt and uncle insisted on her compliance. My aunt had been made ill through the ordeal of shame and anxiety, and my uncle had taken her for a rest cure, but we received their instructions by letter. She was to become your wife, and I was to be sent to live with a distant aunt." Lily took a breath. She saw that Gervase was transfixed by her words, but his face betrayed no emotion. She continued.

"At the eleventh hour, quite literally, my cousin begged me to take her place. She thought it would be possible since we share the same name. She was quite desperate not to be wed."

"And you thought that you would take advantage of the situation, is that it?"

"No my lord. Betsy - my cousin Elizabeth - was so enamoured of Mr Farrington and was convinced he might return for her. I fear you will think ill of her for this, but she had been very greatly misled. She had understood there to be some kind of informal engagement, or she would never have done what she did. I am quite sure of this. To marry another man was to lose all hope of that. For me, to marry someone unknown seemed by far the smaller sacrifice," Lily said.

"Marriage to me was a sacrifice?"

"Oh no, my lord, I did not mean..." Lily struggled to express herself. "Such a marriage is a very wonderful opportunity, I am sure."

"An opportunity that seemed all too tempting, I don't doubt."

He still thought she had set out to trap him. She wished she could make him realise that she had not, to convince him of her genuine reluctance to take Betsy's place. "Before this happened I had given no thought to marriage, my lord."

"Given no thought to marriage? I find that hard to believe, given your cousin's machinations."

"I am a year younger than my cousin, my lord. She had debuted in society but I had not." She saw Gervase's brow furrow in shock at this. "Nor were there plans for me to do so. I had no fortune and no expectations. As I have said, my uncle had arranged for me become the companion of a relative in Scotland. I thought that marriage, to anyone, might be as bearable a prospect."

Gervase almost wanted to laugh. The notion that becoming his marchioness with all the position's associated wealth and prestige should be a merely "bearable prospect" quite took his breath away.

But looking at the girl's pale and terrified face, and the plea in her eyes, he saw to his amazement that she was absolutely sincere. She had truly had no desire to marry him whatsoever, despite her poverty and his high station. If he had had wind in his sails it would have been utterly knocked out.

Other more chilling realisations were dawning. Their wedding night: this, then was the reason for her maidenhood.

All the times he had judged her, the many times he had interpreted her behaviour as that of a coquette or wanton or treated her as such, he had done her an immense injustice. Her only sin, the only deception she had practised, was to substitute a foolish woman with one who was both innocent and wise.

How could he not have known? He should have realised. His self-recriminations were bitter, as were his regrets. All this time he might have been able to simply enjoy her willingness to share his bed, without the shadow of her previous indiscretions hanging over his delight in her. He had assumed that her responses were due to a naturally wanton nature.

But after all, what if she had been a victim of Tom's philandering? Should it really have mattered so much? Her cousin's transgression was but one brief error made by a very young girl in her first season. Sir Stephen Seton's words came back to him and he finally found himself in agreement with his friend. He, Gervase, should more easily have been able to dismiss it.

He regarded her now: still pale, her eyes glittering with unshed tears.

The sight moved him, though his heart grew even heavier. She had made this enormous sacrifice of herself for the sake of another. She had trapped herself in marriage to him - and his godmother was right, he was far too old for her. Her younger age, and now the fact that he knew her to have been innocent and inexperienced, jolted his conscience. She should not be tied to him. Much as it caused him agony to admit it, she should be free to find herself a more suitable husband, and one who was of her own selection.

"It is not right that you are forced to remain in a situation that was barely of your choosing," Gervase said. His earlier anger had rapidly abated though the shock of her disclosure would take some time to get over. Likewise the galling confession that she viewed matrimony with him as less a prize than a prison. He felt a growing horror of the way he had treated her on their nuptials. An innocent maid, whose innocence he had torn away. "I will consult my solicitor in the morning and begin the necessary proceedings."

He meant this as a kindness but Lily's expression was stricken.

"Oh no my lord, I do not seek..." she trailed off.

Gervase thought that she had meant to say "divorce". It would be a stigma for them both and worse for her, he knew. "I will ensure that adequate money is settled on you, so you will want for nothing. Enough for a dowry even, should a suitor of your own choosing one day appear." Just saying this stuck in his throat but he owed her no less.

"It is not that." Lily wanted to weep. He was clearly desperate to be rid of her, even suggesting that she marry someone else. She couldn't blame him, what with all the lies and deception.

"I am aware of the apology I owe you. I have violated you, I have suspected your nature, accused of offences you could scarce have committed. It is impossible for me to express the increasing shame I feel for my conduct, Elizabeth."

"But you have not violated me, my lord." Lily was confused.

Gervase passed his hand over his eyes, rubbing his brow. "The way I treated you on the night we wed was not the way that any man should have treated his bride, regardless of his knowledge of or suspicion of her conduct. It is something I have frequently berated myself for, and with this new knowledge I feel my trespass upon you all the more bitterly."

Lily felt embarrassment suffuse her. "My lord - " she scarce dared to call him Gervase " - you must know that I was not unwilling, on that occasion. Nor - " she struggled to find the words " - unsatisfied."

He looked at her, frowning. She hesitated, waiting for him to speak. When he did not, she continued.

"Though I was still a maiden, and ignorant of such things, still something in my body was not ignorant, my lord. Although it was a sudden union, still, it was a union that was welcome to me." From the first moment his lips had met hers she had felt herself lit by his touch. By his mere presence.

"You cannot mean this, Elizabeth." Gervase had carried the burden of guilt for so long that he thought she spoke only to assuage his conscience.

"My lord, I did at no time attempt to resist you, nor ask you to stop. Had I cried out, I am confident that you would at once have ceased your attentions," Lily said. "Is it not so?"

Of course it was so, even despite the raging desire he had felt for her that night. That he had felt for her every day since. "Indeed it is so."

"Then there was no violation. I was only ignorant as to how to convey my willingness, my lord, and my - " again she struggled for the phrase " - subsequent complete satisfaction."

Gervase might have laughed at this description, were the overall situation not so disastrous. Even so, there was an amused light in his gaze as he repeated: "Complete satisfaction?"

"Quite complete, my lord." She smiled at him, still pale, with sincerity.

He was surprised and felt the stirrings of relief at this. It was no good, however. Nothing was orderly nor fair about this union, to this girl at least. "Still, I must release you. It is only fair. Your poverty and position should never have condemned you to a forced marriage, my dear." Gervase felt weary and resigned as he spoke these words. But he could not force her to remain with him.

"But I... I do not want... I cannot say..." Why was it so hard to express herself? Lily felt her chest and voice constrict.

"What, then? Come, let there be no more concealment between us," Gervase said, seeing that she was reluctant to explain herself. He spoke gently given her invalid state, but with firmness. "The time for that is long past."

Lily tried to find the words. "It is that... I would rather remain married to you."

Just moments ago he had assumed she was desperate to escape. The dark brows drew together. "Why?"

"My lord, I..." Lily closed her eyes, gathering her courage. She felt the presence or memory of her father and knew that he would have expected to be brave, no matter the risk or exposure to herself.

She steeled her nerves. Her heart felt stopped in her chest.

"I love you, Gervase."

She was terrified to use his name but it was a last attempt to show him how she felt. As soon as she had spoken she wanted to cover her face with the bedclothes, to hide away. But she forced herself to remain looking at him.

His eyes showed surprise. There was shock, disbelief.

If Gervase had been taken aback before, now he was staggered. Both at what she said and the fact that she had said it. He might have believed she was acting but no one could act this well. And he knew this was truth when he saw it, because her words echoed in his own heart.

For the first time in many years he felt a hope stir in him that he had long thought impossible. Yet he still doubted.

"You love me? You mean my titles and the home I have provided you?"

Lily felt bolder. "No. With respect, your titles mean nothing to me. Such things never have."

It was true. She had been raised to respect honour and kindness, not rank.

"I see." Gervase was gazing at her, hardly knowing how to react. For his entire life, since his uncle had died suddenly without issue and the title unexpectedly passed to him, he had been used to his primary attraction being his rank and property.

The dozens - hundreds, even - of women jostling for his hand before even meeting him wanted only to be married to the Marquess of Westford. Not Gervase Dainard.

And now this girl, penniless as she was, claimed she loved only him. When she had trembled in his arms, when her body had been aroused by his embraces, this was solely for him. It was not the symptom of a licentious nature that bestowed such favours on any many, but a response to him alone. The thought humbled him and also began to inflame him.

"My father taught me differently than other girls, I have come to realise," Lily told him. "Perhaps if my mother had not died, my outlook might be different." Privately she doubted this, since everything she had been told about her mother painted the portrait of a woman who shunned society and pretension as much as her husband had done. "I realise that I am not what you would seek in a wife. It is selfish of me to have said what I have said. I understand that you must release me for your own sake."

The light in the room seemed to have turned golden to Gervase.

He stopped, and simply looked at the young woman before him. He realised with a surge of joy that he loved her, he adored everything about her. And that there were no barriers between them now whatsoever.

"You are… everything… I would ever seek in a wife," he said, drawing out the words for emphasis. Lily's eyes widened. "If I had even known that such things could be sought."

He took her hands. "I have no desire to release you. I have no desire for you to marry another, be he a prince or a poor curate. I have no desire for anything except to keep you with me for the rest of my days, and enjoy the hope that you may one day bear our children."

She was gazing at him, her grey eyes trusting yet worried.

"I love you, Elizabeth. God help me, how much I love you. Even from the first moment I saw you, though I have been unforgivably slow to realise it."

The expression on her face, the quiet joy and relief, moved him as perhaps nothing else ever had.

But even as he spoke a new shadow fell, darkening his just-found happiness.

For she might not be his after all, at least not legally. And if she were not, then he shuddered to think what their union had been and the implications for them both.

Lily saw the change in him. "Something more is wrong?"

Gervase took her hand, feeling oddly avuncular. "My child, based on what you have told me, I do not know if our marriage is legal. You had not attained the age of majority when we wed, and I did not have your guardian's permission. He may seek annulment. Even though you say you wish to remain married to me, and God knows I could not bear to part with you, the law may force us asunder."

45. The eleventh hour

Feeling a confusing mixture of emotion, Gervase was finally persuaded by Lily that he could leave her for a short while. He had barely bathed and eaten these past few days, and his guests had been sorely neglected.

"There are my cousin, Mrs Hollis and Sarah to relieve you of your vigil, my lord," Lily told him.

Gervase descended to the hall, his emotions a confused but happy turmoil.

She was his. She was entirely his. She loved no other, nor ever had done. Gervase felt almost boyish in his joy. It was only tempered with fears as to the legal status of their union, and he determined to summon his lawyer forthwith.

He found Betsy and Sir Stephen in the parlour. Both turned to him anxiously for news.

"She is well," Gervase told them. "Quite well, and her spirits recovered fully. The doctor says that all danger is past."

Betsy burst into tears and then struggled with embarrassment for doing so. Sir Stephen gave her his handkerchief and she buried her face in it. Sir Stephen himself felt a weight lift from his chest.

"These are glad tidings indeed, Westford. The very gladdest."

Gervase thanked his friend sincerely for all his help but Sir Stephen brushed it off. "I have done very little. The mercy of Nature, a skilled physician and your wife's own fortitude have seen us through this darkest hour."

"Nonetheless, I am grateful to you for your presence here." He turned to Betsy. "Miss Cosgrove, your cousin has made certain revelations to me, which we need not go into at this time. Suffice it to say that if a certain matter has been troubling you, it need do so no longer."

Betsy's brow wrinkled. "Do you mean…?"

"I admit surprise, and while there may be some legal formalities to attend to, I have no wish for the situation to be altered. Please know that you remain our welcome guest for as long as you wish to reside here."

Gervase had already considered Miss Cosgrove's precarious position. Something would need to be done for her, though at present he knew not what. He turned back to Sir Stephen. "Seton, since this must all come out, and you are an old and trusted friend, with Miss Cosgrove's permission I will disclose the news."

Betsy found that she was terrified to lose Sir Stephen's good opinion of her, if indeed he had any. But she could not fairly refuse consent. She nodded, clenching her nails into her palms.

Sir Stephen, who had only managed to guess that Lady Westford might be in a delicate situation for reasons other than her accident, was all ears.

Gervase began. "It seems that there are two cousins with the same name."

He did not get to speak further, as light at once dawned for his friend. For Seton it was the missing piece of a puzzle of which he had been close to guessing the solution. "Ah! You need say no more, Westford. There were times I had wondered about certain matters. I confess that my mind did not run to quite that possibility, but all is now clear. *'We that are true lovers run into strange capers'*," Sir Stephen quoted. "But all's well that ends well, though that is a different play altogether."

"You have always been a better scholar of Shakespeare than I," Gervase remarked, grateful for his friend's ready understanding and acceptance.

Betsy, no scholar at all, was lost by their exchange. "Then you are sure that you do not mind?" she asked Gervase.

"It is indeed something to absorb, I grant you, but I have conceived a deep affection for your cousin and would not wish the situation altered."

Betsy bowed her head in thanks. "If I may take your leave, I am eager to see my cousin."

"By all means, my dear." Gervase spoke gently to her, wishing to further reassure the young woman that he bore no anger towards her.

When Betsy had gone, Gervase sank into a chair. He felt a sudden exhaustion at it all, as happy as he was.

Sir Stephen was regarding him, his face suddenly grave. "Westford, what is Farrington's role in all this? He must have realised the substitution as soon as he arrived here. Has he always known?"

Gervase had given his cousin little thought, save for his gladness that Lily had never bore any affection for him. "He knows, but the rest I cannot say. I have not had time to think on it."

"He has kept strangely apart all this time, from both Miss Cosgrove and myself."

Gervase was relieved that nothing had resumed there, for he doubted Tom's intentions towards Betsy were any more honourable than they had been six months ago. He wondered what Tom's intentions were. He rarely lingered long at Westford Park, once he had managed to get Gervase to pay his latest accumulation of debts.

He feared a difficult conversation lay ahead.

***

Betsy stopped by her room to refresh herself before visiting Lily. She felt quite overwhelmed with it all. The relief that Lily was safe was paramount. Then the release of the terrible dread of their deception. Betsy marvelled that Lord Westford had taken it so well.

But it was clear to her that the Marquess was deeply in love with her cousin, and people in love will perhaps forgive anything.

It had also been kind of him to offer Betsy continued hospitality, for she feared her parents would never offer her a home again.

Yet Betsy could not feel at ease. Tom Farrington still lurked below, and Betsy felt grave agitation to think of him there. Her former affection for him had all but vanished. If she felt a twinge, it was more one of regret, for how misled she had been and for how much time and tears she had wasted on him.

She made her way to Lily's room and for a moment, could hardly believe what she saw.

There stood Nanny Noakes, a pillow in her hands, pressing it down upon the bed.

Her teeth were bared with the effort, her lips stretched back into a horrible grin.

Beneath it, Lily kicked and struggled.

For the slightest fraction of a second Betsy froze, before rushing upon Nanny Noakes and trying to pull the crazed servant off her cousin.

The elderly woman was surprisingly strong. Her thin, bony arms had a wiry strength. "For God's sake, stop!" Betsy cried, wrestling with her. A side table crashed to the floor, a large vase falling from it and smashing on the floor.

Betsy shouted for help. She finally managed to get Nanny Noakes away from the bed, dragging her backwards and knocking over another chair that had been stood hear the bed.

Realising her attempt had been thwarted, the old woman crumpled, standing and clutching her pillow and affecting a feeble air.

"I was only trying to arrange her ladyship's pillows in a more comfortable manner," she wheedled.

"You were trying to suffocate her!" Betsy said.

Lily was still gasping for breath, not recovered enough to speak.

"Such a cruel thing, to accuse an innocent old woman," Nanny Noakes said. She stood there muttering to herself as Gervase and Sir Stephen appeared, roused by the commotion. Mrs Hollis was close behind them.

"What in heaven's name is happening here?" Gervase asked.

"It is this evil, murderous old witch," Betsy said. "She was trying to kill Lily by putting a pillow over her face."

"Oh no, my lord, I only sought to rearrange the bedclothes for my lady's comfort," Nanny Noakes said.

Betsy was outraged. "You're lying! Just look at Lily."

Lily managed to speak, but barely. "I couldn't breathe…"

Nanny Noakes let out a sudden wail and flung herself with surprising speed toward the door. She fled past those gathered there, who were too startled to stop her.

"This cannot be so. There must be some mistake," Gervase said.

"There is no mistake, my lord. Nor is this the first time, but I hesitated to add to your troubles while my cousin lay so gravely ill," Betsy said. She felt bolder than she had ever done before.

Sir Stephen noted the spark of anger in Miss Cosgrove's eyes and the colour in her eyes, and the vibrancy it gave her. He thought for a moment how transformed she was from the wan, fading flower who had first arrived there.

"I fear it is true," he told Gervase, who was now kneeling by Lily, cradling her. "Miss Cosgrove shared such concerns with me, and I regret it was due to my counsel that she did not advise you of them."

"Concerns?"

Betsy explained what had happened. She was reluctant to reveal it all, not wanting to cause Lily any more distress. "As you know, my lord, there have been several strange instances of sickness. I came upon Nanny Noakes in this room, while my cousin was absent, and she made wild claims of adding poison to our cups."

"She is delusional, I am sure," Gervase said. He struggled to believe that the elderly servant would have had the capability let alone the malice to behave in such a fashion.

"There is something else, but I cannot repeat it here," Betsy said.

"Can you disclose it to me privately?" Gervase asked.

"I do not know." Betsy did not want to put him into a difficult position. To relay what had been said was effectively to accuse Tom Farrington of attempted murder.

Gervase stood. "I must know all. Come. Seton and Mrs Hollis will jointly guard Lady Westford. You may share your concern to me in private."

46. The culprit

It was not easy for Betsy to tell Gervase that his own cousin may have been harbouring murderous intentions towards Lily.

"I am sure you must think very ill of me, both for my conduct and for the deception that I practised on you," she began.

Gervase silenced her. "We have all erred. Given my knowledge of Farrington's nature, had I chosen to expose him rather than to pay his many debts and save him from the Fleet, much trouble might have been saved." He spoke candidly to her, for the time for secrets was past.

"It is of your cousin that I wish to speak. I believe - I greatly fear - that he wishes my cousin ill."

Gervase did not appear as disbelieving as Betsy had feared he might, so she continued.

"Nanny Noakes said many wild and troubling things when I first encountered her in my cousin's bedchamber. Among them, as I have mentioned, was that she had sought to poison her several times. But then she also spoke of Mr Farrington 'settling what she could not'. I do not know if she was delusional, my lord, but she spoke of him inheriting Westford Park, and of course if you and my cousin… if there were to be a happy event…"

Gervase understood. "I see. But these may well be the fancies of a crazed old woman. I know that she has doted on him for many a year. What gives credence to her claims of my cousin's involvement?"

Here Betsy faltered. "I am not quite sure. Only when I spoke to him, I felt a terrible fear. There was something in his manner when he returned from searching for her."

Gervase had given little thought to the implications of his marriage on Farrington's expectations. It was a horrifying thought to consider that a man might resort to murder to restore them. Did the old servant have the capacity and will to have acted alone? He resolved to have her room searched and to question the other staff.

He called for the steward and the housekeeper. Mrs Hollis and James Pelham soon stood before him, a trace of anxiety on their faces. It was an unusual summons.

"I wish to know if Nanny Noakes ever receives correspondence," he asked them.

Mrs Hollis frowned, since it seemed an odd inquiry. "Indeed, Lord Westford. On occasion, perhaps no more than once or twice a twelvemonth, she receives a note or card." She looked to the steward for confirmation.

Pelham nodded. "About so often, I would say."

"Do you have any notion of whom this correspondence is from?" Gervase asked. "If you have chanced to recognise the hand, for example."

"I believe a niece writes to her every Christmas, my lord. Then in the past months she has had one or two pieces of correspondence, that I have brought to her," Mrs Hollis said. ' Mr Farrington has written to her on occasion. She has always nursed a fondness for him, as her last charge, and it is a kindness that he remembers her, for she has few visitors."

Gervase knew Tom too well to believe that he troubled himself to write to an old woman out of any sense of kindness. "I would like to recover these letters, if possible. I would have you search her room. I would also have her confined to her room, and her door kept locked at all times."

Mrs Hollis's mouth fell open and Pelham looked no less startled. "My lord!" She quickly recovered herself. "Of course, my lord. Myself and Sarah will attend to it."

This was done at once, for Mrs Hollis understood the matter to be urgent. They found Nanny Noakes in her room in an alarming state, her hair dishevelled, rocking herself and cackling incoherently. What could have happened to her?

"Lord Westford requires that we recover some letters that were sent to you, Nanny. Can you tell me where they are?"

But there was no response from the old woman. She continued her rocking and strange cackling. It was clear that some madness had overtaken her.

They made a thorough search but no correspondence could be found save for the Christmas greetings from Nanny Noakes' niece. Mrs Hollis took these, and when she and Sarah finally turned to leave, Nanny Noakes broke out in a wheezing laugh. Her face was twisted in strange glee. "All in the fire! All in the flames! Just as the young master instructed! All shall be ashes, all shall be gone!"

Thinking she was raving in a fit of lunacy, Mrs Hollis did not mention her words to the Marquess when she handed him the niece's letters. "This is all I could find, my lord."

But Sarah carried the news to Ben when she visited him in the stables. "Such a strange to-do there was with old Nanny Noakes! I believe the old woman has gone quite mad and his lordship will have her sent to the asylum," she told him.

Normally Ben would have chided her for tattling but he had other things on his mind. Sarah took his silence as encouragement to reveal more.

"Lord Westford wanted us to find some letters she had received, but we do not know why. Nanny Noakes sat there, laughing at us in such a strange. I was quite frightened, I may tell you. She started talking about the fire and the young master, by which I suppose she means Mr Farrington?"

A cold chill was settling around the heart of the stable hand. "Something is not right about all this," he said. "See here." He went and recovered the sabotaged tack from under the straw. "There's been a knife put through that. It's what I found on Dido, the day I recovered her."

Sarah was agog. "What can it mean? Is that why Lady Westford fell? You don't mean someone did that deliberately?'

Ben looked grim. "It seems that way."

"But you must tell the Marquess, Ben."

The stable hand was reluctant. Saddling the horses was his responsibility, and he feared being accused of negligence. Or worse, accused of being the actual culprit.

It took all Sarah's powers of persuasion to make him agree to take the tack to his employer.

***

Tom Farrington had planned to flee as soon as he had heard of Lady Westford's recovery. He feared the game would soon be up.

The old hag was getting madder by the day and Tom no longer trusted her silence. She had started to rave and mutter. He contemplated silencing her but he had already taken on too much risk.

For even if Gervase cast the two chits out when he realised their deception, he might be no more inclined to look favourably on Tom.

And Tom was growing less confident that Gervase would cast his wife out. His cousin's reaction when he thought his marchioness was near death was one thing. But the continued concern, and the never leaving her side, did not bode well for Tom's prospects. After all, the deception had left Gervase with a maiden, and a more than comely one at that.

It had been a mistake to threaten her with exposure, Tom saw that now.

It was time to cut his losses. He had a fancy to return to the continent, where some rich mistress could lavish wealth upon him. Or he might find himself a young and impressionable heiress, and induce her to elope. There were always possibilities, if one had enough will and charm.

Thinking these things, Tom cast a glance outside the window to see the stable hand walking towards the house carrying the broken tack.

Damn. He had already left it too late to arrange his affairs. He would need to hightail it to London immediately. Just as he rose, intending to slip out to the stables and make off with the best of the horses, the door opened and Gervase entered.

The Marquess's expression was grim. "Tom," he greeted his cousin. "I regret that an allegation has been made, one that I am loath to credit with any veracity, but of such a nature that it requires me to seek your response."

This was typical Gervase, Tom thought. He never could get to the point. "Lay it before me then, I beseech you," he replied, affecting nonchalance.

"Have you colluded with any of the servants in this house to threaten the safety of Lady Westford or any other persons here?"

Tom decided the best course was to bluster it out. "What an outrageous suggestion! I might take offence, were it not so patently absurd."

Gervase had expected denial either way. "Were you aware that Nanny Noakes harboured ill feeling toward Lady Westford? I am aware that you have exchanged correspondence with her."

Tom laughed. "Really, old boy, you make it sound like some sort of tryst. I've written to the old thing once or twice purely as a kindness. Her mind is clearly growing addled."

Before Gervase could respond, Ben entered, carrying the harness and looking very uneasy. "I wasn't sure whether to trouble your lordship, but I've been worried about the state of the tack found on Dido."

He held it out to Gervase, indicating the severed straps.

300

"These have been cut through," Gervase said.

Ben nodded. "Looks deliberate, is what I thought."

"Indeed. Wouldn't you agree, Tom?"

Tom was entreated to inspect the straps, and attempted to shrug it off. "Hard to say what caused it. A prank gone wrong, I dare say, by some local fellow."

Gervase had a sudden flashback to a broken window and a cricket ball. A younger Tom disavowing any knowledge. *"I dare say it was the gardener's boy."* Except the gardener's boy had been at home, sick.

Tom had been lying then as he was lying now. Gervase knew it in his bones, and felt physically sick. "That will be all, Ben. Thank you for making me aware of this." With Ben dismissed he turned his attention again to Tom, who still stood there with a defiant, half-smirk on his face.

"You surely can't think that I..." Tom began, but Gervase cut him off.

"We have the letters you wrote to Nanny Noakes. I was hoping you would confess it yourself, but I see that it is not to be."

The bluff paid off as Tom whitened, the guilt now glaring over his face. Still he tried to bluster his way out of it. "They were but fantasies for the old woman's sake. She had a notion of me having the title one day. I thought it might appease her, it was nothing but a joke. I never dreamt she would try anything, you must believe me."

Gervase stood there, holding the sabotaged tack. His voice was deadly calm. "You incited an elderly woman to poison half the household. You severed the tack that you knew would be used on my wife's horse. I may have no proof, but I strongly suspect your hand was at play with the cottage and the fire. For the first and final time, I order you to begone from this house forever. I would have you hanged, were it not for the sake of our family name. Go now and never return."

Tom scowled. "At least let me inform you of one thing. That chit that you wed is not who you think she is. She and her devious brat of a cousin duped you, Gervase, they played you for a fool. And how exceedingly easy it was for them."

A muscle clenched in Gervase's jaw. "I would beget heirs by the Whore of Babylon ere you should ever inherit Westford. Know that I will embark on the necessary legal procedures to formally disinherit you. You shall never again have any claim on the estate or the title, now or in the future."

"You are quite welcome to it," Tom said. His flippant air was returning. The worst was over, he was at least free. He was furious to have been discovered, and longed to crack Gervase's skull open with the poker, but he was nonetheless free.

There was no farewell. Tom strode out of the room, through the hall, and the front door clanged shut behind him. He would not darken the halls of Westford Park again.

47. The resolution

The time that Lily spent with Gervase following the revelations was the sweetest time she had known. Finally freed from all deception, they could be as one, with no obstacles or deception between them.

Gervase was hopelessly, absurdly in love with his young bride. "Deranged", as he knew Seton would have termed it. He had little wish to do anything except spend time with her. He still felt occasional compunction that she had not more freely come into his hand. But each day he grew more assured of her mutual affection and desire for him, assuaging any lingering misgivings.

"I can only beg your forgiveness for mistaking the interview between you and my cousin. It is not the first time I have wrongly accused you, and I can make no excuses for my conduct, now or then," he told her.

"It is quite understandable that you thought as you did, given what you believed of me and Mr Farrington at the time. And that was entirely my fault, so no blame should be yours, my lord. But certainly our conversation was very far indeed from what you imagined. Even were it not for my regard for you, he is not a man who might ever have attracted my regard." Lily was still reluctant to reveal the blackmail but Gervase saw the cloud pass across her face.

He recalled Farrington's proximity to her, which now took on a very different light. "When I saw you together, was he threatening you?"

"In some manner, perhaps, but I am sure he did not mean..." Lily trailed off.

"I am quite sure he meant whatever threats he made. God knows his intent was murderous. But it is past, and I can see that it troubles you. We will speak of it no further. He is gone, and certain legal formalities are underway, and he shall not return."

He pulled Lily closer to him. They were sitting by the fire in his bedchamber, and her form beneath her translucent nightgown was distracting him. "So you have 'regard' for me. Is that all I inspire in you?"

Lily saw the gaze that she loved in her husband's eyes. She kept her own expression serious. "Indeed, my lord. I have the very deepest respect for you."

"Only respect? It sounds very cold and formal. I inspire no warmer emotion in you?" He traced his hand over Lily's breast, and she shivered at the sensation through the thin fabric.

"What emotion did you wish to inspire, sir?" It was very hard to maintain her composure but she delighted in provoking him, now that she actually dared to.

"This." Gervase brought his lips down upon hers, and let her know his love and mastery of her.

It was not something his wife could, or wished to, resist.

But there were others considerably less gratified by the newly revealed union.

Sir Robert Cosgrove was incandescent with rage when the news was brought to him. He travelled at once to Westford Park in a fury, brandishing his whip at Lily as Betsy cowered behind her.

"You are a wicked and deceitful brat. That we opened our home to you, for you to lie and steal your own cousin's prospects! It shall not be borne, if I have anything to do with the matter."

They were fortunate that Sir Stephen Seton had called round earlier that day, for only his calm presence managed to prevent Gervase from killing his wife's uncle.

Sir Robert threatened all kinds of retribution, chiefly that he would have the marriage annulled and Lily cast out.

"Little good would that do, sir." Gervase informed him. "For I have no intention of taking of any other bride, even if the marriage were found to be void. Though my lawyer assures me that it is not. Force us asunder and I will simply give your niece the protection of my own roof, until such a time as she reaches the age of majority and the formalities may be once more undergone."

The other man was apoplectic. "You think so little of reputation, that you would take a disgraced and ruined chit for bride?"

Gervase managed to refrain from knocking him to the floor. "If you recall, I was quite prepared to do so once before," he said. "Fortunately a substitution took place that left three people far happier than otherwise."

Sir Robert turned his attention on Betsy. "As for you, you foolish little idiot. I curse the very day of your birth. A black day that was indeed, the last hope of our line to be a worthless girl. You shall be sent abroad. For not even Frances would not have you in these circumstances."

Betsy began crying and Gervase looked confused. "Frances? Is she not your relative who died a month or so back?" He caught Lily's eye and guessed at the truth. The resurrection of a distant relative was insignificant in the circumstances, so he changed course. "There will be no need for Miss Cosgrove to travel abroad, unless she wishes to. She is a welcome guest at Westford Park and the dear companion of my wife and myself for as long as she cares to reside here."

At this, Sir Stephen stepped forward. "If I might be so bold as to make another suggestion, I also can offer Miss Cosgrove a home that she may wish to call her own."

Betsy looked at him and gasped. Lily was also startled. She knew that the two had grown to be friends. Sir Stephen dined with them frequently and they made a very companionable foursome. But wrapped up in her happiness with Gervase, she had not suspected any deeper attachment forming between them.

"What do you say, my dear?" Sir Stephen asked Betsy. "I have lived long enough alone, and Grantlings has been too many years without a mistress." The expression in his eyes was kind but also anxious. He had planned a longer courtship than this but the situation forced his hand.

"You cannot mean it, sir." Betsy was bewildered.

Sir Stephen smiled, his eyes kindly. "Indeed I do. We will talk more of it presently."

Betsy reddened, but Lily was glad to see that her cousin did not seem entirely displeased by the offer.

***

Once they were finally rid of Sir Robert, who had refused to spend a single night in the "deceitful harlot's" abode, Gervase offered his warmest congratulations to Sir Stephen and Betsy. She had accepted his proposal and looked happier than she had done for many months.

"My offer for you to reside here as long as you wish still stands, Miss Cosgrove," Gervase said. "I know that Elizabeth shares my sentiment."

Lily hugged her cousin. "Do stay, dearest. You can be married from Westford Park, should you wish. If my aunt and uncle are still in a temper, Lord Westford can give you away. But I am sure they will come around, once they are used to the situation."

Thus it was decided, along with plans for Betsy to travel to London with Lord and Lady Westford in the coming weeks to arrange her trousseau.

That night as Lily lay in her husband's arms, Gervase yet felt misgivings when he thought of Seton's proposal and the upcoming nuptials. They compared very differently to his own.

"Before our marriage you had never had the opportunity to meet other men," he told her. "I feel that your inexperience has been to my advantage, in that you were never able to consider others. Perhaps you might have chosen elsewhere, had you been given the chance."

Lily regarded her husband and perceived a flicker of insecurity in him. Somehow it aroused a devil in her.

"There were several other men," she told him.

Gervase raised his eyebrows.

"There was my uncle's curate, of course. Many an impoverished relation has married a clergyman," she said.

Her husband frowned, then realised. "You cannot mean that elderly gentleman who married us?" he asked.

Lily kept her expression sweet. "He might have made a very kind and respectful husband. Then there was our dancing instructor, who had a very noble figure and was an excellent dancer..."

At this she saw something flare in Gervase's eyes, which he failed to completely suppress. It gave her a sensation of delight yet she did not want to torment him too far.

"...but I am afraid his preference was for bachelorhood rather than female companionship," she said. This phrase had been used of Claude Belvedere, so she knew he would understand her meaning.

The trace of tension in Gervase's expression relaxed.

"You forget also that I have seen many other men since I married you, and even danced with them, and I am happy to say that none compare to you," she told him.

"So you regarded other men, then?" Gervase asked, giving himself away. Then he was frustrated with himself. "I have no right to feel as I do, Lily, to bristle at the thought of any male you have come into contact with. I do not know what beast has awoken in my nature, but I will do all I can to quell it."

"I hope that you will not do so entirely," his wife said.

"Not entirely?" He was confused.

"For if you do so, I shall fear that I am no longer able to arouse it. And it is a wildness that is sometimes very welcome to me."

Now Gervase looked truly surprised.

"Knowing that your passion for me frequently overtakes your better nature is very satisfying," she explained. She was smiling now, reaching for him. Gervase felt a hardness in his loins that almost gave him pain.

He buried his face in her neck, breathing her in. "Lily..." He felt her body mould against his. What a marvel, that she should seem to want him as much as he desired her.

Gervase tried very hard to be gentle in his ministrations, wanting to cherish her tenderly. But the violence of his feelings overtook him and restraint was impossible. Fortunately her cries and gasps throughout, and afterwards her flushed face and shining eyes, told him that his vigour had not been unwelcome.

He dozed for a while, and when he awoke, Lily was watching him, her face thoughtful.

"Something is wrong?" he asked.

"The one thing I do not know Gervase, is how I compare. For I am sure you must have known other women."

This stopped him short. He hardly knew what to say, and then he saw that she was laughing at him.

"In truth there have been but few. Partly because my heart was hardened for many years. Indeed, it is only falling in love with you that has restored my regard for many of your sex," he told her.

"Your heart was hardened?"

Gervase decided that she should know the truth about his past. After all, he knew everything of hers, precious little of it that there was compared to his. The disparity in their ages and experience still gave him some unease, though Lily continued to reassure him that she wanted no other, younger man.

He began his story.

"When I was a young man, too young it must be said to have seriously been considering matrimony, I conceived an admiration for a certain lady of my acquaintance. She was an heiress and I was but the son of the younger brother of a Marquess. She had higher hopes than me. We were both too young, Lily, and foolish. I believed I had obtained her promise only to find she had promised herself to an Earl. I conceived many hot-headed fancies, to challenge him to a duel among them, though a wise friend restrained me. But it left me bitter for a while, and wary thereafter."

He turned to her.

"Then with the sudden death of my uncle, himself still a bachelor, the title became mine. At once every matron in London seemed to be thrusting their offspring at me. All showed the same false admiration, it was my position and my wealth that ignited their affection. Just as with the woman I have formerly mentioned. So you see why it has been my lot and choice to remain unmarried, and why I struggled with my sense of duty to pay recompense for my cousin's offences. I did not trust you nor any female because that long ago woman had played me false.

"I am sure it was not so, my lord," Lily said.

Gervase raised his eyebrows. "Indeed?"

"That they showed you only false admiration. There is much about your person to admire." A smile danced in her eyes.

"Are you paying me a compliment, wife?"

"If you will accept it, then yes."

He marvelled at her growing confidence in conversing with him. She had never cowered from him, he had long observed that she had too much courage for that. But her earlier manner had been cautious and deferential, burdened by her sense of guilt.

Now she was bolder, and he took advantage. "You say 'much', not 'all'. What parts of my person do you not admire?" he asked her.

Lily looked him up and down. "Very few, my lord."

"Name them. I will have their imperfections addressed forthwith."

She lowered her eyelashes. "It is your lips."

He frowned. "You find fault with my lips?"

"It is their position I find fault with."

He remained confused.

"That they are not on mine," Lily continued.

Gervase was delighted at her daring and gave her what she sought. Then he undressed her, revelling in the soft curves that were now unequivocally his. He traced his fingers past the curve of her waist and across her lower belly.

"I would to see you swell with my seed and bear my children, Lily."

She smiled up at him. "That may require your participation."

"What form of participation?" He knew full well, but wished to hear her say it.

She told him, and her words aroused him so much that he was unable to restrain himself from immediate participation.

Gervase held her afterwards, but Lily rolled onto her side and gazed at her husband. Her face was serious. "I am afraid I have practiced another deception on you, my lord."

Gervase felt some alarm. "You have deceived me? In what regard?"

"Regarding the need for your participation."

Now he was confused. "What do you mean?"

"That your participation was not actually required, in this instance," Lily told him.

He drew his brows together, then saw the teasing light in her eye. "You cannot mean...?"

"It is very early, Gervase, but yes. It is already happening.'

The shock and joy made him feel like a boy again. "It's true?" Then he drew back from her, concerned. "In such a delicate situation we should not perhaps have..."

Lily cut him off. "Yes, we should. I am reliably informed that it is perfectly safe to continue."

Gervase decided it would not be to his advantage to challenge this. Lily was smart enough to know what she was doing, he reasoned. She might be young but she was Edward Cosgrove's daughter, and more than wise for her years.

48. Epilogue

Six months later

With his father's dark hair and his mother's silver grey eyes, Edward Cosgrove Dainard, the future Marquess of Westford, lay in his cradle. He was a healthy and beautiful child, the apple of the entire household's eye.

Looking upon him and the woman who had brought him into the world, Gervase thought that he had never loved Lily more. Throughout her pregnancy he had wrestled between desire for her and wanting to treat her like a tender flower. Lily had repeatedly assured him that there was no need for the latter.

Gervase had heard that some men tired of their wives after they had borne children, but for him it was quite the opposite. The physician had advised a temporary cessation of relations between husband and wife, necessary for the new mother's recovery, and it was driving the Marquess of Westford to distraction. Two weeks so far, and many weeks more to wait.

When the nurse came to bathe the child, leaving husband and wife alone, Lily gave Gervase a very suggestive smile. The fuller swell of her breasts only served to remind Gervase of what he was currently forbidden.

"Do not look at me that way, Elizabeth, for you know it inflames me. Had I less self-control I might be tempted to disregard the physician's advice entirely, which would not be conducive to your well-being."

"My lord, there are still ways that we might enjoy one another."

As ever, Gervase found himself slightly shocked. He still marvelled that Lily matched him in appetite, having believed that a woman would never be as interested in such things as men.

"The doctor has ordered us to remain apart," he said.

"He has advised us not to couple in a way that might result in conception. He has not forbidden me to embrace you, nor to be embraced by you," Lily said. "Come and lie with me."

Gervase needed no further invitation.

"You will think me very wicked, Gervase, but there is something I have read about." Lily had been waiting for a time to try this, but during her pregnancy had not seemed an appropriate time. Now, however, she felt free to experiment as she wished. Unfastening her husband's breeches she showed him exactly what the subject of her study had been.

Gervase cried out in shock and arousal. "Where on earth did you read of such a thing?"

Lily raised her head. "In a book in your own library, my lord. I confess I was most surprised to find it there. But it proved a fascinating topic."

Damned Great-Uncle Henry. Gervase recalled his ancestor's proclivities had included collecting erotic literature, but he had no idea those books were tucked away in his library. Trust Lily to have found them. He had never known anyone to read as much as she did.

Or perhaps blessed Great-Uncle Henry, Gervase reconsidered, as his wife continued her ministrations. He had never expected nor requested such an act from a wife, but nothing seemed more natural or more pleasurable to him now.

He groaned. "You will be the undoing of me. Come here." He drew her back up to him, and turned her over so he was once again above her.

About Noël Cades

Noël Cades is a British writer who currently lives in Sydney, Australia. A fan of romance, particularly historic, some of Noël's favourite authors include Jilly Cooper, Georgette Heyer, Elizabeth Rolls, Anne Mather, Sara Seale and Victoria Holt.

Noël is always delighted to hear from other fans, readers and writers of romance.

You can contact Noël at noelcades@gmail.com

Noël's website is at **www.noelcades.com**

Visit Noël's blog to sign up for exclusive news and the chance to receive new free book giveaways.

More hot, forbidden romances by Noël Cades available in paperback:

Falling From Grace

Gabriel entered the priesthood after a betrayal left him bitter. But when he meets troubled, beautiful Leonie, he wonders if he made the right choice.

His Model Student

When Sera's new art teacher mistakes her for a model and demands that she strip naked, sparks start to fly. Will Mr Marek be able to keep his student at arm's length after seeing everything she has to offer?

Tempting Her Teacher

Catholic school teacher Carl Spencer faces a crisis of faith when he falls for his student Juliet, how can he resist the temptation to be with her? But while he struggles to resist his growing attraction, she's starting to realise that it's become more than just a game for her.

Summer's Edge

When sports coach Stewart Walker finds out the girl he kissed is a student at his school he's furious and determined to keep away. But 18-year-old Alice has fallen hard and won't give up.

Man of the Match

Broken-hearted student Cara has no idea that the handsome stranger who seduced her on holiday is England cricket captain Matt Curran. Shocking twists and sexy action in the glamorous world of international cricket.

Excerpts from *Summer's Edge* by Noël Cades

Alice remained silent throughout this. She was still feeling disappointed and uncertain. She tried to tell herself it was for the best. Really, she should be grateful that he had just decided to move past it.

But she still felt embarrassed. She picked at the grass next to her, pulling off a small flower, avoiding looking at the play.

Then a shadow fell over them. She looked up.

It was Mr Walker.

"I want a word with you. In the pavilion, now," he ordered her. His eyes pierced into hers and he looked furious.

Numb, she obeyed, walking ahead of him.

Inside it was empty and he closed the door behind them and turned to her.

"What the fuck do you think you're playing at?"

He was absolutely incensed. He stood there, suddenly the adult, the authority, not just some guy she had kissed in a pub.

Someone she had compromised. Alice couldn't think of anything to say.

She stood there in front of him. His scent of faint cologne and sun-warmed skin was disturbingly familiar to her, mingling with the dusty wood and sports equipment smell of the pavilion.

"Did you know who I was?" he asked.

"Yes." There didn't seem to be any point in lying.

He glared at her and she looked back at him. His eyes pierced into her, their light grey-blue contrasting with his tanned complexion. He was one of the most devastatingly attractive men she had ever seen. All the more so now as his anger turned his face into carved steel.

As terrified and awkward as Alice felt, she also felt slightly defiant. After all she hadn't done anything wrong or illegal.

Then suddenly he grasped her by the shoulders and brought his mouth down on hers, hard. Surprised, she initially squirmed to escape his grasp then yielded as her forced his tongue into her mouth. His lips were bruising hers, he was almost biting her yet she wanted more.

Her hands, which had pushed against his chest to try and get away, went round his neck and she arched against him.

He was trying to hurt her, devour her. Punish her. All at once. But he wanted her too. She could taste his need, raw and urgent. Feel the hotness of his breath as he nearly suffocated her with his kiss.

His mouth left hers and moved to her neck, half embracing, half biting it. She tasted blood on her lip where he had crushed it with his own. He was gripping her hard and she clung to him. She didn't even care that he was hurting her.

He could have ripped all her clothes off right there and forced himself upon her. She had never wanted anyone so much.

Then just as suddenly he thrust her away from him. He swore under his breath as he tried to recover himself.

"Is that what you wanted?"

"No... yes... I mean..." Alice had no idea what to say. She was shaken and half in misery, half in ecstasy.

His face was like granite, its angles unyielding.

"Get out and don't come back here again. Stay out of my way," he said.

* * *

Alice tried to enjoy herself at the barbecue but she couldn't relax with Mr Walker just metres away, deliberately avoiding her. She had no appetite but knew she needed to eat something to avoid getting completely drunk on an empty stomach.

Graeme was good company and buoyed up by misery, alcohol and perhaps a desire to make a point to Mr Walker she flirted with him a bit. He was the kind of guy you could flirt with without it meaning much. Besides she knew he preferred Jules. She also noticed that Mr Walker's gaze was frequently on her and he didn't look happy about her flirting with Graeme. Or she hoped that was why he looked annoyed.

As the beer went down the revelry increased and someone accidentally knocked a glass full of beer over Alice. It went all over her top.

Feeling as though nothing much more could go wrong with the day she found her way to the kitchen and tried to sponge out the worst at the sink. If the beer dried on it, it would smell awful and probably stain the fabric. Hopefully even though she was getting her top even more wet it would dry quickly in the sun.

As she was finishing getting the worst off someone else came into the kitchen. She knew even before she turned that it was Mr Walker. He looked angry.

"Did you come here deliberately?" he asked.

She faced him. "I came here with Becky. I didn't know you'd be here. Or care," she added.

"What have you done to your shirt?"

"Someone spilt beer on it. I was washing it off."

"You can't go back out like that. You look like a wet t-shirt competition," he told her.

Alice looked down and went red. The wet fabric had gone transparent and soaked through her bra too.

Without a word Mr Walker pulled off his own shirt and handed it to her. He wore nothing under it. Alice was transfixed by his physique. His arms rippled with muscle and his flat, hard chest was tanned a deep gold. He was far fitter than she expected a cricketer to be, really powerful looking.

"Put this on."

The shirt was white cotton and warm from his body. She held it. It smelt of him. She wanted to envelop herself in it but she didn't follow his order.

"You want me to walk out of here wearing your shirt with you following me, topless?" she asked him.

He was silent for a moment, glaring at her. She was right, it would have exactly the opposite effect he intended. The situation was bad enough as it was.

"I don't want them gawping at you."

Alice's stomach gave a secret flip. Possessive and protective. He clearly didn't feel as neutrally towards her as he wanted to.

"The sun will dry it. I'll cross my arms." As she said this, she deliberately left her arms uncrossed and put her shoulders back slightly.

It had the desired effect. He was momentarily transfixed.

"Jesus Christ."

Alice took charge of the situation. "You should put this back on." Instead of just handing it to him she went to put it over his head meaning her arms were raised and her body was nearly against his. He was still for a second before taking a step backwards. A muscle clenched in his jaw.

"Just give me the shirt." She did so and he put it back on.

Then they both stood there. The tension was unbearable. She knew he wanted her and was fighting against it with every fibre of his being.

She broke the ice. "I am sorry you know. We were all just having fun the other night and I just didn't think about the implications."

"You were just messing around with me because I'm employed at your school?"

"God no, that wasn't why." Alice couldn't believe he thought this. Surely he'd realised how much she also wanted him to kiss her that night?

"So even if I hadn't been, you would have still put on your little act?" he asked.

What act? "I wasn't acting, I genuinely..."

"You wanted it too?"

"Yes." It was barely a whisper.

For a moment she thought he was going to kiss her again. He was wavering. Then he stood straighter. "I'm way too old for you, Alice, and I work at your school. Get back outside."

To find out what happens between Alice and Mr Walker, get Noël Cades' thrilling taboo student-teacher romance, Summer's Edge.